CONVICTION

TCKPUBLISHING.COM

MICHAEL CORDELL

ISBN:
978-1-63161-190-2

Sign up for Michael Cordell's newsletter at
www.michaeljcordell.com/newsletter

Published by TCK Publishing
www.TCKpublishing.com

Get discounts and special deals on our best-selling books at
www.TCKpublishing.com/bookdeals

Check out additional discounts for bulk orders at
www.TCKpublishing.com/bulk-book-orders

To my father, Homer Cordell

"Of what worth are convictions that bring not suffering?"
- Antoine de Saint-Exupery

1

When the shiv plunged into his side, Thane didn't even realize he'd been stabbed.

He hadn't seen the knife because he'd had been laying on his prison cot with his eyes closed. It felt like he'd been stung by a giant insect, but by then his eyes were open and he saw the jagged blade raised a second time, his blood dripping off the tip of the blade.

His assailant swung his fist down a second time. Thane managed to jerk just a bit to the left so that the blade didn't enter as deep or as clean. It likely didn't cause as much internal damage, but it hurt a hell of a lot more. From that point on, the adrenaline and the fight for survival took precedence over comparing how much each stab wound hurt, and there were a lot of them.

Thane wasn't sure if the man was trying to kill him, or just cut him up, although the distinction between the two intentions was subtle.

In a matter of seconds, Thane's chest and stomach were soaked in blood. The man attacking him kept muttering "God damn you," and "Why didn't you just stay away?" but he obviously wasn't looking to have a conversation with anyone but himself.

Thane had witnessed other brawls in Forsman

Penitentiary, and the guards were always quick to stop them, at least when there were guards around. In Thane's case, it felt like forever before he heard the heavy stomping of boots racing toward his cell.

Finally, he felt the fellow convict wrenched off of him by a guard who had placed his baton against the man's neck while another guard entered his cell and grabbed the wrist holding the shiv. The two men jerked Thane's assailant away and flung him to the ground, while a third guard called out for medical assistance.

A piercing whistle signaled the other inmates to immediately return to their cells as lock-down procedures were implemented. Everyone in the vicinity moved from one place to another. Everyone except Thane. He laid on his cot, wanting nothing more than to close his eyes and go to sleep, despite someone now at his side yelling at him to stay awake.

But Thane no longer wanted to stay awake. He was ready to leave this place, and now seemed like the perfect opportunity. He had already lost his freedom, had already lost Hannah, so losing his life seemed almost insignificant in comparison.

But fate had other plans for Thane Banning.

Five years later, Thane stood in front of his full-length bedroom mirror, looking at the still visible scars on his chest and abdomen.

He cursed himself for allowing the memory of that day to play itself out in his mind, although it was hard not to think about it when the remnants of the attack were so visible. Besides, if he was going to remember that brutal scarring, this was an appropriate day to do so.

He hurriedly buttoned up his white dress shirt, once again covering up the memories, and started putting on his tie. He was to give a eulogy in less than two hours, and he couldn't afford to stand there reliving the past, even if the man whose eulogy he was scheduled to give was the man responsible for Thane being attacked. If it hadn't been for Joseph Crowell, Thane never would have gone to prison.

But when it was all said and done, Joseph was now dead while Thane remained standing, albeit scarred and more than a little bitter.

Thane looked out at the rows of solemn faces and took a deep breath. He felt more uncomfortable than he expected. Not nervous, but uncomfortable. And more than a little hypocritical—but that was to be expected, given the circumstances.

The mourners at St. Vincent de Paul Roman Catholic Church watched Thane closely, not just to hear him give the eulogy, but because for many, it was their first opportunity to see the man who had all but blown up the L.A. District Attorney's office two weeks earlier. Thane had grown used to being stared at over the past several months, but that was when people thought he was a cold-blooded killer, an unjust reputation he had been branded with more than five years ago.

People now watched him with respect, viewing him as a man vindicated after serving years for a murder he didn't commit. Of course, the irony wasn't lost on Thane. After all, he was now speaking at the funeral of a man whose death he helped orchestrate.

"Joseph Crowell was a force of nature," Thane said to the rapt onlookers. "More of a tornado than a hurricane. With a hurricane, one can predict its arrival, track its path. A tornado, on the other hand, is a surprise. Unpredictable, unexpected, and traveling a course known only to itself. That was Joseph."

Of the thousands of churches in Los Angeles, St. Vincent's was the most beautiful; Joseph had loved buildings that made a statement. The church seated over a thousand, but Thane guessed there were more than that in attendance, with people standing packed together at the back of the church and along each side. If any funeral was considered the social event of the season, it was this one.

Thane spent several evenings writing, then discarding, draft upon draft of Joseph's eulogy. It shouldn't have been that difficult: it was obvious which things to talk about, and which to avoid.

Of course, he would note how Joseph gave him his first job, convincing him that real estate law was the direction to go after he'd graduated law school. Thane would talk about the friendship that had developed over the years between them. How Joseph often went far above and beyond the role of a boss, acting more like a mentor—

perhaps even a father—and giving him his job back after Thane had served five years on death row before getting himself released.

It was Joseph who had been responsible for the murder for which Thane had been convicted. "When I got released from prison, Joseph believed in me when few people did. There was Joseph—and of course my wife Hannah—and that was about it."

Several in the congregation dropped their eyes toward their programs or their feet... anywhere but at Thane.

"Joseph was there for me at the beginning, and he was there for me at the end, and that pretty much sums up my friend. If fact, in a way, it was his commitment to helping me that got him killed."

Thane hesitated as he looked down at his notes, taking a deep breath while everyone looked on. He didn't pause to remember his next line, or to summon the strength to carry on with the eulogy. He did so to show despair at the death of his friend.

It was the role he needed to play.

"I wish I hadn't told Joseph I'd be working that night," Thane said, as he looked down at the podium in front of him. "Or that I'd decided to pack one more box before leaving so Joseph wouldn't have been out on the street trying to get into my office to see me."

Thane looked up and saw Hannah sitting in the third row, her eyes moist, watching him with compassion. He remembered his wife's stunned expression after Thane had been informed by the police about Joseph's death. She'd held him tight, sharing what she assumed was his need for solace. She was there for him.

She'd always been there for him.

"I tell myself that Joseph lived more in his fifty-eight years than most people do who live to be a hundred. He was the lawyer most developers turned to for the largest and most beautiful construction projects in this great city of Los Angeles."

Thane couldn't help but smile.

"When I was in college, I had an opportunity to spend a few days in Washington D.C., where I saw the Washington Monument and the Lincoln Memorial, majestic tributes to incredible men. I know I'll think of Joseph every time I drive past the one-of-a-kind buildings here in L.A. he helped make possible."

Thane paused, then added, "Not that he would feel comfortable being compared to Washington or Lincoln. Knowing Joseph, I'm guessing he'd feel I was selling him a bit short."

The church flooded with laughter.

Thane smiled as he looked out at the packed pews. He figured even Joseph would have enjoyed that line, assuming he wasn't pissed at how it all went down.

He slowly scanned the crowd and noticed Detective Vince Struthers sitting near the back of the church, watching Thane with a hardened stare.

Prior to having spent five years in Forsman Penitentiary, Thane likely would have made eye contact with the detective. But Thane had learned not to reveal anything while in prison: not surprise, not confusion, and definitely not fear.

But that didn't stop his pulse from ramping up a few beats.

Struthers was the lead detective assigned to Joseph's murder. Thane had first encountered Struthers during the trial of Scotty "Skunk" Burns, the case that had exonerated Thane. The detective had testified in that case, and Thane had been impressed by the man, who struck him as one of the top detectives on the L.A. police force.

Thane secretly wished that any other detective had been assigned to Joseph's case.

While Joseph had worked with a wide range of people, he mostly associated with the richest and most powerful developers in the city which, unfortunately, meant most of the people in the church that day were white, male faces. But Struthers didn't stand out solely because he was Black. He had a presence about him. He was a force to be reckoned with, and it unsettled Thane to see the detective studying him so closely.

"So to my friend," Thane concluded, "I say we will miss you. We will mourn for you. But mostly, we will celebrate you. Like a tornado, you were impossible to miss as you swept amongst us. But rather than causing destruction, you simply carried many of us along for the ride, swirled around by the force of your personality, and leaving us a bit dazed—but exhilarated—by the ride. I will never, ever forget the impact you had on my life."

As he spoke this final line, Thane felt confident everyone listening would interpret it one way, but Thane knew what it meant to him. Now, however, he wondered if Detective Struthers would hear the words the way Thane wanted everyone else to hear them, or if he took them in differently.

Thane knew this was not the time to be clever.

2

FIVE MONTHS LATER

Thane parked in front of the decrepit apartment building that had always reminded him of photos he'd seen of grim, cheaply made communist housing complexes in Siberia from the 1950s. The apartment on Crenshaw was where he and Hannah had lived for the past year, the same apartment where she had landed almost five years earlier when Thane was sent to prison.

But despite the decay that defined the place, they had started their life anew in that small, dark apartment. And while he wouldn't miss the place, it had served them well, providing them refuge from a hostile city.

Besides, after spending five years in Forsman Penitentiary, the apartment was like moving into the Ritz. Or at least a Holiday Inn.

Thane stepped off the elevator on the sixth floor and went to their old apartment one last time to pick up the few remaining boxes that hadn't yet been moved to their new home. He stood in the tiny living room and thought about how far he and his wife had come during this past year. It was a life he hadn't believed possible while on death row, yet here he was.

"I'm surprised you want to spend any more time than you have to in this place."

Thane turned and saw JoElla Williams standing in his doorway. A stocky Black woman in her mid-60s, JoElla lived directly across the hall, having lived in her tiny apartment for over thirty years. Her bright blue apron clashed with her lime green house dress, a streak of flour dusting the bangs of her hair.

"Hard as it is to believe," Thane said, "there are things about this place I'm going to miss."

"You're right, that is hard to believe." She looked around at the peeling wallpaper as the sound of old man Watkins bellowing at his wife in the apartment below filled the room for a moment. "How many things you think you're going to miss?"

Thane laughed. "Well, there's you. And..." He paused, struggling to think of a second one.

"Yeah, that's what I thought," JoElla said, stepping into the apartment. "I'm so glad I caught you. I wanted to wish you nothing but the best, and to say I'm going to miss having the two of you around. Don't get me wrong, though, if the city gave me the money they gave you, I'd be getting the heck out of Dodge, too."

JoElla had been there from the start, as Hannah made her transition from living in a gorgeous home in Brentwood Heights with a husband who was a real estate development lawyer, to having to move into this fire hazard by herself after Thane was convicted of murder. JoElla had consoled Hannah, watched out for her, was always a shoulder for her to lean on.

On top of that, she had never judged Thane.

9

"I read about you in the paper the other day," she continued. "About the law firm you opened up. Sounds like you're going to be doing some good things. Lot of people given the sort of money you were given would probably just go buy an island or something, so good for you for trying to help people."

JoElla walked over and looked out Thane's living room window. Then, she sighed.

"So I suppose you're going to focus on helping people charged with murder, or big crimes like that? The sort of thing you went through?" she finally asked.

"I want to try to help people who need it." He watched JoElla nod as she continued looking out at the street below. "Are you by chance in need of some help?"

She brushed her hands on the front of her apron as she turned back to him. "Truth be told, I am, but this is such a piddling bit of nothing compared to what you're going to be doing now, I'm embarrassed to say anything. But it is worrying me something fierce."

"If there's anything I can do to help you, I'd love the opportunity. You were always so gracious to me when everyone else made me feel like Ted Bundy."

"You're rich now. Maybe you can thank her with money," a tall, skinny ten-year-old girl said. She leaned against the door frame looking satisfied and exuding a self-confidence Thane didn't think he'd achieved until he was well out of college.

JoElla walked quickly over to the girl. "Hush! Haven't you already caused me enough embarrassment?" She put her arm around the girl's shoulder and ushered her into the apartment. "Mr. Banning, this is my granddaughter, Cricket. She moved in with me two weeks ago and has already managed to cause two years' worth of problems."

Thane smiled at the girl. "Nice to meet you, Cricket. How'd you get your nickname?"

The girl looked at her grandmother and raised her eyebrows, as if they had just encountered the village idiot. She then turned back to Thane, unamused. "That's not my nickname. That's my name. My mama named me Cricket. You got anything else funny you want to say about that?"

Thane flushed. "Sorry. I didn't mean anything by it. It's just a very unique name."

"Well, Thane isn't exactly Joe or Bob. You named after the god of thunder or something?"

"I believe you're thinking of Thor."

"Thor. Thane. Same diff." She pulled a phone from her front pocket and started looking at something she obviously found far more interesting than Thane, although he figured that could include a blank screen.

Thane turned his attention back to JoElla, more than happy to get back to an adult conversation. "So what sort of problem are you dealing with?" He glanced toward Cricket. "Besides the obvious."

Cricket raised her eyes away from her phone just long enough to fire a visual dagger his way.

"Cricket here is a bright young lady, which makes me very proud most of the time, but there are occasions when she's a little too bright. When it comes to hacking into things, for example, she can be a bit of a troublemaker."

"I prefer the term 'prodigy,' Grams."

"I'm sure you do, dear," JoElla said. "And apparently, unbeknownst to me, she found a way to hack into our cable system in order to get us free television."

"That's because you don't get any of the premium channels," the girl scoffed. "And that's where 'Chip and Chad' are."

"Who're Chip and Chad?" Thane asked.

Cricket looked at him like he was speaking in tongues. "Who's Chip and..." She slapped a hand to her forehead. "Sorry, I forgot. You probably didn't get premium channels in prison either, did you? Guess you and I got that in common."

"Cricket!" her grandmother exclaimed.

"Chip and Chad do home makeovers," the girl explained. "They're white guys—like you couldn't already tell by their names—and they usually fix up homes of rich white folk who already live in mansions. Why don't those shows ever come to places like this and do a makeover for people like us who really need it? But whatever. Anyway, what the cable company charges is stupid, and since Grams always tells me when I see something I want, I should go for it—"

"In an aspirational way, not by stealing!" JoElla shook her head. "The other day I got a letter from the cable company saying they're pressing charges and that they'll do everything in their power to make sure Cricket gets a harsh punishment."

"It's a bluff, Grams. Let's call it."

"Mr. Banning, I can't afford to hire a lawyer, and I can't afford to pay any penalty. What happens if the cable company decides—"

"Let me look into it and I'll see what I can do. I'm guessing we'll be able to figure something out."

"Or you could just pay off the cable company," the self-proclaimed prodigy said, shrugging her shoulders.

"You're rich now, ain't you?"

"Or we can try to get you enlisted in the army and sent overseas," Thane countered. "The cable company likely wouldn't be able find you in another country."

Cricket looked at her grandmother, surprised, then set fiery eyes back on Thane. "You're supposed to be more patient with kids. I'm going out on a limb here and guessing you don't have any."

"Yep, and right now I'm feeling like that was a smart decision."

Thane struggled to hold a large cardboard box while attempting to open the front door to his and Hannah's new home. Rather than put the box down, he lifted one knee and balanced it on his leg, trying to hold it steady with his left hand while his right hand fished around helplessly for the key in his pocket. It would have been easier to set the box down, but by now it was a matter of personal pride.

In the end, physics won. The box tumbled onto the porch. He finally found the key, opened the door, and kicked the box through the doorway.

Their house, which they had moved into a few weeks earlier, was a gorgeous Tudor-style two-story. Following Thane's settlement with the city, they could have afforded something considerably larger and far gaudier, but neither Thane nor Hannah wanted anything too over-the-top. This house was considerably more modest than their first home, but exponentially nicer than the hovel they had just moved out of.

Other than having Hannah with him, his most important requirement was that the house have a lot of windows. This one had floor-to-ceiling windows in the living room and their master bedroom, as well as a sunroom that looked out onto their back yard.

Spending twenty-three hours a day for five years inside a prison cell that looked out at a jaundiced cement wall made windows a top priority.

He was about to call out to Hannah when he heard her talking quietly in their bedroom. He walked down the hallway and leaned against the doorframe, watching his wife in her black slip as she put on ruby earrings and a beautiful gold necklace she had gotten from her mother ages ago. She was talking to herself as she looked in the mirror, fiddling with one of the earrings as she spoke, unaware of Thane's presence.

"Muhammed Ali said that 'service to others is the rent you pay for your room here on earth.' So, through your participation in tonight's gala, you are not only providing a service to others, but you are also helping provide a room for abused women who have turned to East L.A.'s Shelter for Assistance. Thanks to you people…" She paused, shook her head, and emitted a growl of frustration. "Thanks to people like you…"

"Actually, I prefer 'thanks to you people,'" Thane said, startling Hannah as he walked into the room.

"Of course you do."

"Or, even better, maybe 'you's peeps.' Really show them that you're just plain folk."

"Great," she said, laughing. "Now you know there's probably a fifty-fifty chance it will come out 'you's peeps.'"

14

"I'll give you a dollar if you do it," he said and sat on the edge of their bed.

"And I'll give you a fat lip." She put her face in her hands and sighed, then looked back up at herself in the mirror. "Why did I agree to do this? I'm not a public speaker. What if I mess up? What if people absolutely hate it? What if they hate *me*?"

"They're not going to hate you. They wouldn't have asked you to be the keynote speaker if you weren't their superstar volunteer. Besides, I've experienced universal hatred by large groups of people. Yours doesn't feel so bad."

"Are you going to do that every time I get frustrated with something? Compare my troubles to what you dealt with? If so, then no fair." She walked over and kissed him on the top of his head. "Besides, people don't hate you anymore, whereas there's no guarantee the people attending this gala won't despise me for the rest of my life."

She walked back over to the mirror and picked up a tube of lipstick.

"Did you get the rest of the boxes? Were you at least of *some* use to me?"

"Mission accomplished. I also had a chance to say goodbye to JoElla, and I met her granddaughter."

"Granddaughter? What was she like?"

"Let's just say it might be best we don't have kids." But the second Thane said it, he wished he could take it back.

Hannah looked over her shoulder at him and spoke matter-of-factly, "Our child wouldn't be any trouble at all. Our child would be perfect."

15

"Is that right?" Thane wanted desperately to change the subject, but didn't know how to do so without being obvious.

"How could she not be?"

"Oh, it's a she?"

"Or a he. I always pictured a little girl, but whatever the case, she or he will be perfect." Thane couldn't help but notice the warm smile that appeared on Hannah's lips whenever she talked about having a child.

"A little girl who would grow up thinking the proper term is 'you's peeps,'" Thane said with a grin.

"Stop that!" Hannah shouted, then started to laugh. "If I say that tonight, you're going to be sleeping out in the shed."

"We don't have a shed."

"Then I'll hire someone to build one, and trust me, mister, you'll be sleeping in it. Now go take a shower. We need to be out the door in an hour."

"Yes, ma'am."

Thane hopped off the bed and headed toward the bathroom, happy to make an escape. This wasn't the first time Hannah brought up the topic of having kids, and Thane always felt awkward—and more than a little guilty—making light of it and trying to steer the conversation to something else. He knew Hannah wanted to talk more seriously about it, but she wasn't pressing it. He could see that time coming, though, when they would have to discuss it without making jokes.

They had decided it was time to start a family a few months before Thane was sent away to prison. They both talked excitedly at the prospect before their plan—their entire world—was blown apart. Then Thane got himself released, and from that point on he and Hannah had slowly and deliberately worked to try to reclaim their lives.

Now that they were in their new home, it was almost starting to feel like they were ready to resume their normal life together, which made the question of kids an understandable one.

But the possibility of being sent back to prison weighed heavily on Thane. He knew Hannah sensed his fear that their life could be uprooted once again, but she assumed it was a reaction to the trauma Thane had experienced. She never blamed him for feeling that way, but also believed it was based on emotion and not something concrete.

But it *was* based on something concrete. Joseph's murder was concrete. Thane's role in it was concrete.

And he couldn't explain that to Hannah.

3

Gus and his two friends leaned against a brick wall under the awning of Jackson's Pharmacy, desperate to get out of an October sun that was far hotter than usual this time of year. It was too hot in South L.A. to do much of anything but watch the movement of their neighborhood, which looked as lethargic as they felt in the heat.

But sometimes lethargic was good. Sometimes lethargic meant fewer gunshots in that part of town.

Eighteen years old, Gus was tall and slender, with wholesome good looks that would likely stick with him as he grew older, given he didn't fall into the wrong crowd and get his cheeks sliced. He wore a generic pair of blue jeans, a white Fruit of the Loom t-shirt and old Nikes. He didn't come from a household with much discretionary income, but he also didn't feel the need to be flashing the latest fashion to be comfortable with himself.

Andre, on the other hand, looked like he belonged in a Kendrick Lamar music video. A gold chain dangled from his neck, catching the sun whenever he leaned outside the safety of the awning's shade. Gus was fairly sure the chain was real gold, especially if it turned out to be a gift from Andre's brother.

Jamie, a short white kid, was dealing with a case of

acne that looked like a biblical plague. His clothes were similar to Andre's, although on Jamie, the baggy jeans and extra-large t-shirt made him look like a Shar Pei.

"So I told her, you oughta stick close to me, baby, 'cause I can show you what's what around here." Jamie grinned as he talked about the new girl in the neighborhood who he had immediately latched onto. "I said if she didn't stick close, she might find herself in all sorts of trouble. So she should stick close. That's what I kept saying: stick close."

"Subtle, man. You thinking that's some sort of subliminal shit? That she'll suddenly want to be close to you?" Gus couldn't help but laugh.

"Just wait and see. That girl will be all over me."

"She'll be over you all right, soon as she gets to know you." Andre shook his head. "And what do you mean, you can show her what's what around here? You think you're plugged into things around here?"

"What are you talking about? I'm just as street as you guys."

Gus burst out laughing. "Says the rich white kid."

"First of all," Andre added, "the fact that you're saying you're street shows you ain't street. Only people using that term are ignorant white kids trying to sound cool."

"Hey," Gus jumped in, "maybe you can get a t-shirt that says 'I'm Street'. That would be bitchin'. Or at least, I'm assuming you also still say things like bitchin'."

Gus and Andre burst out laughing while Jamie stammered.

"Why you all up in my ass about this? Just cause I'm white doesn't mean I don't know things."

"Yeah, but what you know is probably about fiduciary bonds and Dow Jones," Andre said.

"Damn, man, why you gotta—"

"Ah, lighten up," Gus said and lightly punched Jamie on the shoulder. "We're just having fun."

Gus and Andre had been friends since they were five and had brought Jamie into their fold a couple of years ago. Jamie's family was relatively new to the area—part of the gentrification of the neighborhood—but he was okay. A little privileged, but okay.

"You're good, man," Andre agreed. "We wouldn't hang with you if you weren't." Andre looked at his phone and pushed himself away from the store front. "But seriously, man, you have to stop saying you're street."

"You out of here?" Gus asked.

"Yeah, it's too hot to be hanging outside. Plus, I gotta go sign up with some SAT tutor my mom thinks I should use. School counselor says I'm going to be fine without it, but mom doesn't want to take any chances."

Jamie grabbed his backpack from the sidewalk and pulled out a brown paper bag. "Hey, Andre, I need you to do me a favor. I borrowed these video games from a guy and I promised I'd get them back to him today, but I gotta meet my dad downtown. Mind dropping them off for me?"

Andre shook his head. "Man, I look like Uber Eats to you? Take 'em back yourself."

"I would, but my dad works in the other direction from this guy and I'm already running late. Besides, you remember the other day when you were short on cash at lunch, and I covered you? You said you owed me, so I'm just asking you for this small favor. He's on the way to your house."

"But I ain't heading home. I was going to—ah, shit. Give me the damn games." Andre snatched the bag.

"Where's he live?"

"Just across Woodlawn on South Harlan. Small purple house. It's like three blocks from your place."

"Yeah, but again, I wasn't going home. But whatever. Don't start acting like I'm one of those guys carrying a 'will work for food' sign."

"You know it's not like that. If I wasn't meeting my—"

"I'll take 'em," Gus said, reaching over and taking the bag from Andre. "I'm heading that way."

"N—no," Jamie stuttered, then fell silent.

"Really?" Andre asked Gus. "Appreciate it. Sure it's not a problem?"

"But Andre owes me." Jamie's face flushed between the already crimson patches of acne.

"What's the big deal?" Gus asked, snatching the bag from Andre. "This way he'll still owe you. Maybe he can teach you how to be more street."

Gus cut through Woodlawn Cemetery, relishing the shade provided by the trees and taking in the smell of fresh cut grass. The small cemetery bordered an industrial area north of the 91 freeway which, combined with an ever-growing homeless presence, defied the phrase 'Rest In Peace.'

He looked in the bag and saw an old X-Box version of Mortal Combat, two versions of Call of Duty, and a Grand Theft Auto that looked like it dated back to the Playstation 2 era. He was surprised Jamie even had a console that would still play these relics. If he got jumped in the cemetery, whoever grabbed the bag was going to be sorely disappointed.

He exited the cemetery and hit Harlan Avenue. All the houses up and down the street looked like they'd been designed by the same disinterested architect—tiny single-story, wood-paneled houses with one small living room window in the front.

He immediately spotted a dirty purple house that looked like it should have been torn down years ago. At least a quarter of the paint had peeled off, with the rest appearing to be held on solely by the dirt coating the wood. A white cable company van sat across the street from the house.

Gus made his way up to the front door and knocked, then took a step back and held up one of the games from the bag, holding it next to his chest so it would be visible through the peephole. He wanted to do whatever he could to reassure anyone on the other side who might be wondering why a young Black man was knocking on their door.

The front door opened just wide enough for a bald head the size of a bowling ball to lean out. The guy wore a dirty, sleeveless undershirt and red and blue striped boxer shorts. The stench emanating from the living room smelled like a day's worth of farts and Del Taco.

"You Jamie's friend?"

"Yeah. He asked me to drop these off."

As Gus handed the bag over, the back door of the cable van across the street burst open. Four of LAPD's finest poured onto the street and rushed the front door. The guy in the house froze, lurched away from the bag, and ducked back inside.

"Freeze!" two of the cops shouted. Their drawn guns made more of an impression on Gus, who knew to immediately raise his hands in the air and not take so much as a breath, despite his sudden urge to run.

One of the cops dragged Gus onto the front lawn while the others knocked on the front door, then kicked it in before giving the guy inside a chance to answer. Within a minute, the bald guy was shoved out the front door, hands cuffed behind his back.

The cop who stayed with Gus cuffed him and started pulling the plastic boxes out of the bag.

"They're video games!" Gus shouted.

"That bag ain't mine," the bald guy said. "It's the kid's. I've never seen him before. Ask him, he'll tell you."

The cop opened one of the video game boxes and pulled out several small bags of white powder, holding them up like he was appraising a diamond.

"Funny," the cop said. "The games I buy don't ever seem to come with coke in them. This a special edition?"

"They're not mine," Gus stammered. "I was just dropping it off for a friend."

"Right," the cop said as he lifted Gus up off the ground and directed him toward one of the police cars that had pulled up during the bust. "Your brother is going to be so pissed at you."

Gus turned his head around as far as he could, trying to look at the cop behind him. "My brother? I don't have a brother."

"Of course you don't," the cop said, chuckling as he pushed Gus forward. He then leaned closer and lowered his voice. "But you and I both know he's not going to be happy about this."

Gus sat handcuffed in a claustrophobic interrogation room, a chain linking his cuffs to a metal ring bolted to the table.

He had only been in a room like this once before, when he was twelve and a woman accused him of stealing her cell phone, a phone she'd conveniently found in her purse after Gus was hauled off by a neighborhood cop. The woman acted as though Gus should be grateful she even came down to the station to tell them it was her mistake—a lot of people wouldn't have taken the time to make the trip.

And Gus had actually said thank you.

He hadn't been handcuffed at the time, however, and the cop sitting across from him hadn't acted as though he legally owned Gus. The same couldn't be said of the narcotics detective now leaning back in his chair, looking like he had all the time in the world.

Detective David Mahone stared at Gus as though he was trying to classify and categorize him for a high school project. Mahone was dressed far more fashionably than any of the other plainclothes detectives Gus had seen around the station. He had the cocky good looks of someone who had been star quarterback in high school and president of his fraternity in college, although Gus doubted he'd gone to college. He seemed like the kind of guy anxious to get out into the world and get started, rather than spending four more years trying to learn impractical things.

Mahone had been questioning Gus for the last half hour, but whenever Gus got to certain parts of his story, Mahone shook his head ever so slightly.

"I need you to clarify your story a bit more for me," Mahone said, expressionless.

"What else do you want me to say? I already told you everything I remember."

"No, all you told me was that some punk named Jamie gave you the drugs."

"I didn't know they were drugs," Gus said for what he felt was the fiftieth time. He wasn't looking to rat out Jamie, but these charges were serious enough that he wasn't going to take the blame for drugs that weren't his.

"But they *were* drugs, and you were caught delivering them. What I need from you is to admit that it was your buddy Andre who gave them to you to deliver."

"No, like I said before, Andre didn't have—"

Mahone held up his hand. "No, you took the bag from Andre. Andre gave you the bag, and you took it. You delivered the contents of the bag for Andre. Notice how there is no Jamie in this story. There is only Andre, and there is you, and one of you is in a shitload of trouble."

"Andre didn't have anything to do with it."

Mahone sighed, closed his eyes, and lifted his head toward the ceiling like he was trying to get a tan from the overhead lights.

"Let me try one more time to summarize where things stand. You delivered a sizable amount of coke to a small-time dealer. An amount that makes it a federal offense, which means you're looking at twenty years easy. I also have the guy you gave it to willing to sign an affidavit testifying you are a fairly major drug distributor in that part of the city."

"What? I've never had anything to do with drugs in my—"

Mahone held up his hand. "I can only go on what he's saying".

"Just like you're wanting me to tell you Andre gave me the drugs, even though it's not true."

"Then don't tell me he did it, but you and I both know he has connections to drugs. He knows some mighty bad people, and you'll be doing the time instead of him. Although, neither of you have to do any time if you just play nice and give me what I want."

Gus looked at the detective, the pieces finally falling into place.

"You're after Andre's brother, aren't you? That's why the cop said what he did about my brother being pissed. He thought I was Andre. You know I didn't do anything wrong, and you probably know Andre didn't do anything wrong. You want his brother."

"What I want is to get as many drugs off the street as I can, and if that means putting you away and making sure you don't get out until you're well past your mid-life crisis, then that's what I'll do. But you and I both know there's a better play here that you can make. Andre gave you the drugs. It's a short story, but usually those are the most powerful."

Gus didn't like being bullied, and he didn't like being set up, but he also didn't like the idea of being sent to prison for decades. He knew far too many stories on the street about guys like himself who were doing a hell of a lot of years behind bars because they wouldn't give the cops what they wanted.

And because they were Black.

But Gus couldn't say Andre gave him the drugs. He wouldn't. Not just because Andre was his friend, and not because it wasn't true. Gus also wanted to stay alive, and falsely ratting out Andre was not the way to accomplish that.

Not as long as Andre's brother was involved.

"I want to call my mom."

Mahone looked at Gus with disappointment. He sighed and rose from his chair.

"Fine. Call your mama. But be sure to tell her that with any luck, the next time you'll be able to give her a hug will be when she turns eighty."

And with that, Mahone left the room and slammed the door behind him.

4

The International Ballroom at the Beverly Hilton was packed, although emitting a different vibe from when it hosted stars from the Grammys each year. Fundraising for a shelter for abused women brought a different dynamic. For one thing, there weren't any 60-year-old men wearing leather pants, which was a positive thing.

Thane and Hannah had been placed at a table with four other couples, the men in tuxedos and the women in expensive gowns. Since Hannah was one of the main speakers, their table was right next to the stage, with the remaining seventy-five tables set up anywhere from eight feet to a lightyear away from theirs.

Thane considered the lackluster meal in front of him: a generic chicken dish that epitomized hotel banquet dinners across the country, although compared to what was offered in prison, it was like dining at a 5-star restaurant. Whenever possible, he tried to avoid comparing everything with his time in prison, although it did keep him grateful.

But even focusing on his dinner plate, he knew he was being watched.

From the moment he entered the ballroom, dozens of eyes followed him, people nudging their partners as he passed. He wondered if movie stars ever got used to the constant surveillance.

Evie Cannon, the executive director of East L.A.'s Shelter for Assistance, and her husband were seated at their table, as were three other couples who were major donors to the cause. The donors appeared pleased to be seated at the same table as Thane, as if that was one of the perks that came from writing large checks. While their pedigree kept them from asking him about his experience, they now had a story to share with their rich friends.

"So, Thane," Evie said, "I'm assuming you know how much of a godsend Hannah has been to the Shelter. While we greatly appreciate all our volunteers, sometimes it's a bit of a crapshoot in terms of the level of commitment and competency people have. But on the first day of her orientation, I could tell Hannah was going to be our, shall we say, informal leader."

"I know I'd follow her anywhere," Thane agreed.

"Not to yoga," Hannah said, turning to Evie. "I've been trying to get him to come to a yoga class with me. He focuses solely on weights at home, and I think it would help him to work a bit more on flexibility."

"Yes, I'm afraid I'm a bit inflexible when it comes to flexibility."

The conversation eventually withered away, and everyone went back to working their way through the chicken. As Thane studied his plate to see if he wanted to take one more shot at it, a hand clamped solidly onto his right shoulder. The tight grip caused Thane to react out of instinct—his left hand swept over his shoulder, firmly grasping a thick wrist. His right hand reached for his steak knife.

Fortunately, Hannah quickly placed her hand over Thane's wrist, her soft touch enough to make him aware of the situation.

Thane let go of the wrist, and the large tuxedoed man took a half-step back, obviously caught off-guard by Thane's reaction. Thane turned and stood, immediately extending his hand and offering up his warmest smile.

"Sorry about that. You startled me."

The man flinched, then cautiously took Thane's hand and tried offering up a smile of his own, although his lips quivered.

"No, I'm the one who should apologize. I just saw you over here and wanted to say how much my wife and I have been cheering for you ever since you were released from prison."

"Thank you. That's very kind of you." Thane was fairly certain the man and his wife actually supported him after it was proven he was innocent, and not right when he was released from prison.

Nobody had.

"And I wanted to congratulate you on your settlement with the city. What happened to you was terrible, but given how things turned out, there's a small part of me that wonders if in the long run it didn't turn out alright. I mean, all that money, you know? In a way, you made almost five million dollars in jail, not counting the funding for your new firm. That's a pretty healthy wage, regardless of the work environment, am I right?"

Thane stared at the man, trying to come up with a response that wouldn't make anyone feel awkward.

"You've never been to prison before, have you." Thane shook the man's hand again and gently turned him, like a dancer guiding his partner, letting him know it was time to be on his way. "Enjoy the rest of your evening."

As Thane sat back down, Hannah leaned over and whispered in his ear, "Thank you for not stabbing him in the neck. Although I suppose that would have taken the focus off my speech."

"Anything for you, sweetheart. I guess I need to keep reminding myself that people here probably aren't trying to sneak up from behind to kill me."

"No, tonight I think the chicken is the only thing you need to worry about."

"And I want to conclude by saying it's easy to only focus on what's wrong with the world—on all of the unfairness that exists—but we can't stop doing whatever we can to make it better."

Hannah stood on the main stage behind a podium, the spotlight illuminating her in the otherwise darkened room.

"We can't just complain; we need to contribute by doing whatever is within our ability, whether that's the gift of time, or by contributing money."

The crowd chuckled at her transparency in emphasizing the need for donations. She paused as she looked up at the audience, knowing as well as anyone that none of the big donors in the room were going to be showing up at the Shelter the next day offering to take out the trash.

"I have seen others with less than I have, helping others, not wavering from the moral compass that directs their actions. It's people like you," she glanced down at Thane, "who keep me doing what I can to help those less fortunate. Thank you, from the bottom of my heart, for your continued support of the Shelter."

Hannah stepped away from the microphone to a wave of applause. Thane gave her a thumbs up as Evie walked onto the stage and gave her a hug.

Thane wished he could be half the person Hannah was. He felt like his moral compass was spinning out of control as he searched desperately for his true north, and he wondered how long her image of him as a good man would last. After Evie thanked everyone for coming, the lights went up and most of the people stood, some taking the opportunity to get one last drink for the road. Thane nodded to the donors at his table as they said goodnight and wished him well.

Hannah remained on the stage, talking to a small crowd gathered around her, so Thane waited nearby, nursing his second glass of wine.

Then, he heard a voice soaked with hostility.

"I want you to know you ruined a good man."

He turned and saw a 60-something, rotund man holding a cocktail and an apparent grudge. His face was flushed and sweating, even though the air conditioning was on full blast. The man walked up to Thane and stood a little closer than was comfortable.

"I'm Barry Warlick, Associate District Attorney for the city of Los Angeles. I worked with Bradford Stone for over twenty years. He was a good man, and now he's been run out of office because of you."

The last thing Thane wanted was to cause a scene at Hannah's event, so he kept his cool, despite wanting to tell this man that Bradford Stone was out of office because of decisions he himself had made.

"Brad Stone is a good man, and was a hell of a good DA," Warlick continued, the alcohol turning 'hell of a good' into one slurred word. "You didn't know him like I did."

"I'm sure that's true," Thane said. "My only direct experience with him was when he sent me to death row for a murder he knew I didn't commit, and then later when he falsified evidence against my client who, once again, he knew to be innocent. But other than those two interactions, I don't really know him all that well."

Warlick looked as though he wanted to throw his drink at Thane's face, but probably didn't want to part with something so important. Instead, Warlick wobbled ever-so-slightly and took a deep breath.

"Well, you ended up doing alright financially, so maybe you don't have all that much to complain about."

"So I keep hearing."

Warlick shook his head in disgust. "I can't believe the city settled with you so quickly. If it had been me, I would have dragged this out as long as possible. Kept you from your big payday for years."

"Well actually, my big payday was getting out of prison. But as for the settlement, if you were in charge of negotiations, I would have insisted the entire twenty-million-dollar check be made out directly to me, which would have resulted in far more negative press for you and your department. Instead, the city was able to say that the vast majority of the money was earmarked to create a law firm to represent people at risk of falling through the cracks, which made your department actually look like it was part of the solution."

"Maybe the cracks are there for a reason. Maybe some people deserve to fall through them."

Thane started to respond when a calm voice interrupted them. "And maybe it's time for a cup of coffee."

Thane and Warlick turned and saw a tall, Black woman in a gorgeous, dark red dress. Her bright gold jewelry wasn't quite enough to draw attention away from her eyes, which seemed to reflect as much light as her necklace. She looked like she had stepped directly from the pages of the L.A. Times' annual "Power Issue" highlighting Los Angeles's movers and shakers.

Warlick nodded at the woman. "Angela," he said, then turned with a huff and headed away toward the bar.

"I sort of figured he wouldn't go for the coffee suggestion," Angela said as they watched Warlick weave between the various tables on his way toward the exit and, hopefully, a designated driver.

"I apologize for my colleague," she said and extended her hand, which Thane shook. "I'm Angela Day. I replaced Brad Stone as the new DA."

"I know. I've read about you. I was planning to reach out to congratulate you, but figured I'd give you some time to settle in."

"That might be a while. Thanks to you, I'm afraid there's quite a bit of settling that still needs to be done."

"Well, that was the other reason I hadn't reached out yet. I wasn't sure how any messages from me would go over in your office. Based on my brief interaction with

Barry, I'm guessing not so well."

"It's safe to say there's a wide range of opinions, but my sense is the vast majority in the DA's office are angry at Bradford, not you. He embarrassed them and made it that much harder for them to do our important work. People were appalled at what happened to you and don't wish you ill, nor should they. Of course," she said, looking across the room toward the exit through which Barry Warlick had walked, "there are outliers."

"Well, I appreciate you intervening."

"I believe that's your wife up there?" Angela looked up at Hannah, who was still surrounded by coworkers from the Shelter. Hannah glanced over at Thane and smiled, then gave Angela a nod of the head.

"Yep, that's her."

"You're a lucky man."

"Never a doubt in my mind."

"I'll leave you to go congratulate her, but I would love the opportunity for us to sit and talk sometime soon. Perhaps we can collaborate on something as we work to improve the overall system. I'm sure we're both in agreement that the process needs to be improved. You especially should agree with that."

She shook his hand firmly again and walked toward the exit.

Thane knew better than to judge anyone based on a five-minute conversation, but given what he had just witnessed, his sense was that the DA's office was in far better hands than it had been under Bradford Stone.

At least, he certainly hoped so.

5

Venice Beach wasn't crowded. Yet.

It was too early for tourists to be up and about, so Thane could run without needing to dodge people walking down the middle of the boardwalk with their eyes glued to their phones. He was nearing the end of his five-mile run and breathing hard.

He looked forward to his morning runs. They helped him maintain the fitness level he had acquired while in prison, but mostly he treasured the freedom he felt as he ran—a contrast to Forsman, where his only option was running around the rock-hard dirt courtyard, between the hours of 3:00 - 4:00 PM and supervised by men with rifles.

He didn't listen to music or podcasts while running. He wanted to hear all the sounds L.A. had to offer—couples laughing, seagulls crying, dogs barking, and people just living life. These weren't noises to block out. They were sounds to embrace.

As he kicked up his pace, Thane approached Venice Beach's outside workout area where a group of preening, grunting bodybuilders each lifted the equivalent of a small grand piano. One man bench-pressed a giggling, bikini-clad girl over his head, using her as a bar bell.

Thane thought that for all their bulk, most of these

guys wouldn't last two minutes in a prison fight.

He then noticed three older men wearing baggy, old t-shirts, working with another set of weights apart from the other lifters. He could tell immediately they'd likely done time, not only from certain tattoos they sported, but simply by how they carried themselves. In prison, the purpose of weights was to increase strength and power. These men weren't looking to draw attention to themselves. They wouldn't be caught dead lifting another person over their head to show how strong they were. They simply showed up, put in their work, then called it a day.

Thane finished his last fifty yards at an all-out sprint, trying to outrun thoughts of prison. When he crossed his imaginary finish line he stopped and bent over, hands on his knees, sweat dripping off his forehead like a soaking hose.

"Want some water?" a familiar voice asked.

Thane froze.

Bradford Stone, L.A.'s former District Attorney, sat on a bench facing the ocean. Thane almost didn't recognize the man wearing a light pink polo shirt and white linen pants. He had never encountered Stone, or even seen a picture of him, without a prim and pressed suit and tie. Stone looked like he hadn't shaved in days, but he looked healthy, displaying a tan he probably hadn't had in years, given the insane number of hours he had spent working in his office as District Attorney.

Stone offered up his water bottle. "You can check the seal. It hasn't been broken. No poison."

"Thanks, but I'm fine."

"Oh come on, take it. Who are you kidding? You've already sweated more in the last minute than is in this bottle. Hydrate. It's good for you."

Thane shrugged and took the bottle, surprising himself by surreptitiously checking the water bottle's seal. "Thanks."

Neither man spoke as Thane chugged down half. Stone leaned back on his bench and looked out at the ocean.

"I come down here most days lately," Stone said. "I had no idea it could be so enjoyable to just sit and watch the ocean and think. Or not think, depending on the day." He stared at the waves crashing onto the beach. "Don't get me wrong, it's probably not a solid long-term plan, but it's been good to have the chance to step away and sort things out."

"You have a lot of sorting to do, I imagine."

"You should know better than anyone, although I suppose after our last encounter, pretty much everyone knows."

Thane offered the remaining half bottle of water back to Stone, but the ex-DA waved it off.

"I've seen you running down here before," Stone said. "At first, I hoped you wouldn't notice me, then eventually I found myself wanting to have a chance to speak to you, but you always ran on past. I figured you saw me and didn't want to stop, but now I'm thinking I just blended into the surroundings."

"I've only seen you wearing things that are overly starched, so you're a bit out of context like this."

Stone smiled and nodded, looking down at his outfit. "Used to be I'd wear a button-down shirt even on weekends. I'm trying something new, although the temperature will have to go above 150 for me to put on a pair of shorts."

"Baby steps," Thane said. "This is a coincidence, because just last night I encountered a former colleague of yours who wasn't too happy with me. He apparently blamed me for everything that's happened to you. Associate DA Gary something?"

"Barry Warlick?"

"That's him."

"I worked with Barry for a long time. Funny thing is, I never really liked Barry, although for whatever reason, he was always rabidly loyal to me. But I obviously don't need—or deserve—anyone sticking up for me. In fact, the reason I started hoping you'd stop is that I wanted to apologize to you. I know that doesn't do a frog's pecker's worth of good to you, but I still at least owe you that."

Thane simply nodded, not disagreeing with anything Stone said, but not knowing how to respond.

"I read about your settlement with the city. That was a clever angle, having them fund your law firm for the next several years. They somehow even came out looking noble, which was no small feat after what I did."

"So what have you been up to, other than sitting by the ocean thinking? It sounds like you aren't going to be charged for what you did."

"No, I don't think so. There was a bit of plea bargaining going on. Obviously, I was fired, publicly flayed, flogged, and fried, but I don't believe there will be any actual charges brought by the city. That would only keep the whole sordid affair in the news. Plus, as ex-District Attorney, I know about a lot of skeletons that others wouldn't want exposed. I'm not saying it's fair, but that's sometimes how it works in a rigged system."

Stone looked as though maybe he felt he'd said too much, so he paused, then looked up at Thane.

"Does that disappoint you?"

"Not really. I wasn't necessarily looking for an eye-for-an-eye. I was just looking for the truth to come out." That, of course, wasn't necessarily true for everyone in the case. Thane took far more than an eye from others—like Joseph, who ended up paying with his life.

"I recognize you could still sue me in a civil trial. You would most likely win."

"I'm not looking to do that, if that's something you've been thinking about as you stare out at the ocean."

"It's been on my mind. And thank you. It's more than I deserve." Stone looked back out at the ocean, lost in thought. "I remember you telling me that if I had done the right thing as far as your client went, you would have been willing to move forward. I have to tell you, I'm a bit skeptical about that."

"It's true."

"But I'll bet you weren't disappointed when I gave you the opportunity to bring me down."

Thane couldn't argue. He relished the opportunity to expose Stone and his actions. And while he told Stone he would have let it drop if he had done the right thing, Thane wasn't sure that was actually true.

"I prefer to think you brought yourself down."

Stone nodded, a sad smile on his face. "I would not argue with that."

"So what do you think you'll do next?"

"I don't know. Maybe I should take up running?" Stone chuckled. "I have time to figure it out. I'm a complete cheapskate, so we've lived pretty frugally for the past several years. Don't get me wrong, I don't have a savings account with the sort of money you recently came into, but I don't have to worry about my next act for a little while."

Thane finished the water and tossed the bottle into a trash can. "I better go. Thanks for the water."

Stone looked up.

"I know there's no reason why you would believe this, and I don't even know why it's important to me to say it, but I want you to know I didn't do what I did solely to save my reputation or for political reasons. I understand that that in no way excuses what I did. If there's one thing I've come to clearly understand these past few months, it's that. But while one likes to think they will always do the right thing, when faced with certain situations, people might be surprised. It's not always a black and white world out there."

"Sometimes it is, though. Sometimes the right thing is very clear."

"But that doesn't mean it's always easy," Stone said, sounding as though he was getting ready to argue. "Sometimes people can justify doing the wrong thing to the point where it feels like the right thing to them. Or at least where they feel it's what needed to be done."

"But that doesn't make it right."

"No, that doesn't make it right. But humans aren't always as good at doing the right thing as we like to think we are. Perhaps you've never really been tested."

"Oh, I feel like I've been tested more than my share," Thane said, stating the obvious.

"And how'd you do?"

But that was a question Thane didn't want to answer.

6

Thane sat in one of the four chairs at the small, round table in his office, once again reminded of how far his practice had come—at least in terms of work environment.

Instead of sitting on a sofa that looked like it came from a crack house, he sat on a leather-cushioned chair with wheels that actually rolled, and at a table that was level, not to mention polished.

Thanks to the generous settlement with the city, Thane moved himself and his team into a far nicer office building. The office wasn't opulent by any stretch of the imagination, but Thane and his team had everything they needed.

Kristin Peterson entered his office at her usual power-walking pace, dropping herself into the chair to the right of Thane and exhaling dramatically.

"Sorry I'm late," she said, "although that's one nice thing about working with Gideon—I never have to worry about being the last one here."

As if on cue, Gideon Spence lumbered into the conference room and slowly lowered himself into a chair. "No need to get here 'til the Queen Bee arrives, otherwise there wouldn't be any agenda items."

"Good morning, team," Thane said, smiling.

"As a matter of fact, I do have an agenda item," Kristin responded to Gideon.

"What are the odds? Don't answer, I was kidding. The odds are a hundred percent."

Kristin ignored Gideon and spoke directly to Thane. "We need to speed up efforts to hire someone to help with the phones. They're ringing non-stop and I'm usually the one stuck answering it."

"I know," Thane said. "I try to pick it up when I can, but—"

"You're often in meetings or fending off interview requests. Yeah, I get it, and I know we're still getting our act together so I'm willing to do more than my fair share, but I don't want to be expected to answer the phone just because I'm a woman. We're not the only two people who work here."

"Gideon doesn't answer the phone, but that's not because he's a man," Thane said. "It's because he has absolutely no social skills." He turned toward his friend. "No offense."

"When you're right, you're right," Gideon replied.

"I've interviewed several applicants but haven't found the right person yet."

"What are you looking for?" Kristin asked.

"Well, I already have an open fire and a canister of gasoline working here, so I thought maybe hiring someone who didn't add to that combustible combination might be nice."

Gideon looked over at Kristin. "Which one you supposin' you are: the fire or the gas?"

"I'm assuming the fire, because I'm hot, and you just sort of smell."

"I have a couple more applicants coming in later this morning," Thane said before things could get out of hand. "Maybe one of them will be a good fit." He turned to Gideon. "You coming across any interesting requests for our services?"

"Nah," the big man said. "Half are dudes who got a DUI. I tell 'em we only take the big splashy cases so Little Miss Sunshine here can get on the news."

After the last case, Thane was glad the two of them had stayed with him. He had no doubt Gideon would stick around. An ex-con with limited employment opportunities, Thane knew his friend would end up back at Forsman if he had to work at a fast-food joint or some other minimum wage gig. But Thane was able to offer him a very good salary, a routine, and respect, all of which he hoped would be enough to keep him out of trouble.

Thane was especially pleased that Kristin had decided to continue working with him. She had graduated from USC Law and passed her bar a couple of months earlier. She was also taking the lead role in helping their previous client, Scotty "Skunk" Burns, with his lawsuit against the city.

Thane first met Kristin when she volunteered to help him with Skunk's case. She felt the exposure she got would help her start off with a corner office after she graduated. When they won Skunk's case, Thane thought there was a good chance she realized there was more to law than a corner office. But in honor of her contributions, he gave her the lone corner office in their leased space. Granted, it was a small office on the second floor of a non-descript building overlooking a Chuck E. Cheese, but it was a corner office, nonetheless.

"And ol' Tick Thompson called," Gideon continued. "Wants you to represent him at his upcoming murder trial. You remember Tick, don't ya?"

Thane sighed. "That's just what we need. Did you tell him we wouldn't be able to help him out?"

"I told him I hoped he got the chair, so I'm guessing he understood we wouldn't be offering no help."

Thane looked over at Kristin. "He may not have any social skills, but he's to the point."

"You know Tick not only probably did it, he's likely gotten away with a hell of a lot more murders than he was ever caught for," Gideon continued. "I didn't think that was the kind of person you was wanting to represent."

"He's not," Thane said. "But I don't know that you needed to add the bit about hoping he got the chair."

"Don't you? That cat's a psychopath."

As they worked through requests for representation, their main goal was to help people who didn't have the means to hire a lawyer who would fight for them. People who were being unfairly prosecuted, whether due to their economic status, race, or because they were unfortunate and got caught up in the bureaucratic cogs of the legal system.

"The first few cases we take are going to be especially important," Thane said. "We got a lot of publicity about us trying to help good people, so a lot of eyes are going to be on us. Keep sorting through the requests. I know lawyers are supposed to represent anyone who needs one, and that it's not our job to worry about whether clients are guilty or not, but I want to work with people I truly believe are innocent."

"I haven't come across too many of those," Gideon said with a shrug.

"Yeah, but you don't exactly have an optimistic view of humanity," Kristin said. "You think everyone is guilty of something."

"Only 'cause they are."

"Okay," Thane said, closing his laptop, the international sign that the meeting was over. "Kristin, I'll try to be better about answering the phone, but hopefully I'll find someone this morning."

Gideon got up and walked out of the room, carrying himself like a man who wasn't looking forward to sifting through more requests for help, but Thane knew he was glad to be part of a team.

Kristin closed her MacBook and headed out as well, then stopped in the doorway.

"Oh, I almost forgot. I heard from someone I know over at the Central Community Police Station that they got some new intel about the murder of your friend. Sounds like they might be close to making an arrest, although none of this is on the record yet."

This news hit Thane like a Mike Tyson left hook. He took a deep breath. "Any word on what they found?"

"No, she couldn't give me any details. Just said she sensed they had some sort of breakthrough. I'll let you know if I hear anything more."

As soon as Kristin left, Thane reopened his laptop. He wasn't exactly sure what to look for or how to get the answer he desperately wanted to find. He searched the news for updates to Joseph's murder, but nothing new came up. Then, on a whim, he did a search for Russell McCoy, the father of the murdered woman in Skunk's trial—and the man who actually killed Joseph—in case there had been any arrest.

What he found surprised him. Russell McCoy had passed away a couple of months ago. He had apparently spent a couple of painful days in the ICU at UCLA Medical Center before succumbing to the effects of a severe stroke.

Thane sat, stunned, and wondered if Russell had made any sort of deathbed confession, and if so, if that confession included him. Or if his widowed wife had come across anything he left behind that exposed them.

It felt like too much of a coincidence that new evidence had surfaced so quickly after Russell's death.

The two men had only spoken once following the night in his office with Joseph, but the topic of what happened to Thane's former boss wasn't broached. Instead, Thane had reached out to McCoy after receiving a settlement for his false imprisonment. Thane offered to give some of his money from the city to the grieving father, but McCoy's only question was whether or not the money would bring Lauren back.

When told no, McCoy said he wasn't interested in the money.

Thane swore as he looked at his laptop, then quickly deleted his search history. He was angry at himself for having searched Russell McCoy minutes after searching for updates on Joseph's murder. He wasn't sure if deleting the search history would truly erase that lapse in judgement: he always assumed most everything was retrievable in the world of digital information.

He just hoped no one would think to look.

As soon as the most recent interview hit the ten-minute mark, Thane thanked the applicant for stopping by. He usually thought that if someone took the time and effort to come in for an interview, he could give them at least thirty minutes of his time, even if he knew from the start it wasn't a good fit, but in this case, he was doing them both a favor. The applicant started by listing all of the things he didn't want to do—answer the phone, paperwork, research, welcome visitors—which was most of the job description.

Kristin then appeared with a Black woman in her early twenties. Although young, she carried herself with the poise and confidence of a seasoned litigator thirty years her senior. Thane had noticed that some applicants stood at the door until invited in, but this woman walked right on in and handed Thane a copy of her resume.

"In case you misplaced mine."

"I didn't," Thane said. "But I appreciate the consideration. Come on in..." he glanced at the resume, "Letitia."

As Letitia walked over to the small table in his office, Thane looked over at Kristin for any silent feedback she might have. Kristin held her hand out flat and twisted it back and forth, signaling it could go either way.

"I can see your reflection in the window," Letitia said matter-of-factly, without turning around.

Kristin immediately shifted the movement of her hand into a wave. "Good luck," she said, then hurried out of the office, shutting the door behind her.

"Can I offer you some water, or coffee, or anything?"

"No, thank you. Miss '50-50' out there already offered, but I'm good. Thanks."

Thane couldn't help but smile at her directness. He took his seat and positioned his legal pad and pen in front of him. "I appreciate your interest in our job opening."

"Actually, I'm here to learn more about it to see if *I'm* interested. I have a few questions to ask, if you don't mind. That way if it's not a good fit, I won't be wasting your time or mine."

"That's great," Thane said. "Sometimes when I meet with—"

"First of all," Letitia said, cutting him off, "let me first say I like what you appear to be doing with your firm. Or at least how it's portrayed. Problem is, a lot of organizations say one thing but do another. Like the Fortune 500 companies who stress their commitment to diversity but don't have a single board member of color. Their statements make good press, but they don't mean jack."

"I can appreciate that, but I do feel like what we're trying to do here—"

"But what helps is your background. If anyone is going to truly understand being unfairly chewed up by a corrupt legal system—well, it still probably wouldn't be you since you're white and a lawyer—but if anyone from your demographic understands, then it would most likely be you."

Thane sat back and took a sip of coffee, sensing that trying to speak would likely be futile.

"May I speak candidly here?" she asked.

"You mean you haven't been?"

"I'm not crazy about working for some sort of white

49

knight out to assist all the poor, put-upon people of color. On the other hand, if your intentions are legit, then who am I to look down on anyone trying to help others? So I decided I'd like to learn more about your firm."

"That's a very reasonable—" Thane started to say, before catching his mistake.

"So I did some research and talked to a couple of people, and I liked what I heard. Getting the city to finance your firm was a stroke of genius. If you had taken all the money yourself and just said you wanted to help those in need, I wouldn't be here, but having three-quarters of the settlement go directly into funding this practice, that gives you skin in the game."

Letitia got up from the table and walked over to the small refrigerator in Thane's office. She opened it and helped herself to a bottle of water.

"Changed my mind about the water, if that's alright," she said as she sat back down. "So, here's my story. I'm twenty years old, but I've been working and basically fending for myself since I was fifteen. I'm actively trying to make a difference, so it's important that any job I take is one that moves the arc of the universe further towards justice, as the saying goes."

Thane nodded to let her know the reference wasn't lost on him.

"I plan to go to law school someday. Not sure how I'll swing it financially, but I'll find a way. But for the purpose of this interview, I'm a hard worker and if I'm treated fairly, you'll get my all. I don't mind doing scut work, but it has to be scut work for a reason, and not because you're disorganized or plain lazy. I get that phones need to be answered, so as long as the people calling are people in need and not some rich asshole who needs a lawyer because their dog Mitsy bit the mailman, I'm happy to pick up the phone and say, 'Good morning, how can I help you?'"

Letitia leaned back in her chair and studied Thane as she took a long drink of water. Thane knew it wasn't his turn yet, so he let her look for whatever it was she was looking for. Finally she leaned forward again.

"You're not going to find anyone more committed to helping people in need, and let's face it, this firm would benefit from another face of color. You had an experience unlike ninety-nine percent of rich, white people, but you still haven't lived as a Black person in the inner city. You'll benefit from my perspective, and I'll benefit from seeing the inner workings of a law firm doing the sort of law I hope to practice one day. So as long as the pay is fair and the benefits aren't predatory, I'll take the job."

She lifted the water back to her mouth then stopped as she remembered something else.

"Oh, and if you hit on me or behave in any way inappropriate, I'll sue your ass and I'll win." She sipped her water and nodded at him. "But I have a good sense about that sort of thing, and you don't seem like the type that would be a problem. So, when would you like me to start?"

Thane smiled. He had settled in to enjoy the monologue and had to bring himself back into having a two-way conversation.

"I have to be honest, Letitia, usually in job interviews, I've found it helpful if I ask some questions too. Plus, for whatever reason, I always envisioned actually offering the position before it's accepted."

"Oh," she said. "Are you still uncertain whether or not I would be a good fit?"

Thane thought about it, then laughed. "That's a good point."

Thane glanced over her resume again, then turned it face down.

"Truth be told, these pieces of paper don't mean a lot to me. A lot of what I'm looking for probably isn't going to be found on a resume. One thing that's important to me, for example, is having someone who will be steady if things get bumpy. When I represented Skunk Burns a few months ago, everything pointed to his guilt. Public opinion was hostile, the establishment played rough, and no one in their right mind thought we had a chance, but my team stuck together, and we were vindicated. That's what I'm looking for in whoever I hire. In fact, I even got shot at, but I'm hopeful that was an isolated incident."

"Just out of curiosity, are we allowed to shoot back?"

"I'm pretty sure it won't come to that. And I don't really have a doubt as to whether or not you're the type of person who will stick around if things get tough. But I do have one question for you: what do you think the difference is between doing what's legal and doing what's right?"

"Are you asking me that because you're afraid I'll be too much of an activist?"

"No," Thane said. "I'm asking because I'm trying to figure it out myself."

Letitia looked at Thane curiously, then took another sip of her water.

"I don't think there's a strong correlation between the two. At one point, it was legal to send Black children to a school that looked like a condemned building after it got hit by a tornado. It was legal to deny West Virginia coal miners health coverage, even though the union had

52

bargained for it. And it was legal to not hire a woman because she was pregnant. And none of those things were *right*. But they were legal. So I'm afraid I haven't always been able to make the direct correlation between legal and right."

Thane nodded in agreement. "I'd ask when you can start, but I get the feeling you already have."

"Not until we discuss salary, but if it's a fair wage, then yeah, consider me started."

7

The only non-tech-related item on Kristin's desk was one manila file holding two inches of documents. Otherwise, the desktop only served to hold her MacBook, two monitors, a wireless keyboard, mouse, and a phone.

She always marveled at Thane's desk, which was covered with torn sheets from a legal pad and various stacks of papers that made his desktop look like a giant squirrel was in the process of making a nest. But that was still better than Gideon's, which looked like an un-bussed table at a fast-food restaurant.

Kristin's lone file was from the city and pertained to the settlement agreement with her client, Scotty "Skunk" Burns. After Thane exposed the former District Attorney's efforts to falsify evidence against their client, Mr. Burns was in a good position to cash in. Kristin and the city's attorney were quibbling between $750,000 and a $1,000,000, which Kristin guessed would end up somewhere around $900,000. It made her smile every time she thought of Skunk being settled in a nice place to live.

She glanced up and saw a worried-looking, middle-age Black woman enter the reception area. The woman looked around hesitantly, as if tempted to quickly turn back around and leave before anyone approached her. All of their offices had a glass panel that looked out into the reception area, but Thane was on the phone, and Gideon had turned his desk so that he faced away from the window—God forbid he should be expected to help—so Kristin sighed and walked out of her office.

"Good morning. Can I help you?"

The woman brushed nonexistent wrinkles from her gingham dress, looking for something for her hands to do.

"Hello, thank you, although I think I'm probably in the wrong place," the woman said, glancing around the nice waiting area. "I was wondering if a Gideon Spence works here?"

Kristin was surprised. For whatever reason, she never thought of Gideon as someone anyone outside prison walls would know, let alone ask for, unless he was in trouble. But now here was a nice-looking woman around Gideon's age asking for him. Kristin smiled broadly at the woman.

"As a matter of fact he does. Let me get him for you."

Kristin started toward Gideon's office, then turned back toward the front desk. She picked up the phone at the reception desk and pushed the intercom button that sent her message through an overhead speaker. "Mr. Spence. You have a visitor at the reception desk." She figured if this woman was a potential girlfriend, she'd pull out all the stops in trying to make a good impression for her colleague.

Thane opened his office door, still holding his cell phone up to his ear and looked out into the reception area. He made eye contact with Kristin after noticing the woman who was now taking a seat, and raised his eyebrows.

Kristin grinned and nodded.

Gideon hesitantly opened his office door. He looked around and stopped when he saw the woman, then cautiously stepped out into the waiting room, pausing for a long moment as he and the woman stared at each other.

"Pearl. Hey. Nice to see you."

"Hello, Gid. It's been a while."

"It has at that. Whatcha doing down here?"

The woman glanced at Kristin, who quickly found something of interest at the reception desk that needed her immediate attention.

"I was wondering if I could talk with you a minute?"

"Sure. What about?" Gideon glanced at Kristin as she tipped her head a couple of times toward his office. "Oh yeah. How about you come on into my office and we can talk there?"

"You have an office?" Pearl asked with raised eyebrows, as though Gideon had just told her he owned a unicorn.

"I know. What are the odds, right?" He smiled and escorted Pearl into his office. "Gotta warn you, though, it smells a little bit like French fries."

When they reached his office, she stopped. "You have an office?" she repeated, sounding no less surprised than the first time. They then entered and closed the door.

Thane finished his phone call and looked over at Kristin, his eyebrows once again raised. "Who was that?"

"I don't know, but I'm wondering if Gideon has a girlfriend," she said with a sizable grin on her face.

Fifteen minutes later, while Kristin sat at Thane's

office table updating him on Skunk's settlement offer, Gideon appeared in the doorway, with Pearl standing beside him.

"S'cuse me, you mind if I grab the two of you for a minute? This is Pearl, and she needs our help."

Thane and Kristin stood and waved for them to join them at their table. Pearl hesitated, but Gideon placed a hand on her shoulder and guided her into one of the empty seats.

"I'm sorry to be interrupting," Pearl said, "but I need a lawyer and you're the first one I thought of, because of Gid."

"How long have you two known each other?" Kristin asked, not even trying to hide her curiosity.

"Known each other?" Gideon asked. "I've known her all her life. Pearl's my little sister."

"Sister?" Thane said, noticing that Kristin looked a little disappointed. "Really?"

"You sound surprised. It not occur to you I might have a sister?"

"It's not that," Thane said. "It's just, she's so..." he paused, trying to find the right word.

"Nice," Kristin said.

Thane smiled. "Please ignore us, Pearl. You probably didn't come here to listen to us kid each other."

"I wasn't kidding," Kristin said.

Pearl looked around at them but couldn't seem to find any words.Gideon cleared his throat and said, "Pearl's son, Goose—I mean, Gus—got busted for drugs, but he says he didn't know what was in the bag. Said it belonged to someone else." Gideon looked at Thane and shook his head. "Trust me, I know better than anyone how that sounds. I never met a dealer in prison who didn't say the same thing, but this kid's different. If Pearl says he didn't know what was in the bag, then he didn't know."

"Tell me what happened," Thane said.

Pearl took a deep breath, then proceeded to tell them about the bag of video games, the police bust, and how her son was being pressured by a narcotics detective to claim it was some other kid who gave him the drugs, but that Gus didn't want to do that. The cop said if Gus didn't cooperate, he'd end up doing hard time. They couldn't afford a lawyer, at least not a good one, and she and her husband didn't know what to do.

"What's your son's full name?" Thane asked, his legal pad at the ready.

"August Royden Cleveland." She glanced over at Gideon who looked like he was getting ready to roll his eyes. "Don't you start." She turned back to Thane. "He turned eighteen last month."

"He's even trying to get into college next year," Gideon added. "I haven't seen the kid in maybe twelve, thirteen years, but I believe Pearl when she says drugs ain't his scene."

"We'd be happy to talk with him," Kristin said, and Thane nodded.

"Is he being held at Twin Towers?" Thane asked, playing the odds since L.A.'s Twin Towers Correctional Facility was the world's largest jail.

"Yes, sir," she said. "I spoke to someone who said his lawyer can check in at the main office anytime between 10 AM and noon, and they can make him available."

Kristin looked at her watch. "If we leave now, we can get there by 10:30. How do you want to handle this?"

"How about you and I go see what we can find out?" Thane said.

"And leave Gideon with the phones?" Kristin asked with mock horror. "Whatever shall become of our little law firm?"

As Thane stood and reached for his briefcase, he noticed Detective Vince Struthers walk into the reception area, looking around for someone to help him. Thane froze, only long enough for Gideon to likely pick up that something was wrong.

He took a deep breath. If Struthers was there to arrest him, he would have been accompanied by more men, but it still bothered him to see the detective so soon after Kristin mentioned a potential breakthrough in Joseph Crowell's murder investigation.

"Actually, I should speak to Detective Struthers," Thane said as he held up his hand to Struthers through his office window. "Gideon, if you think you can play nice with the guards at the jail, you and Kristin go together. You'll have a better idea of what sort of non-legal questions to ask Gus anyway."

"I can't tell you how much I appreciate this," Pearl said. "Whatever it takes, my husband and I are willing to do it. I don't know how much you charge, and it might take us awhile, but we'll make good on it."

"Don't worry about that," Thane said. "One of the fringe benefits we offer here is legal representation for nephews of our team. We'll do our best to get this straightened out as soon as possible. The detective was likely trying to scare Gus into giving him what he wanted, but these sorts of arrests can usually be dealt with fairly quickly."

Pearl stood and shook Thane's and Kristin's hands, then turned to Gideon. She looked like she wanted to give him a hug, but didn't appear comfortable doing so. Instead, she rested her hand on Gideon's shoulder and gave it a squeeze.

"Thanks, Gid. I appreciate this more than I can say. I probably don't deserve it, but I appreciate it."

After everyone had left the office, Thane waved Struthers in to join him. The detective's every movement was smooth, like a finely calibrated machine. It wasn't that he moved slowly, it was that he moved deliberately, as if taking everything in and giving it time to process.

"I apologize for stopping by unannounced," Struthers said, "but I kept getting your answering machine." Even his voice was smooth, like Morgan Freeman after a couple of glasses of warm brandy.

"We're a little short-staffed right now, but I just hired someone to help us. Please, have a seat."

He directed Struthers to sit in one of three padded chairs that were across from his desk, with Thane taking one of the other chairs.

"What can I do for you?" Thane asked, trying to get a sense as to whether or not the detective was closing in on him. He knew he had to be on his guard and to quickly consider each answer he gave to ensure he wasn't being set up or caught in a contradiction. But he also didn't want to come across as being too deliberate in how he talked to the man.

"Mr. Banning—"

"Please, call me Thane."

"No," Struthers said matter-of-factly. "Mr. Banning, I had a couple of questions about Mr. Crowell that I wanted to ask you."

"Fire away."

"Forgive me for jumping right to the point, but that's how I prefer to do things. Did Mr. Crowell do drugs, that you know of? Hopefully it goes without saying, but everything I'm going to ask you is directly related to the murder investigation, nothing else. There's obviously nothing you can say that will get Mr. Crowell in trouble. Being murdered is pretty much the top of the trouble pyramid."

"I understand, but as for your question, I'm afraid I can't be of any help. It certainly wouldn't surprise me if he smoked a little pot. I suppose I also wouldn't be shocked to learn he did cocaine from time to time, but it's not something I ever saw, and it's not anything he ever mentioned to me. It certainly wasn't noticeable at work."

"But it wouldn't surprise you?"

"Very little would surprise me about Joseph. He pretty much marched along his own path. Whether something was legal or not wasn't usually his first concern, at least in his personal life. I don't mean to imply he took this same approach in his work."

"I understand. Then can you tell me what you know about a man named Kyle Miller? I believe you're acquainted with him."

Thane thought hard but couldn't make the connection. "I'm afraid I don't recognize the name."

"You did time together at Forsman. I think you even had a conflict or two with him. You may have known him by the name Kilo."

Thane frowned, as if he'd suddenly experienced a severe case of indigestion.

"At Forsman I knew a psychopathic, white supremacist, drug-dealing Neanderthal who would make a piece of shit look like a work of art in comparison. His name was Kilo."

"OK, so you do know him," Struthers said.

"We had a run in or two, but I'm pleased to say I don't know much about him other than the Cliff Notes I just gave you. Mind if I ask how he plays into any of this?"

Struthers looked at Thane a little longer than he felt was comfortable, then nodded. "Don't give this more weight than it deserves right now, but we're looking at Kilo for the murder of Mr. Crowell."

Thane focused on making sure he kept his emotions in check. If Struthers was telling him this to see how he reacted, he didn't want to appear too anxious to support the detective's case.

"Really? I'm surprised their paths would have even crossed. I take it Kilo—Kyle—is out of Forsman?"

"Six or seven months now, yeah," Struthers said, looking at his notepad. "As for possible connections, we have some intel that points to Mr. Miller. Please know this is extremely preliminary. It's very possible it will turn out to be nothing, maybe even likely, but right now he's our prime suspect."

Thane nodded, although no part of him thought it made sense. Not just that Kilo was the murderer, but that he was even a suspect. He couldn't figure out what sort of evidence the police could have that would lead them to a thug like Kilo.

Thane had conflicting emotions. After having served time on death row for a murder he didn't commit, the very reason for the existence of his law firm was to help others from being wrongly convicted of serious crimes such as murder. And yet at the same time, he wasn't able to totally push down the part of him that was happy to think of someone like Kilo taking the rap. That would take away Thane's fear of being connected to the murder, and there was definitely no love lost between the two men.

Thane wanted to feel ashamed of having these thoughts enter his mind, but he wasn't quite there yet.

"Can I ask what the evidence is, or can you tell me?"

"I can't share specifics yet, but we're assuming Mr. Miller has once again returned to the pharmacology business, and was providing your boss with cocaine or heroin. At least, that's what Mr. Miller always dealt in the past. It's possible it was a drug deal gone bad. And, as I believe you know first-hand, Mr. Miller trends on the violent side."

Thane knew that side of Kilo far too well. Had scars to prove it.

"I think that if Joseph was actually doing drugs," Thane said, "Kilo wouldn't be the kind of dealer he'd use. You know as well as I do that someone of Joseph's wealth usually has a more upscale dealer."

Thane felt this was the best way to play it. Telling Struthers he didn't think Kilo had anything to do with it would not only possibly soothe Thane's conscience, but it also might make Thane look like he had no stake in someone else being charged with the murder.

"Maybe so," said Struthers, "but sometimes these sorts of things don't always end up making sense. Mr. Miller dealt out of that neighborhood in the past. If Mr. Crowell was coming to see you that evening, maybe he simply ran into Mr. Miller and violence ensued. Or, given your history with Mr. Miller, maybe he was there to settle some prison score with you. But since you weren't around, Mr. Crowell somehow was the recipient. I don't know yet. Right now, I'm just following up on possible angles."

"I saw you at Joseph's funeral. Was that another angle you were following up on?"

Struthers shrugged. "It's something I do. The hope was to learn something about the victim that was relevant. I figured maybe someone would say something that caught my ear. It's me trying to be thorough."

"So did you learn anything?" Thane asked, regretting the question as soon as it left his mouth.

"I almost always learn something, Mr. Banning," Struthers said. He closed his notepad, slipped it back into his sports coat pocket, and stood. "I'll see myself out."

8

Gideon and Kristin approached the main entrance of the Twin Towers jail. Kristin walked at a faster pace, occasionally glancing over her shoulder and waiting for him to catch up.

He was apparently in no hurry to enter the prison.

Over a million square feet of correctional facility located between Los Angeles' Chinatown and Little Tokyo districts, Twin Towers was light tan with dark brown horizontal stripes running the height of the building. Apart from the relatively low concrete and metal fencing that ran around the perimeter of the building, it didn't really look like a jail—more like an enormous hospital designed by someone with a vendetta against windows.

Kristin entered the building without a second thought, but Gideon had been there enough to at least cause him to pause. Granted, before he'd always been there as an occupant, never as a guest, but just the same, the thought of walking through the front door on purpose made him anxious.

Kristin leaned outside, looking at him. "You coming?"

"I ain't a fan of places like this," he sighed, then joined her.

"Don't worry, I won't let them keep you. Of course, part of that is up to you. I can't help you if you hit anyone."

After checking in, emptying their pockets, and being searched—a far less invasive search than Gideon was used to—they were escorted down a long, sterile hallway with harsh fluorescent lighting. Gideon looked through a glass door and saw a line of six new inmates getting ready to go through processing. He became tense as the guard directed them to a small interview room, but noticed a level of courtesy shown to them by the guard, something he hadn't experienced in previous visits. The guard opened the door to the room and asked them to wait while he went to get the inmate.

Gideon walked over and, out of habit, sat on the side of the table that had metal rings bolted onto the tabletop. Kristin touched his shoulder and directed him to sit on the other side of the table, next to her.

"How long has it been since you saw your nephew?"

"I don't know. I think he was maybe five, something like that."

"You haven't seen him since you got out?" she asked, unable to hide the surprise in her voice.

"Haven't been invited. It's okay, though. I understand."

Before Kristin could ask any further questions, the door to the interview room opened and Gus was escorted inside. He wasn't handcuffed or under any sort of restraints, but he moved as though he was being held back by something, most likely exhaustion. He nodded blankly at Kristin, then stopped and looked with surprise at Gideon.

"How you doing, Goose?" Gideon said as the guard left the room.

Gus managed a small laugh. "Man, nobody's called me that in probably thirteen years."

"Sorry. That's all I really knew you as."

"Gus, I'm Kristin Peterson. Your uncle and I work with Thane Banning. Your mother came to see us and told us about what happened. If you're open to having us represent you, we'll do everything we can to get you out of here."

"So you really work at a law office?" Gus asked, looking at Gideon like he'd just learned his uncle performed open heart surgery.

"Proof that miracles happen."

Gus turned back to Kristin and sighed. "I don't belong here. I've done everything a guy is supposed to do to be on the right side of things, but here I am. I don't know how much longer I can do this."

"You'll be able to do it as long as you have to," Gideon told him. "A lot of people go through this. You get locked up and it's like walking into some sort of bizarro amusement park where all the rules have changed and you don't think you'll last five minutes. But until we can get you out of here, you gotta stay strong."

"I don't know what I'm supposed to do."

"Just do what the guards and anyone in authority tells you to do. That wasn't never my strong suit, but it's the best way to play it. And don't act like some kind of tough guy in front of any of the other clowns in here. That don't mean you should act like a punk, but if you just mind your own business, that's your best bet."

"Gus, your mom gave us a sense of what happened," Kristin said, "but can you tell us in your own words?"

And so Gus did. He told them about his two friends,

the bag, the fat man at the smelly house, and the bust. He provided a detailed account of his conversation with the narcotics detective, Mahone. He was calm while he spoke, like he was telling a story that had happened to somebody else.

"And you told this detective that it was your friend Jamie who gave you the package? You made this clear to him?"

"Yeah, but no matter how many times I told him, he didn't care. He wanted me to say it was Andre who gave it to me."

"So then did—"

"Who's this Andre kid?" Gideon interrupted. "He deal?"

"No, he's cool. He's my best friend. We've always had each other's backs."

"He run with a gang?"

"No, Dre's on the up-and-up. He and I steer clear of the drug scene. We're looking to go to college, get good jobs." Gus's head dropped to his chest. "Or at least I was."

"I'm still gonna want to talk to him," Gideon muttered, unconvinced.

"No, *I'll* reach out to him," Kristin said firmly. "But first, I'm going to push to get you released on bail."

"That detective said he was going to make sure there was no bail. Said he'd be telling the judge I'm a threat to the city and that the judge would believe him over me."

"'Course he would," Gideon said with a hint of venom.

"Well, I'm going to talk to Detective Mahone and get him to change his mind," Kristin said. "Your mom said you haven't been in trouble before, so I don't know why they would fight bail."

Gus looked at her skeptically, then glanced over at Gideon.

"I know she don't look it," Gideon told Gus, "but this one's a force of nature. You gotta trust her. She's good at what she does, and she's going to do whatever she needs to do to get you out of here."

Gus started tearing up. He looked away and wiped his face with his shirt sleeve. "Sorry. Don't mean to be acting like some sort of baby."

"You got nothing to apologize for, Goose. Ain't no shame in a few tears."

Kristin reached over and took Gus's hand. "We're going to get you out of here, okay? You didn't do anything wrong, and we'll get the right people to see that."

The guard knocked then entered the interview room. "Time's up."

Gideon put his hand on his nephew's shoulder. "Stay tough. You just gotta stay tough."

"Easy for you to say," Gus said as the guard escorted him out of the room. "You've always been the tough one."

After Gus was gone, Kristin put away her MacBook. "I'm going to set up some time with that detective. I'll get him to work with us."

As Gideon turned to leave, Kristin grabbed hold of his arm.

"You need to let me do this the right way. If you go out there and start threatening potential witnesses like this kid Andre, or shift into vigilante mode, it's going to come back and hurt Gus. I know your first instinct is to break something, but don't be messing things up just because you're mad."

"You do what you need to do. I'll keep out of your way, but if it starts looking like your way isn't getting the job done, I may need to do some breakin'."

They walked out of the interview room, then Kristin smiled.

"Hope you didn't pull a muscle back there, complimenting me."

"I meant what I said. That don't mean you don't get on my nerves, but you got fight in you, and I respect that."

"Well, you've got fight in you as well. Unfortunately, that doesn't always work to your advantage."

Thane stood at the far end of a liquor store, staring at a bottle of whiskey. Wearing an L.A. Dodgers ball cap pulled low, he positioned himself in the back aisle and waited while the guy behind the counter rang up several bottles of wine for the only other customer in the store.

Thane struggled all afternoon with the thought of Kilo possibly being arrested for a murder he didn't commit. However, it was at least a small consolation that the man in question was a violent, drug-dealing white supremacist. Kilo had blood on his hands, some of which, at one time, had been Thane's.

That was another consideration he wasn't strong enough to completely ignore.

After having taken so many liberties with what was legal and what was moral, he always felt his line in the sand would be fighting to never have someone sent to death row for a murder they didn't commit. But perhaps that was why it was called 'a line in the sand,' something easy to move or simply brush away.

The customer buying the wine finally left the store, leaving Thane as the only customer. The liquor store was a run-down place squeezed between a pawn shop and an auto parts store in a dimly lit strip mall. The odds were good they had a lot of shoplifters there, which meant it was likely he was being observed by at least one security camera monitor, so he decided it was time to see this through. He grabbed a random bottle of whiskey and walked up to the counter.

Pulling out his wallet, he looked up and feigned surprise when he and the cashier made eye contact, but in fact, neither looked surprised at all. Instead, they stared at each other for a long, tense moment.

Thane had scripted out what his first words were going to be, but standing so close to Kilo, he now found himself wanting nothing more than to smash the whiskey bottle over the man's head.

Kilo stared at Thane with dead eyes. His once shaved head was starting to grow bristles of hair since Thane last saw him, giving him the appearance of a marine rather than a skinhead. He wore a black tank top and faded blue jeans, and Thane noticed a wide bandage wrapped around his enormous bicep. Perhaps the store owner drew the line at swastika tattoos.

"Kilo. I didn't know you worked here," Thane lied. He had, in fact, tracked down someone he knew in prison who was still connected with a lot of fellow ex-cons. The man asked if Thane was planning to kill Kilo, but Thane assured him he only wanted to talk, so the guy told him about the liquor store. Thane figured the man would have told him where Kilo worked even if Thane had said he was planning on killing him; he just would have asked for more money before giving up the info.

"Banning, how long were you in Forsman?" Kilo asked him, sounding almost bored by Thane's act.

"A little over five years."

"And during those five years, are you telling me you didn't learn to know when you were being watched, even if you didn't see the person?"

Thane saw where this was headed and didn't answer.

"Yeah, that's what I thought. So don't be hiding over there in the corner watching me, waiting for the place to clear out and then walking up and acting all 'hey, man, I didn't recognize you.' As many times as this place has been held up, you're lucky I didn't pull a gun on you, so say what you came to say."

"A detective came to see me earlier today," Thane began. "A guy I know was murdered, and the detective wanted to talk with me about a possible suspect."

"I'm going to take a wild guess that I'm the suspect."

Thane nodded. "Any thought as to why you would be?"

"Why not me? I'm an ex-con with a history of violence. But what are you now? A junior detective? If that cop wants to ask me questions, he can come talk to me."

Kilo tried looking nonchalant, but Thane could see he was uncomfortable with this new information.

"You want the whiskey or not?" Kilo said. "If not, take it back; don't be leaving it here for me to deal with. I ain't one of your servants."

It wasn't too late for Thane to simply return the bottle back to its rightful place, leave, and let the legal system play out however it might. Maybe he could even console himself by saying he had tried.

But he stood stock still. He had already decided what the right thing was to do.

"The guy who was murdered was a friend of mine. A friend and my former boss. And while I'm the first person who would raise a glass at the thought of you going back to prison, I want the right person to do the time for his murder, and I don't see you being the guy. But since we're being all candid and everything, let me ask you outright: did you kill a guy a few months ago?"

"You think if I did, I'd say so?"

"I think if you did, you wouldn't say anything."

Kilo stared at Thane, then shook his head. "I'm doing things different this time around, Banning. I got me this job, crap job that it is, and a couple of other crap jobs, too. But I'm done with my old life, including no longer associating with ex-cons like you. So either get the whiskey or get the hell out of here. I'll even take it back to the shelf if it means getting you out of here sooner."

"I don't know if you're aware, but I've gone back to practicing law."

"Really?" Kilo said with mock surprise. "You mean like the high-profile shit that made the front page of every newspaper for the past two months? No, I hadn't heard. Guess I've been living under a rock."

"My point is, if you find yourself needing help, let me know."

"Because we're bestest pals, right?"

"Like I said, I want the right guy to get caught, and if that means helping out someone like you, then that's what I'll do."

"You know nothing about me," Kilo muttered.

"I know enough." Thane took out thirty bucks and put it on the counter. "If you need help, don't let your macho pride get in the way."

"Yeah, well, I don't see that happening."

"I don't either. You never struck me as being too smart." Thane grabbed the bottle. "I don't need a bag." He walked toward the door.

"Hey, Banning," Kilo called after him. Thane turned and waited while Kilo tried unsuccessfully to look unconcerned. "Did the cop tell you why I'm a suspect?"

"No," Thane said. "Probably because you're an ex-con with a history of violence, remember?"

And with that, he let the door slam shut behind him.

9

Kristin waited in an uncomfortable interrogation room at the 77th Street police precinct in south Los Angeles that had all the personality of an old refrigerator box.

A large one-way mirror on the wall made the room look twice as dull as it actually was. She saw her own reflection and sat up a little straighter. She wondered if Detective Mahone was watching her from the other side, then decided she was being paranoid.

But that was the purpose of the room.

After a twenty-minute wait, Mahone finally breezed inside, bringing with him a cup of coffee, but no apology for making her wait. He flashed a frat boy smile and held up his cup.

"You want one? I can get you one."

"No, thanks. I'm good," she said, even though she would kill for a hit of caffeine.

Mahone was dressed in a dark, Hugo Boss sport coat, black jeans, and a pair of Timberland boots. The man's cologne reached her before the smell of his coffee did. He appeared to notice her taking in his wardrobe as he sat across from her.

"I have to appear in court later this afternoon. I usually dress more casually, but what can you do? I find that the better I dress, the more I get what I want."

"I appreciate you taking the time to talk to me," Kristin said, already strongly disliking the man. "I'm sure meeting with lawyers isn't something you particularly enjoy."

"On the contrary, I love talking with lawyers. That's a common misconception about cops and lawyers. Usually a perp's lawyer is going to understand the situation a hell of a lot better than they do, and a lawyer can explain it in a way their client will understand. When I tell them the situation, they're not going to trust me. I'm just the big, bad cop who wants to bust them solely because I'm an asshole."

"Well, in the case of Gus Cleveland, I do think there are some circumstances that are worth us talking ab—"

"Let me guess. He didn't know there were drugs in the bag. A friend gave it to him, and golly gee, Your Honor, he didn't know there were drugs in there. If he'd known that, he would have called a policeman over right away. That's going to be your entire defense, am I right? Let me know how seriously the judge takes good ol' Gus, especially after I testify."

Kristin watched Mahone as he sat back and chuckled.

"I'm sure you hear that a lot, and I can see where you would immediately assume this is just another case of someone you've arrested claiming to be innocent. But I think if I could share with you a couple of—"

"No," Mahone said, then sipped his coffee.

"No?"

"No."

"But I haven't even—"

"You're wanting to explain to me that this case is

different. That there are extenuating circumstances and that this boy is actually a good kid and it's all been some misunderstanding."

"Actually I do believe he's a good young man and—"

"Look, I'm trying not to be rude here."

"Well try harder," Kristin said, clenching her jaw. She probably should have asked for that cup of coffee after all.

Mahone smiled. "Listen, I'm not trying to waste our time here, so forgive me for being blunt. Your client showed up at a low-level drug dealer's house with a bag of coke. The dealer says the kid moves a lot of product. We arrested him after he handed over the drugs to the dirtbag whose house we were staking out."

"But a friend of Gus's—"

"Okay, see, now we're heading toward some common ground where we can talk. Yes, I do believe a friend gave him the bag, but he's telling me the wrong name. The friend who gave him the bag is named Andre. Gus keeps saying the guy who gave him the drugs is called Jamie."

"Because that's who—"

"Look, this is the part where, as a lawyer, I was hoping you would understand the situation here. I hold all the cards. You and your client don't hold any cards. I don't know if you know anything about poker, but in poker, high hand wins, so if I have cards and you don't even have any, by the game's very definition I'm going to win. If your client doesn't do what I'm asking him to do, then he's going away for twenty to thirty years, guaranteed. Guar-an-teed. But if he works with me, I'll get the charges dropped. And don't even waste your time trying to get him bail, cause that ain't going to happen."

"So let me get this straight. You're going to send him

to prison unless he lies and says what you want him—"

"Whoa, whoa, whoa. I'm not saying I want him to lie. I'm saying he needs to tell me Andre gave him the drugs."

"But that would be lying, dumbass."

Mahone cocked an eyebrow and smiled. "Okay, we're talking in circles here. You know, when I first walked in here, I thought, now here's a pretty girl who will be able to see what's what."

"And when you first walked in here, I thought, now here's a boy who looks willing to listen."

"See, this is what breaks my heart. You've got spirit, and you're attractive as shit. But then you have to spoil it by being all indignant when you have a client caught red-handed delivering drugs, and you act like I'm the one being the jerk. Here I thought perhaps there was a chance we could grab a bite to eat sometime, or maybe have some drinks. You know, get to know each other a little better."

"That wouldn't work," Kristin replied, holding his gaze with her own. "I'm afraid my sexual preference is for men."

"Ouch. Good one, but I've been a detective for almost fifteen years now and I can size up people in about a second and a half. You're not nearly as tough as you think you are. You think you're some sort of hot shit lawyer because of that murder case you worked on a few months ago, but *you* didn't win that case. You're just a newbie law grad who probably still wears her college law sweatshirt around on weekends and who was only seated at the defense table to serve as eye candy for the male jurors. So if you want to get your client out of jail, you'd best get him to tell me what I already know to be the case, and that's that Andre gave him the drugs. He does that, he goes home. He doesn't do that, by the time he gets home his mama and daddy are going to be in a nursing home. Those are his only two options."

Mahone stood and calmly picked up his cup of coffee. Kristin watched him, feeling like all the words she wanted to say were logjammed in her throat, all clamoring to get out at once.

"Ah, you're not going to cry now, are you, girl?"

"You mean because of your cologne? No, I've smelled worse. Or at least I'm assuming I have. How many bottles of that you go through a week, anyway?"

Mahone laughed. "See? I love your fight. You really are a little spitfire, but I'm afraid you're playing with the big boys now."

"I'd be surprised to learn you were big."

"Take me up on my offer of drinks, girl, and maybe you can find out."

"I'm not surprised the only way you can get someone to go home with you is to get them drunk," she said, looking him dead in his cold, dark eyes. "And if you call me 'girl' again, you'll be wearing that cup of coffee to court."

Mahone smiled and turned to leave. "If your firm wants to talk more about this case, tell them next time to send a grown-up."

Thane walked into his house a little after 7:30, still frustrated by his conversation with Kilo. He didn't want anyone going to jail for a murder they didn't commit, but deep down he was happy it might take any suspicion off him. It obviously complicated things that the person who was the prime suspect in Joseph's murder was a guy like Kilo.

He stopped and listened, but couldn't hear Hannah. The living room and upstairs lights were off, but when he went into the kitchen he saw her out on the back patio. He poured himself a shot of Jack, downed it, then poured himself another.

He went outside and noticed Hannah was on the phone.

"No, I do appreciate it, Evie," she said. "It's just something I'd really need to think about. Mostly I'm so sad to be losing you."

Thane sat in the pine green Adirondack chair next to Hannah. Their backyard was immaculate, the outdoor setting having been one of the biggest selling points of their new house. If there was one thing he needed to catch up on, it was being outside.

"You'll definitely have to let me take you to lunch sometime before you leave," Hannah said into the phone. "Maybe even cocktails." Hannah listened and then laughed. "Thanks again for calling. And despite trying to lay a guilt trip on you, I really am very happy for you."

She hung up and looked over at Thane.

"Evie Cannon is leaving the Shelter next month. She's taking a job somewhere in the Midwest."

"That's too bad. Seems like she did a lot of good things there."

She paused for a long moment, as if trying to process something. "She thinks I should apply for the CEO

80

position. Obviously, there's no guarantee I'd get it, but I've developed a good reputation there while volunteering, and once she learned I had an MBA from Wharton, she seemed to think there's a good chance I'd get the offer."

Thane looked over at her, surprised. "Is that something you'd think about doing?"

"I don't know. I love the bookstore. Granted, it's getting tougher for independent bookstores, although I do like the idea of keeping the good fight going, especially since I don't exactly have to make much of a profit for us to have a good life."

"That's true."

"But I've had the bookstore for ten years now. The Shelter does such great work, and to be honest, I'm a little envious when I see what you're doing with your firm. You're making a difference in people's lives, helping those who aren't getting a fair shake. That's the sort of thing I could be doing."

Thane looked at Hannah and knew exactly what she would end up doing. Over the past several months, he saw her enthusiasm whenever she had volunteered at the Shelter. He knew she loved the bookstore and everything it represented, but if given this opportunity to help those in need, he didn't think she would pass it up.

"Any idea when you have to decide?"

"The board is going to need to move quickly since Evie was only able to give a month's notice. They'd want her to bring the new person up-to-speed, if possible." She sighed as she took a long sip from her drink. "Do you see a downside to me doing this? Anything I need to consider?"

"I think a change would be invigorating. Is there

anything holding you back?"

"No," she said, in a tone that Thane knew meant yes. He waited her out. "The only thing is, before everything that happened to you, we had been talking about having kids. I know we were joking about it the other day, but if we still think we want to try to have a baby, I don't know that I would want to take on a position like CEO."

"Women do it all the time."

"I know. I'm not saying I wouldn't, but it's a factor."

It was now her turn to out-wait him. The idea of having a child scared him. Not the usual concern that some people might have about the responsibility that comes with having a child, but the fear of being torn from his family again because of what he had done to Joseph. He wasn't sure he would be able to handle it.

"I think it's a good opportunity that you should at least explore," he finally said. "If you don't even give it a shot, I think you'd regret it. Besides, you could always apply and see if you even get the offer. And if you do, you could still decide not to take it on."

Thane felt Hannah studying him, trying to figure out if he was telling her to go for it because it was a great fit for her, or if he was trying to delay the conversation of having children. Or both—which was, in fact, the case.

Hannah apparently decided not to push the topic any further.

"You're home later than usual. Busy day?"

"Detective Struthers stopped by earlier to see me. Seems they have a suspect in Joseph's murder, although he was quick to say it might not pan out."

"Oh my God, it would be so great if it did."

"Yeah, except I knew the guy when I was at Forsman.

He was a pretty miserable excuse of a human being, but to be honest, I don't think he killed Joseph. The cops think it was a robbery gone bad, and that's just not this guy's style."

"Did you tell the detective that?"

"Yeah, I shared my thoughts."

"Then you did what you're supposed to do. Let the detective do his job and see how it goes."

Thane stared into his glass of whiskey like he was waiting for an answer from a Magic 8-Ball.

"You're thinking of getting involved, aren't you?" Hannah asked.

"No. Well, yes, I was, and I guess I sort of already did. I went and talked to the guy today."

"Thane! No. Why would you do that?"

"Because I'm not convinced he did it."

"But you're not the one who needs to be convinced! It's not your job to solve Joseph's murder. Let the police do that."

"I know, but Joseph was my friend."

"*Our* friend."

"He was our friend, and I want the right person to be caught, not just somebody to take the rap so the cops can mark the case as solved."

"I know that, baby, but..." Hannah paused. "What could you do?" She waited for an answer, but none came. "Oh God, please tell me you're not thinking of representing him."

"He didn't want my offer to help anyway, so it's a moot issue."

"Good. What you're doing has generated so much goodwill in the city. People feel there's a need for your resources, but if you were to represent a guy accused of killing your friend—well, I can see that goodwill disappearing quickly."

Thane knew helping Kilo would make little, if any, sense to anyone. He knew it would be next to impossible to explain, although it *wasn't* actually impossible to explain.

People would understand… if he told the whole story.

It just wasn't a story he wanted to tell.

10

All night, Thane was plagued by a nightmare.

The dream started with Thane being led down the hallway of Forsman's death row, toward a room with an oversized electric chair sitting on cinder blocks. He was terrified, but the guard escorting him acted nonchalant as though the trip wasn't a big deal. Thane wore his nicest suit and tie, and in the dream, he was worried about what the electricity would do to his expensive clothes.

When they reached their destination, the chair was already occupied. Kilo was strapped in, with an oversized metal bowl placed on his head. Wires and fuses ran to a large metal box, looking like something one would see in a low-budget B-movie. In a voice like he was speaking underwater, Thane told the guard he thought California used lethal injection. The guard said they were making an exception in this case.

The guard walked Thane to an oversized, bright red lever. He quickly realized what he was expected to do.

Thane glanced over at Kilo, who stared back.

"I know what you did," Kilo muttered. Thane didn't know how to respond. Instead, he glanced around the room to see if anyone else had heard, but the guard had left, and the Chaplain was wrapping up the Last Rites in preparation for Kilo's final journey.

Thane turned and saw a large window that looked into the adjacent room where witnesses to the execution sat, but the only person there was Hannah. She looked at him strangely, uncertain what was taking place.

After completing the Last Rites, the Chaplain started to leave the room, but before closing the door he nodded to Thane. It was time.

Thane looked at Hannah. She banged her fists on the glass, screaming at him not to throw the switch.

"I'm sorry," Thane whispered to Kilo. "But I have my life back. I can't lose her again."

"You're just getting revenge for what I did to you," Kilo said. "That's why you're doing this."

"It's not. I swear. I offered to help you and you turned me down."

"You could tell them who really killed Joseph."

"I can't."

"Coward."

Thane opened his mouth to argue, but he knew Kilo was right.

"If you're not going to tell her, I will." Kilo looked up at Hannah and shouted, "You want to know who really killed your friend? It was—"

"No!" Thane shouted, then threw the switch.

Bolts of electricity blasted through Kilo. His shaved head jerked back, body wildly convulsing. Yet somehow, he never broke eye contact with Thane. After an eternity, Kilo's eyes finally closed, and Thane flipped off the power. He looked at a wide-eyed Hannah, her hands pressed to her mouth. The room stank of charred flesh, and he wanted to throw up.

He thought he would feel guilt, but instead, he felt a strong tug of relief. He smiled, and it terrified him.

The door suddenly burst open. Four policemen, led by Struthers, ran in and grabbed Thane, slamming his chest against the wall. They handcuffed his wrists tightly behind his back, the metal cutting into his flesh.

"What are you doing?!"

"You're under arrest for the murder of Kilo Miller. You just electrocuted an innocent man, and we saw you do it."

"But I was told to throw the switch. They told me do it."

"Nobody told you to throw the switch. You *chose* to."

Thane looked back at Hannah, who was crying hysterically and banging harder on the window. Thane struggled with the guards, trying to wrench himself free.

"I can't go back there! I can't do it again!"

But the guards didn't care. They grabbed him under his arms and started dragging him down the hall.

"Hannah!" he screamed. "Hannah!"

"You still with us?" Kristin asked, jolting Thane out of the memory of his nightmare. "If so, you're welcome to join us."

Thane looked up and saw his team—now including Letitia—seated at his office table, watching him closely. He grabbed his mug of coffee and gulped it down.

"Let's get started," he grunted. "Kristin, how did your

meeting with Detective Mahone go?"

"I wish I could say it could have gone worse, but I'd be lying."

"What happened?" Gideon asked, unusually attentive. "Goose at least getting bail?"

Kristin reluctantly shook her head. "Mahone's a major dick. He wants Gus to tell him what he wants to hear, otherwise he's going to play hardball."

Kristin relayed her conversation with Mahone. As she updated the team, Gideon's scowl became permanently chiseled onto his face.

"I don't think there's anything we can do or say to get him to change his mind," she concluded, "other than having Gus lie about who gave him the bag."

"Do we have any sort of defense, other than Gus telling the judge he didn't do it?" Thane asked.

"It's too early to say right now," Kristin said.

"If Detective Dickhead ain't going to let Goose out unless he says this Andre punk gave him the drugs," Gideon said, "then he can tell him Andre gave him the drugs."

"And let the cop win?" Letitia spoke up. "This sort of thing happens far too often. Cop arrests someone with drugs and tells them to rat out someone higher up, whether that person was involved or not. They can't keep getting away with that."

"If we don't let the cop win," Gideon said, his voice growing angry, "then Goose is the only one who's going to lose. You think Mahone not getting what he wants is going to teach him a lesson? Goose needs to tell him whatever it is he wants to hear. Someone else can take on the establishment and be the lost-cause poster piñata."

Letitia set up straighter, her ire rising as fast as Gideon's. "No, we've got to stop this. I didn't join up here to roll over when a cop becomes a bully. Too many men—especially Black men—are doing time because they didn't agree to read the prepared script. And it's not just men."

"And I'm not looking for Goose to be another one of those men. He's got a lot to lose."

"So'd my brother, but he stood strong." Letitia started to say something else then stopped abruptly, looking as though she had already said too much.

"What about your brother?" Thane asked.

"Nothing."

"Letitia, did your brother do time for something like this?"

"*Doing* time," she corrected him. "Probably another ten years."

Everyone looked at her, but she didn't appear ready to offer any more.

"Why didn't you mention this when I interviewed you?" Thane asked.

"Because I didn't want you thinking I was trying to get the job just to get him out of jail. There's nothing can be done for him, but I can damn sure try to keep others out."

"Then don't say Goose shouldn't give the man what he wants," Gideon said. "I mean, I respect what your brother did, but Gus don't need to be another sacrificial lamb."

"Hang on," Thane said, trying to take back control of the meeting. "It's too early for this. We don't even know what sort of case we have yet. Maybe the kid who gave him the drugs will testify Gus didn't know what was in it."

"You think this kid would rat himself out?" Gideon scoffed. "I don't know too many people that stupid."

"What I'm saying is, we just don't know yet. There are a lot of questions that need answering."

"I'd like to take the lead on this case," Kristin said suddenly, looking as surprised as the rest of them. "Obviously we'll all be involved, but I'd like to own this case."

"That cop is doing everything he can to make sure he gets what he wants," Gideon said. "Even if he's got to lie to get it. You going to do whatever you can to get Gus out? Or you just going to do whatever the law says you can do?"

"If you're asking if I'm going to break the law, then no. That would make me no better than that detective."

"Can we save the moral high ground for some other client? This is my nephew. He's not 'a matter of principle,' dammit. He's an 18-year-old kid who was going to go to college. I want someone on this case who's going to do whatever it takes to get him out. Whatever it takes."

Gideon glanced at Thane, as did Kristin. Finally, Thane cleared his throat.

"Take the lead on this right now," he said to her, followed by a groan from Gideon. "But I want to stay involved. And if we get to the point where I feel I need to take the lead, then that's what will happen."

Kristin opened her mouth to object, but Thane cut her off.

"You only passed the bar a few months ago, so forgive me if I'm not going to guarantee you the chance to see this through to the end, but take it for now and do a good job and it will be yours."

Thane turned to Letitia. He could tell from her expression that she wasn't used to a law firm with this sort of dynamic.

"Letitia," Thane said, "I want you to work with Kristin. Provide whatever support she needs. You've obviously spent a lot of time learning about these sorts of cases, so you might have some insight regarding an approach we can take." Thane leaned back in his chair and rubbed his eyes. "Anything else we need to cover today?"

When it was obvious no one was going to say anything, Gideon glared at Thane and trudged out of the office. Letitia nodded at Kristin, then followed Gideon out.

Kristin stayed at the table, even after Thane stood. When he noticed she wasn't getting up, he sat back down.

"I'm not saying you won't be the lead on this all the way through, but—"

"It's not that." She furrowed her eyebrows. "In school, every case we learned about worked under the assumption that everyone followed the rules. The cops played their part, the prosecution, the defense, the judge. Everyone tried their best, but they did it right."

She clenched her fists. Thane expected her to slam them down on the table, but instead she took a deep breath and relaxed her grip.

"I'm not saying I don't realize there are bad players here and there, but I guess I just didn't know they were so upfront about it. That detective steamrolled me and didn't look back."

"You're a good lawyer," Thane said.

"I didn't feel like one today."

"Did you punch him in the face?"

She looked at him to see if he was serious, then smiled and shook her head.

"Then you did better than Gideon would have done."

"Seriously? Can't we set the bar a little higher for me?"

"Look, you're one of the good ones. You're in this for the right reasons, and you care. If I thought you wanted to take the lead on this just to get back at Mahone, then I might have second thoughts, but my sense is you're wanting to do this to help Gus. Am I right?"

"Yeah," she said, then added, "but I also want to get back at that asshole Mahone."

"Good," Thane said. "That's a killer combination."

11

"Banning. Hold up."

Thane turned toward the voice as he left his office building. Kilo pushed himself away from the side of the brick wall where he'd been waiting.

Letitia had left the building right before Thane and was walking in the opposite direction, but she turned to see who was hollering out to her boss. Thane saw her eyebrows furrow as the rough-looking man approached, so he waved his hand to let her know everything was fine. She turned and continued on, glancing back another couple of times.

As Kilo approached, Thane reflexively tightened his fists, as if preparing for a street fight, then remembered he was no longer in prison. He relaxed a little, although not completely.

"You on your way to lunch?" Kilo asked.

"Thought I'd grab a quick bite. You want to join me, or we can go back up to my office if you'd rather."

Kilo looked down at the sidewalk. Thane was certain their entire conversation was going to be awkward.

"Sure," Kilo finally said. "Lunch is fine."

Thane took them to Max's, a sports bar down the block, to get a burger. He was originally planning to get a salad at a nearby health food store, but he assumed Kilo would be more comfortable with burgers. Thane noticed he was making decisions he thought would make Kilo more comfortable. That was ironic.

After sitting at a tall two-top in the bar section and placing their order—Thane ordered a bacon cheeseburger, and Kilo ordered a salad—Thane, at the last minute, asked for a glass of Jack on ice. He looked at Kilo and said it was his treat. Kilo said that drinking during the day was a violation of his parole, then nodded to the waitress to make it two.

"What's up?" Thane asked.

Kilo silently stared at Thane for a long moment, but apparently couldn't find what he was looking for.

"A cop stopped by the liquor store last night an hour or so after you left. I forget his name."

"Black guy in his late fifties? Relaxed, in no hurry?"

"Yeah."

"Likely Vince Struthers. Did you tell him I'd told you that you were a suspect?"

"It's not my habit to offer cops information I'm not asked about."

"Struthers is the guy who told me. I doubt he'd be happy with me telling you."

"Here's the deal," Kilo said. "Struthers didn't come right out and say it, but I can see how this is going to go down. Unless something new comes up, right now I'm the guy in the rifle scope, and that trigger's going to be pulled sooner or later. This is a high-profile case, which means the cops are antsy to put a bow on it and sweep it under the rug."

"For what it's worth, I think Struthers is a pretty

straight shooter. I don't think he's going to be pressured to hang a murder charge on someone unless he thinks he's guilty."

"Yeah, but I can tell he thinks I might be the guy. So I reached out to a couple of public defenders I had in the past, but they can't do anything until I'm formally charged, which is probably for the best because both of them probably got their law degrees from the internet. And I can't afford a real lawyer; I mean the type that charges more money than I make in a year. Might surprise you to learn that working in a liquor store doesn't bring in the big bucks."

The waitress brought their lunch orders and their whiskey. Kilo downed his in one long swig.

"You told me earlier you'd be willing to help me," Kilo continued, "but what I'm trying to figure out is whether I can trust you. I know you said you wanted the right guy to do the time for the murder of your friend, and maybe that makes sense, but it's still not sitting right with me. How can I be sure you're on the up and up?"

"There isn't a way. But just so we're clear, I haven't agreed to help you yet. You and I both know I have every reason to set you up, but that's not an option for me. All I can say is if I decide to help, then I'll be all in, and if I don't think I can do that, then I'll pass, and you can find somebody else. But I doubt there's anything I can say to make you believe that."

Thane had come to this conclusion as they were walking to the bar. He knew the right thing was to help Kilo not be sent to death row for a murder he didn't commit. He also knew there were arguments to be made to let Kilo help Thane get away with what he and Russell McCoy did. Granted, those weren't moral arguments, but that didn't make them any less enticing. But the one thing Thane couldn't do was to take the case and then set things up so Kilo was sent away.

Maybe his moral compass wasn't as out of control as he thought.

"You don't know me," Kilo said. "I know you think you do, and I'm not even saying I blame you for how you see me, but you don't know me. And I don't deserve any of this. I don't mean in a 'karma' sort of way. If you're looking at it that way, then yeah, I probably deserve this and thirty more years of bad shit raining down on me. What I'm saying is, I don't deserve it because I'm trying to do things right this time around. I've stepped away from dealing and from all the trash I used to hang out with, and let me tell you, there are a lot of people pissed at me for getting out, but I don't care. I'm trying to play by the rules this time, but I get the feeling that don't mean shit for guys like me."

Thane had no interest in listening to Kilo play the victim. At the same time, though, he knew the game was usually stacked against ex-cons. He saw the struggles Gideon went through, especially when first paroled from Forsman. Thane knew if he hadn't been able to pay his friend a good wage, the big guy would more than likely have already been locked up again by now.

"Did Struthers give you a sense of why they're looking at you?"

Kilo focused on his glass, staring at it so hard Thane was surprised the ice cubes didn't melt from the heat of his frustration. Thane could tell Kilo felt helpless, and for a man like him, that was probably one of the worse things he could experience.

"He asked me about being at a bar on a particular

night. I'm assuming it was the night of the murder, and the bar must have been nearby."

"Which bar?"

"Gulliver's."

"Yeah. That's a couple of blocks from my old office. That's where Joseph was killed."

"He was killed at your office?"

"Outside it. He stopped by thinking I was there, but I'd already gone home."

Kilo looked at Thane a little longer than Thane felt comfortable with. Kilo seemed to smell something, but wasn't sure what it was. But some of that was likely the result of having spent several years in prison. It didn't take long before you assumed everyone was involved in something. Trust was in short supply behind bars.

"Anyway," Kilo finally said, "Gulliver's is a dive, but you worked around there so you know pretty much everything's a dive in that neighborhood. I live about half a mile from there, so that used to be the bar I went to when I was out. I also used to deal out of it before I got busted."

"Were you there to…"

"I told you I don't do that shit anymore," Kilo said, raising his voice.

"I was going to ask if you were there to meet anyone, or were you just there to have a drink alone."

"First off, I don't even know when the guy was killed. It was some weeknight that I was there, and apparently your friend was killed several months ago, but I'm guessing the cop must have some information saying I was there that night, or else he wouldn't be questioning me about it."

"So did you still go there a lot, or just from time to time?"

"Not often. I'm trying to avoid the old places. I was hoping to catch someone I used to run with who also used to hang out there. He'd been calling, giving me a hard time about not returning his calls even though I'd told him I'd moved on from that part of my life, so I figured maybe it was a discussion best had in person. So I hung out there for a while, then went home when he never showed. It was a shot in the dark anyway."

"Did the detective ask anything else?"

"Just the usual crap. Was I back to dealing, like even if I was, I'd tell him. Asked me how long I'd been working at the store, if I'd heard anything about the murder, things like that."

"Just being at the bar wouldn't be enough to put you on their radar."

"With my record, they don't need a lot."

"But Gulliver's is usually packed with people who would make just as good of a suspect as you. It's pretty much the local bar for lowlifes. No offense."

"You're not wrong. But like I said, I don't hang out there anymore, although when I did, I suppose I was one of those lowlifes you're talking about."

"What I don't understand is why it took so long for Struthers to approach you. Just being at the bar wouldn't be enough to make you a suspect, and even if it did, why'd he wait this long to question you? They either had your name right away or they didn't, and if they didn't, then how'd they get it all this time later?"

They sat in silence as Thane tried putting together the pieces, but it felt like jigsaw puzzle pieces from different boxes were all tossed around, and Thane was trying to come up with one coherent picture.

"So you think you can help me or not?" Kilo asked sharply. "I'm not begging you, if that's what you want."

Thane was surprised this wasn't something he needed to think about anymore. It wasn't that he realized helping Kilo was the right thing to do; that was never the question. It was whether or not Thane would do the right thing. And while he'd be the first to admit he wasn't doing it enthusiastically, he was at least happy to see it was still within him to do it.

"I'll help."

"I can't pay you much."

"The city is giving my firm more than enough money to help people who I believe are being prosecuted unfairly. Besides, if all they've got is you being at a bar, I doubt you'll even be charged."

"So, we wait and see?"

"No, I want you to come by my office and talk more about this. Can you make it this afternoon around 4:00?" Kilo nodded. "Try to remember any of the other questions Struthers asked you, and I'll come up with questions you may be asked if this doesn't get dropped. We'll get a jump on figuring things out so that if you're charged, we're not playing catch-up."

"Why are you doing this, Banning?"

"I already told you why."

Kilo looked at Thane hard. "He must have been a hell of a good friend for you to be helping someone like me."

"He was. And even if he wasn't, having been on death row for a murder I didn't commit, I'm also not a fan of people being charged with murder if they're innocent."

"Even someone like me?"

Thane offered up a small shrug. "I'm not saying I'm not open to exceptions, but fortunately for you, that brings me back to Joseph having been my friend." Thane stood and pulled some bills from his wallet. He left behind his half-eaten hamburger, although he'd finished off the whiskey. "But if it's all the same, I'm not interested in eating lunch with you just to catch up on old times."

"If you were, then I'd know for sure you were trying to set me up."

"And then what would you do? Stab me again?"

Thane felt his anger rising, but instead of throwing a punch like he wanted, he figured it'd be best to throw the money on the table and get out of there before things got out of hand.

Thane called everyone into the firm's conference room for an impromptu team meeting. It was unusual for them to meet in the modestly furnished conference room with its table for eight, since the four of them easily fit around the smaller table in Thane's office, but he wanted a bit more space between them when he told them the news.

When everyone was seated, Thane jumped right in.

"I wanted to give everyone a heads-up that we're likely getting a new client, although he hasn't been charged yet, so it may turn out to be nothing."

"If he hasn't been charged," Kristin said, "why are we taking him on now?"

"Because if he is charged, this case is going to be—

complicated." Thane wanted to find a better description, then decided 'complicated' was as accurate as anything else. "So I'd rather get a jump on things now. Plus, maybe we can keep him from even being charged."

"Is it that tatted up biker dude I saw you talking with outside the office?" Letitia asked.

"His name is Kyle Miller."

Letitia immediately started searching the name on her phone. Thane hoped he'd be able to provide more background before she found too much, although he knew Google would be far faster than him.

"Tatted up biker dude?" Gideon said. "Someone from Forsman?"

Thane hesitated, not wanting to say, but also knowing he had no choice. "Afraid so. Kilo."

Gideon's eyes opened wide. "Kilo? You mean *Kilo, Kilo?*"

"How many Kilos you know?"

"I thought you said his name was Kyle."

"His name *is* Kyle. Did you think his real name was Kilo? Who names their baby Kilo?"

"Hey, I wouldn't have thought anybody would have named their baby 'Thane' either, but here you are."

"What's up with everyone giving me grief about my name?"

Letitia looked up at him from her phone, a red-hot flame flickering behind her eyes. Thane knew she'd had success with the search.

"Oh hell no," she said. "We're representing this guy? This drug-dealing, murdering white supremacist? Are you kidding me? Hell-and-No. I didn't come here to try to keep the Klan on the street."

"He's a suspect in a murder and I don't believe he did it," Thane said. "That's the sort of case this firm was created for."

Letitia started reading from her phone. "And he did time for manslaughter. Care to guess what color the victim was? I'll give you a hint: he wasn't pasty white." She quickly placed her phone face down on the table, angry with what she had seen. "I'm obviously in the wrong place because I'm damn sure not helping you keep your redneck, prison biker friends on the street."

At that, Gideon laughed so loudly that Kristin knocked over her bottle of water in surprise.

"Friend? Yeah, Thane's good friend Kilo, the asshole who stabbed your boss so many times it took the doc a minute to figure out which wound to work on first. There were so many cuts on his chest he looked like he'd been attacked by a bear."

"He stabbed you?" Kristin said, amazed.

Gideon chuckled. "That's an understatement. Kilo told Thane to stop hanging around me because I was the wrong color, and ol' Kilo and his gang didn't like that: you know, the whole race mixing thing, like maybe Thane and I were going to have a baby together or something. But Thane didn't stay away from me—hell, even I thought he was being stupid stubborn—so Kilo knifed Thane one day in his cell. Thane's mattress looked like a sponge that had soaked up a case of red wine. So yeah, that's Thane's good friend Kilo." Gideon looked directly at Letitia. "And just so you know, this idiot here kept on hanging out with me after he got out the hospital."

Kristin looked at Thane, confused. "I understand our mission is to help people wrongly accused of serious crimes, but there are a lot of people like that out there who need our help. Why in the world would you want to help this guy?"

"Amen, sister," Letitia added.

Thane started massaging his temples with his thumbs. Having to talk about all this was giving him a headache.

"So this is where it gets complicated."

"You mean representing a violent felon who tried to kill you isn't the complication?" Kristin asked.

"If he gets charged, it will be for the murder of my friend and former boss, Joseph Crowell."

Again Gideon laughed, this time slapping his knee for emphasis, and again Kristin and Letitia looked at Thane as if he'd just stripped down and was dancing on the table naked.

Kristin nodded slightly. "I have to admit, I didn't see that one coming."

"Yeah, but now that you're thinking about it," Letitia said, "you're starting to get a little excited, aren't you?"

"What's that supposed to mean?"

"I mean you're thinking about all the cable news coverage that'll come with a case like this. Another chance to be in front of the camera. Look at you! Somebody says the words 'cable news' and your eyes light up like a flashbulb."

"They do not!"

Kristin looked over at Thane for support, but he just shrugged and delicately said, "They sort of do."

"Just a little spark," Gideon added, shaking his head. "Nothing too obvious."

"Well, for the record, I think we'd be jumping the

shark on this one," Kristin said. "You representing the guy who's accused of killing your friend? And a drug dealing racist on top of it? You said the other day we need to be particular in our first few cases since people will be paying attention to what we're doing here. Why would you take on someone like this?"

"Because Joseph was my friend and I want the right guy caught. Look, Kilo's coming in later this afternoon. If at any point I feel there's even a ten percent chance he did it, then I'm going to tell him I can't take the case. The only way I'll fight to get him freed is if I'm convinced he didn't do it."

"I didn't think lawyers were supposed to worry about whether or not their clients were guilty," Kristin said.

"Well, I do."

"Maybe the city would be a better place with this Kilo guy off the street," Letitia muttered to herself.

"There's no 'maybe' about it," Thane responded. "It definitely would be better off, and if Joseph wasn't my friend, I'd be the first to put together a going-away party for the guy. But not if he was going to death row for a murder he didn't commit. Been there, done that, and I'm not letting that happen if I can do anything about it. I don't care who it is."

"I don't want to help on this one," Letitia said.

"Well, I'm going to need your help, but I'll keep it to a minimum. Kristin and Gideon won't be here when he comes in, so I'd like you to take notes so I'm sure I don't miss anything."

"You want me to be in the same room as this asshole? That may not be the best idea, for everyone involved."

"Listen, we're too small a group to pick which cases

we want to be a part of. You need to be colorblind on this one."

"But I'm not colorblind! I'm *here* because I'm not colorblind. I want to practice law because I'm not colorblind. You're white," she said pointing at Thane before turning and pointing at Gideon, "he's Black, and she's..." Letitia paused as she studied Kristin, "...and she's some sort of artificial tan." Kristin glared at Letitia, then glanced down at her arm to check out her skin tone. "I can pick out different colors just fine. And this Kilo guy is the whitest of white, and he once killed a man who was Black. I may not know all the colors, but I know the ones I need to know."

Thane slid his chair back from the table. "I know this has the potential to put us in a bad spot. I understand what the press might say and that we might find ourselves in the middle of a hurricane, but it's not as though we haven't been the focal point of hostility in the past, and we came through that just fine. I think the odds are strong Kilo won't even be charged, but this is something I need to do. It's something I'm going to do. I wish I could explain it better, but unless you've gone through what I've gone through, you're never going to totally understand."

"I'm not fetching water or coffee for him," Letitia said. "I'm not a dog. I don't fetch."

"Nor will I ask you to."

Kristin looked at her watch and slid her chair back as well. "Gideon and I are scheduled to meet with Gus, so we have to head on over there, unless there's anything more you need to tell us."

"Anything more?" Letitia said. "You think there could be anything more?" She turned toward Thane.

"Oh, wait, let me guess—he's also your brother."

12

Kristin couldn't tell if they were waiting for Gus in the same interview room they were in last time, or if the rooms all just looked alike. Gideon sat beside her but didn't speak. He didn't usually say much, but he was particularly quiet when they came to the Twin Towers jail. Whether that was because his nephew was here, or simply because he was in a jail, she wasn't sure, but she assumed it was a combination of both.

When Gideon finally spoke, she wished he hadn't. "You tell Gus he ain't getting bail?"

Kristin's stomach clenched as she remembered how confident she'd been telling Gus she'd be getting him out of there soon. "I connected with him over the phone. He thanked me for trying and acted like it wasn't a big deal, but I knew he was upset." She started clicking the top of her pen repeatedly, a nervous habit.

The door to the interrogation room opened and Gus limped in, moving like he'd just played a game of soccer and he was the soccer ball. Gideon took one look at Gus and shot up out of his chair.

Gus turned his head so that the slightly less bruised side of his face was toward them, but it wasn't much better than the other side. His lower lip looked like a plum, and his right eye was bruised. Flakes of crusted blood were still at the base of one nostril, but what appeared to be the biggest injury was the look in his eyes. He had been beaten down, and not just physically; he was hunched over, like a puppy afraid of being kicked.

Kristin lightly put her hand on Gus's shoulder as she gently guided him over to a chair.

"What happened, Gus?" she said softly.

"Yeah, what the hell happened?" Gideon echoed, far less softly.

"I don't want to talk about it," Gus said.

"It don't matter if you don't want to talk about it or not," Gideon responded. "We're talking about it."

Gus refused to make eye contact.

"Gus," Kristin finally said, "you need to trust us, even if you think we can't help you. Sometimes you might be surprised by what we can do."

"You mean like my bail?" he asked bitterly.

Kristin sat back in her chair, looking like she was now the one who had been punched. "I'm sorry. I was wrong to say I could get you out of here, but I want you to know I'm going to do everything I can to get this cleared up. But in order to do that, I need to know what's going on, so let's start with your injuries. Tell us what happened."

Gus put his finger to his bruised eye, then jerked it away like it was red hot. He flinched at the pain, and his eyes started to water.

"I was told not to say anything."

"Who told you that?" Gideon asked. "Actually, that's not even the question. The question is, what do they think you're going to say?"

Gus stayed quiet and stared at the tabletop.

"Goose, this isn't the time to cower. This is the time to stand up. What did they tell you not to say?"

"They said not to talk about Andre," Gus said, raising his voice.

"Who's Andre?" Gideon said.

"Andre. My friend the cop wants me to say gave me the drugs."

"Yeah, I know that, but who *is* he? Why's everyone so focused on that kid?"

Gus squirmed in his chair, then let out a heavy sigh. "He's Stick Sturgess's brother. You know Stick?"

Gideon paused, then nodded. "Not personally, but I heard of him." He turned to Kristin. "Stick is a drug dealing, pimpin' psychopath. I thought maybe he was raised by a pack of jackals, then I realized that was an insult to the jackals." He looked back at Gus. "So that's why that cop is pressuring you to say it was this Andre punk who gave you the drugs?"

"He's not a punk. He's nothing like his brother. He's one of the few people in my class with a higher GPA than me."

Kristin inserted herself into the conversation. "Why didn't you tell us he was the brother of that guy?"

"Because that's not fair to Andre. He's a good guy. Like the polar opposite of his brother. I didn't want to drag him into this."

"Goose, look around," Gideon said. "You're in jail now. You need to stop acting like you'll be rewarded for being a stand-up guy. Don't get so caught up in doing the right thing that you end up spending thirty years in here."

"So you want me to tell the detective what he wants to hear just to get out?"

"I'm not telling you to be a rat. I'm not. But quit hiding things from us. It's time you stopped acting like a boy and start acting like a man."

"If you want me to act like a man, then quit calling me Goose. Nobody's called me that since I was six."

"I'm sorry."

"So the guy who hit you said not to talk about Andre?" Kristin asked.

"It was three guys. They took turns hitting me. Said they'd kill me if I worked with that cop, but I'm not looking to lie and say it was Andre who gave me the drugs. I'm not."

"I understand."

"Well I don't," Gideon said. "Lookit, right now your goal is to get out of here. If Andre didn't do nothing wrong, then let someone represent him in court. He can be proved to be innocent."

"You mean like I'm about to be shown to be innocent?" Gus shook his head, looking like he was about to break into tears. "Besides, if I say Andre gave me the drugs—especially when he didn't—Stick would not only go after me, but he'd also go after my mom and dad. The guy is ruthless. That'd be a death sentence for me."

"Do you think Andre would at least be willing to testify that you didn't know what was in the bag?" Kristin asked.

"Judge won't care about that," Gideon said.

"He might. If Gus and Andre told the same story about Jamie giving him the bag, that might be enough."

Gus said to Kristin, "Andre probably would testify. We're best friends, but I was warned not to involve him in any way."

"Would it be alright if I spoke to your friend? I won't force him to testify. The police already know he was with you prior to your arrest, so it's not as though anyone will know you gave me his name. I'd be talking with him anyway since he was there when you were given the bag."

"I guess, but you better be careful. Stick's not someone you want to mess around with. I once saw him cut off a guy's middle finger with a meat cleaver after the guy flipped him off."

The rest of their time with Gus went quickly, in part because they didn't see any new options than they had before. After Gus was escorted back to his cell, Kristin and Gideon walked out of the jail, Kristin stopping before unlocking her car doors. She looked over the roof of the car at Gideon as he tried opening the door but still found it locked.

"I know that what happened to Gus pisses you off," Kristin said, "but if you try to fix things your way, you'll just make things worse."

"I'll make your car door worse if you don't unlock it."

Kilo sat at the conference room table, with Thane and Letitia flanking him. Thane figured they would all be more comfortable at the larger table, rather than having to sit close to each other at his office table.

Letitia, in particular, put considerable space between herself and their new client. She had been the first to greet Kilo, although 'greet' was being generous. She made eye contact, got up, and told him to follow her. She hadn't said anything else so far, not even during Thane's introductions.

Kilo didn't appear to take it personally. He was likely used to being shunned.

Kilo had dressed up a little for the meeting. He had changed out of his t-shirt with the hole in one shoulder and was now wearing a nice polo shirt, albeit one that looked two sizes too small. He was still wearing jeans, but they appeared to be cleaner than the ones he had worn when he talked to Thane at lunch. It was a small thing, but it still surprised Thane.

Kilo was making an effort.

Since small talk didn't seem like a viable option, Thane jumped right in, first summarizing the situation, then starting in on his questions.

"So are you still not sure whether or not you were at that bar the night Joseph was murdered?"

Kilo shook his head. "I looked through my credit card statements, but I usually paid cash there. You're not supposed to drink the first six months after getting out on parole, so I didn't want that on my credit card."

"There would have been at least a couple of police cars around the murder scene. You didn't see anything like that any of those nights when you left Gulliver's?"

"No. The bar is around the corner and a couple of blocks from where the guy was killed. I live the opposite direction, so even if I was there that night, I wouldn't have seen anything. Besides, me seeing a police car in that neighborhood is probably like you seeing a minivan in your neighborhood."

Thane found himself struggling to think of questions to ask. There were certainly things he wanted to say, but he couldn't do so without revealing his knowledge of the killing.

Finally, Letitia spoke up. "Did you know the victim? Ever have any encounter with him in the past?"

Kilo looked at her, surprised she spoke. "I was wondering if anyone was going to ask me that. No, I never met him, at least not that I remember. He didn't seem like the kind of guy who I'd have interacted with."

"Because maybe you thought he was Jewish?" she asked with a frosty tone.

"No, because he was successful."

Thane realized he should have asked Kilo at the beginning whether he knew Joseph. Now he was concerned Kilo would wonder why he hadn't pressed his story in any way whatsoever.

"I'm assuming you've seen a picture of Joseph?" Thane asked.

"Yeah, I went online to read more about the murder."

"And you didn't recognize him? Didn't maybe deal to him? That's something Struthers was thinking."

"No. Like I told you before, I stepped away from that life."

"Then can you think of anyone who might be trying to set you up?" Thane asked.

Kilo looked blankly at Thane for a moment, then coughed up a laugh. "You mean besides you? Yeah, I seem to have pissed off a number of people since getting released, but I don't think this is how they would come at me. Usually a bullet or a brick over the head is how they would make their move."

"Or a knife," Letitia added, not looking up from her notepad as she wrote something down. Kilo glanced over at

Thane, then back at her.

"Yeah. Or a knife."

Thane wanted to ask if Kilo knew Russell McCoy, the man who actually carried out Joseph's death sentence, but didn't know how to do it without raising questions. Kilo probably wouldn't think anything of a random name or two being tossed around, but Letitia would take note and likely do a search after their meeting. Asking about the father of the young woman who Thane was falsely convicted of murdering would have raised questions.

"Okay, I don't think we're going to know why the police have you as a suspect until they come at you again. Maybe they just approached you because of your record and because someone saw you at the bar the night of the murder, but that seems like a stretch. On the other hand, it's been a few months since the murder, so maybe they're at the point where they feel they have to start shaking the bushes. If they're just cornering people like you for questioning, then knowing Sullivan's, they're going to have a lot of suspects to corner."

"So you don't think there's anything we can do right now?"

"I honestly don't know what it would be. You don't even know if you were there that night, and if you were, there doesn't appear to be any reason why you'd be considered a suspect, unless someone is setting you up. So unless you think of anything else, we wait and assume there's a good chance you won't hear from the cops again."

"Okay," Kilo said, sounding unconvinced. He turned toward Letitia. "Thank you for your help."

"I'm not helping you because I want to."

"You hide it well," Kilo said, with a hint of a smile.

They rose and walked out of the conference room

as Gideon and Kristin were returning from seeing Gus. Kristin glanced up and paused when she saw Kilo, then continued into her office and shut the door harder than usual.

Kilo nodded at Gideon, then looked over at Thane. "I see you two are still hanging out together."

"Yeah," Gideon said. "He may be a lawyer, but that don't mean he's very smart."

"That's always what a guy wants to hear about his lawyer."

"Yeah, well, I'm not having a good day, so maybe we can chit-chat some other time."

"Understood. But I'm glad to see things are working out for you. I really am."

"Fuck you, you spineless, redneck piece of shit."

Kilo didn't flinch. "I'll leave you to your bad day."

Kilo turned and headed toward the door, stopping first at a water dispenser in the reception area to pour himself a paper cup of water.

Gideon continued stomping toward his office when Thane called out to him. "Something happen at the jail?"

Gideon stopped and scowled, looking like he wanted to spit on the new carpet. "Goose's—Gus's—friend turns out to be Stick Sturgess's brother."

"Who's that?"

When Gideon didn't answer right away, Kilo spoke up. "Stick?" Thane turned and looked at him. "If you took a baby and dropped it on his head ten or twenty times, then taught it how to be mean, it'd likely grow up to be Stick."

Thane looked at Gideon for confirmation. Gideon nodded. "I don't think anyone had to teach Stick how to be mean, but otherwise, that's a fair description."

"How do you know him?" Thane asked Kilo.

"I used to work with him from time to time back when I was dealing. He was a major supplier. I heard he started running women too. The guy's a sociopath. I once saw him take a nail gun and shoot a four-inch nail into both eyes of one of his crew when the guy wouldn't tell Stick what he wanted to know. Turned out the guy didn't know anything about what it was Stick was asking. Stick didn't even offer so much as an 'oops' once he realized that. That's when I decided I needed to start thinking about another line of work, but then prison made that decision for me."

Gideon walked back into the reception area. "That's probably why that Mahone dickhead is playing hardball with Goose. He's after Stick."

"Mahone's working that case? Hell, he's almost as bad as Stick, 'cept he has the law on his side."

"What do you mean?"

"Just that he's been after Stick forever. He even tried threatening me, but I told him to blow me."

"What'd he do?" Thane asked. When Kilo started to wave him off, Thane said, "It might help Gideon's nephew."

Kilo glanced at Gideon and shrugged. "Mahone approached me about a minute and a half after I got paroled. Said if I didn't help him get something on Stick, he would go out of his way to make sure I went back to Forsman if I messed up on my parole. He also tried busting me awhile back, but that blew up in his face."

"What happened?"

"A neighbor of mine had borrowed a few tools. I met him out on the street when he was bringing them back to me in a gym bag and suddenly Mahone and a couple of his stooges appeared out of nowhere."

"They think you were in the middle of a drug deal?"

"Probably. Or it was his way of showing he could make my life complicated if I didn't help him."

Thane felt like he was back in the prison courtyard, standing around talking with other felons, getting dirt on new arrivals. Seemed like everyone knew everyone else's business in that world. Usually it was one or two degrees of separation. Even Gideon tolerated listening to Kilo, because you never passed up information that might help you.

Thane looked over at Gideon to see if he had any questions, but he'd already turned and started back into his office. Kilo nodded at Thane, then walked out the door.

Thane was about to return to his office when he saw Letitia staring at him.

"What's up?" he asked.

She offered up a shrug as though what was on her mind wasn't all that important, but it didn't stop her from telling him.

"It's just you didn't ask a lot of the questions I thought you would when we were in there. And you didn't try to poke holes in his story. You said if you even thought there was a ten percent chance he did it then you wouldn't take the case, but you acted like you had absolutely no doubt as to his innocence. I guess I was wondering if you're really that gullible, or do you have the world's best shit-detector?"

Thane hesitated. "I have a good sense about people, which usually turns out to be accurate. I just don't believe he murdered Joseph. It doesn't ring true to me, so I don't feel the need to convince myself. I believe him."

"So you're gullible then," she said, nodding to herself as she returned her attention back to her computer screen. "Thanks. That answers my question."

13

As soon as Gideon got back to his apartment after work, he knew he wouldn't be there long. He said he'd let Kristin take the lead, but it wasn't in his nature to do nothing. Of course, there were numerous times when 'doing nothing' would have served him better, because 'doing something' often resulted in him serving time. But this was family, and he didn't have much of that. At least not many who acknowledged him.

Until Gus got arrested, he wasn't sure he had any.

Gideon grabbed a couple of pieces of pizza from the fridge and tossed them in the microwave, then pulled a plate from a cupboard—and not one made of paper. Even more amazing to him, all the plates in the cupboard matched.

He could now afford to live in a nice apartment with more than three rooms, working appliances, and a refreshing absence of cockroaches. The kind of place where neighbors nodded at each other when they entered the elevator, an acknowledgement Gideon was still trying to get the hang of.

He felt like he had a chance this time around, a feeling he never experienced before. He knew a lot of his behavior was still driven from reflexes developed in prison, which wasn't good, but he thought maybe he was finally starting to get the hang of this whole freedom thing.

At the same time, he didn't want to lose the edge he developed behind bars, especially now that he was trying to free Goose. Gus. Whatever.

After scarfing down the pizza, Gideon headed over to his sister's place. He didn't have a car yet—he wasn't yet comfortable driving, given his lack of practice and his tendency toward road rage—but Kristin had taught him how to use Uber. It was like having his own chauffeur, albeit one that charged each time.

As soon as he got out in front of Pearl's house, he realized he should have called first, although he didn't think he had her number. She and her husband lived in Leimert Park, a predominantly Black neighborhood made up of mostly lower to middle class families. Most of the houses were small and fairly basic, but well kept.

After he knocked on the front door, the curtain over the door window slid to the side and he saw the startled look on his sister's face, then heard two bolts click loudly before the door opened.

"Gid," she said, sounding startled.

"Hey, Pearl. Sorry I didn't call. I realized when I got here that I should of."

"No, that's fine. Really. I'm just surprised."

"I guess I thought maybe it was okay for me to come to your house now since, you know, I'm trying to help Goose."

"Gus."

"Yeah, right. I'm working on that. Gus."

A man's voice came from inside the house. "Who is it, babe?"

"It's Gid."

There was a long pause, then Pearl's husband came and joined her. For the life of him, Gideon couldn't remember the man's name, or whether or not they had had any bad blood between them.

The tall, lean man wore a Raider's t-shirt, blue jeans, and steel-toed work boots, looking like he was fresh off a construction site. He looked Gideon over, then extended his hand. "Roland. I know we met once years ago, but you know, in case you forgot my name."

"Nah, 'course I remember. How's it going, Roland? I was telling Pearl I'm sorry to be barging in like this."

"Not a problem, man. We appreciate what you're doing. Please, come on in." After Roland invited him, Gideon glanced over at Pearl to make sure she was alright with that. She stepped to the side and waved him in.

"Can I get you a beer?" Roland offered, as Gideon carefully lowered himself down onto a padded reading chair in the living room.

"I can't remember a time when I've turned down a beer."

As Roland went into the kitchen, Gideon saw Pearl looking at him with a hint of concern on her face.

"Don't worry," Gideon said. "I like my beer, but I know when to stop. I'm not like the old man."

Pearl sat on the sofa, relaxing at least a couple of degrees. There was an awkward silence, so Gideon looked around the living room. He was struck by its warmth. At first, he wasn't sure what it was about it that made it so comfortable, then he figured out it was because it looked like a home, and not just a house.

His new apartment had nice furniture, a large

TV, and pretty much everything you'd expect to see in an apartment, but Pearl's house also had things like knick-knacks, each likely with a memory attached to it, and small touches like framed photographs. A number of photos were on display on side tables, the fireplace mantel, and on the wall.

Gideon realized he didn't own any photos.

He got up and walked over to look at the framed pictures on the mantel. He picked one up and examined it, then turned to Pearl.

"Tell me this ain't Rose!"

Pearl smiled. "It is."

Gideon stared at it a moment longer, then turned it back toward her. "Our sister's blond?"

"At least when that photo was taken. Hard to say what she is now. She's been in Philadelphia about five years now. On her third husband, and likely already got number four already lined up. We don't talk but maybe three or four times a year, but I think she's doing good."

"That's three or four times more than I've talked with her." He set down the photo, then picked up another, his eyes widening. "Goddamn, how many kids did Bella crank out?"

Pearl walked over next to him and looked at the picture, joining him in his laughter. "Seven."

"Seven?! She and her husband must really like each other. Just out of curiosity, how many nieces and nephews do I got?"

Pearl looked at Gideon with a bit of sadness. He wasn't trying to make her feel bad about being estranged from his three sisters, but he was curious.

"Their seven, plus Rose has two—she had three, but

122

her eldest boy got killed in a car wreck couple years ago—and August makes ten."

Gideon whistled as he gently put the photo back on the mantel. "Goddamn. Would you look at the three of you. Good for y'all."

Roland returned to the room with two bottles of beer. Gideon took one and walked back over to his chair.

"Like I said," Roland said, "Pearl and I both appreciate you and your friend trying to help Gus. I'm not sure either of us have slept more than a couple of hours since he was arrested."

"That's why I stopped by. I wanted to ask you some questions to try to get a better idea of what's what. Get to know my nephew a little better. I'm guessing he's changed a little since he was five."

"Ask anything you want to know," Pearl said.

"First off, this is just us talking, okay? Goes without sayin', I ain't the police, I ain't a schoolteacher, I'm just family, so if there's anything you wouldn't normally tell anyone else, you need to be comfortable telling me, alright? It's important I get the straight shit in order to do my job."

Pearl and Roland glanced at each other, then both nodded.

"Is there any possibility at all Gus could be involved with drugs?" Gideon lifted his hand to stop Pearl, who was starting to answer the question before he finished it. "Before you say anything, I want you to know I'm committed to helping the boy whatever the story is. The way in which I go about helping him might change, depending on what we're talking about here."

Pearl immediately responded. "I know a lot of times

kids are caught doing something and their parents are surprised, saying they had no idea. But I promise you that Gus isn't involved in drugs or anything like that. And this isn't just a mother speaking, this is someone who has seen some shit in her day and isn't naive about how life works, okay? There's no way Gus was involved in that drug deal."

Gideon looked at Roland, who nodded. "Gus is doing things right. A hell of a lot righter than I did growing up."

"That's sort of what I figured, but obviously I don't know the kid very well. So tell me everything you can about these two friends of his who he was hanging with that day. Andre and that punk-ass kid who gave him the drugs. Jamie. You know much about either of them?"

"We know Andre real well," Roland said. "I'm assuming Gus told you who Andre's brother is?"

"Yeah, although he wasn't quick to offer it."

"Andre's a good kid. It's like he was raised by totally different parents," Pearl said.

"The parents are good folk," Roland added. "I just think an electrical circuit in his brother's brain shorted out. That kid ain't right."

"What can you tell me about Jamie?"

Pearl shook her head. "I met him a couple of times. I don't think Roland ever did. He was alright. Always struck me as being a white kid from money who wanted to hang out with kids like Gus. Maybe he thought it made him look cooler. He was always polite enough, didn't seem like trouble. I always thought he was a bit of a poser."

They then talked some more about Gus and his plans for college. When Gideon got up to leave, he handed his empty beer bottle to Roland. He'd been offered a second one, and usually would have taken it, but he didn't want to make Pearl uncomfortable.

Roland thanked Gideon yet again before heading back to the kitchen to finish cleaning up, giving his wife some time alone with her brother.

Stepping out onto the front porch, Gideon glanced at the old iPhone Kristin had given him, checking the status of his Uber driver. The small screen showed his ride was six minutes away.

"You don't have to wait out here with me," he told Pearl. "This little car here is coming to pick me up." He showed her his phone screen. "Look at that: I can just stand here and watch it coming to me. Ain't that the shit? Didn't even need to make a call or nothing."

Pearl smiled and studied her brother. "I appreciate your help, Gid. I really do. And I'm happy to see you doing what you're doing. I'm very proud of you."

Gideon tried responding, but didn't know what to say. He wasn't used to getting compliments, so he just nodded his thanks.

"Looks like you married yourself a good man, Pearl. I'm glad. You and him seem to have yourselves a right nice life, and you did a hell of a job with your boy. You ought to be proud of yourself."

Pearl looked down at the front lawn. Her voice caught as she tried to respond, so she took a deep breath. She then managed to look back up at Gideon, although she struggled maintaining eye contact.

"I'm sorry I didn't reach out on those occasions when you were out of prison. I should have called. Should have offered to try to help you, but I was a little scared bringing you around the family. I'm ashamed to say it now, but I want you to know I'm sorry."

"I understood. I always understood why you didn't."

"But that doesn't make it right. I shouldn't have kept you away. I should have let you see your nephew more than I did. It's just I was afraid you'd turned into our father, and I couldn't take the chance of letting that into my house. I just couldn't."

She wiped her hands a couple of times on her dress, grabbing a handful of fabric each time.

"I get it, Pearl. I do. But I hope you believe me when I tell you that while I know I inherited some of the old man's anger, I didn't end up with his meanness, and for that I'm grateful. I'm not like him. Not like that."

Pearl put her hand on Gideon's shoulder and squeezed it. He was surprised how much that simple touch meant to him. "I can see that now, Gid," she said. "Really."

"So you don't need to apologize, sis."

"It's more than that. I feel bad because you always watched out for us. You always took your job as our big brother seriously. And don't think I don't know how many times you took a beating that belonged to one of us girls. You confessed to more things than you should have, just to keep us from getting hit. And then when you needed a helping hand, I kept mine in my pockets."

"It turns out all that confessing was good practice for my future career in crime."

"Our so-called father is probably the reason you ended up in that 'career' of yours. And then there was that night…"

Pearl looked so deeply into Gideon's eyes that he suddenly felt completely exposed. He shook his head firmly.

"That's ancient history."

Neither spoke for a long minute. Gideon checked his phone screen, watching the tiny car creeping ever closer to his location.

"You ever go visit Mama?" Pearl asked.

"If I could visit her, I'd dearly love to do that, but that's not her. It's just a slab of marble with her name on it. Not much visiting going to happen there."

He had been tempted a couple of times to visit where his mother was buried, but never ended up doing so. He knew what he'd say; knew what he'd ask her. What he didn't know was what she'd say in return, and he wasn't going to find that out by standing over a plot of dirt.

At last, he saw his ride turn the corner and pull up to the curb. As he walked toward the car, Pearl called out to him.

"I know that what you did that night, you did for us. We all know it, Gid. And then all three of us just shut you out once you started spending time in prison like it was your second home. I think all of us felt like it was partly our fault."

"None of it was your fault, Pearl. It was all his. And mine. Don't you ever forget that."

He opened the car door, wanting only to be driven away before his sister could say anything else, but he wasn't fast enough.

"No child should ever have to do what you did."

Gideon looked back at his sister.

"I was never a child."

14

After working a couple of hours re-shelving books at Hannah's bookstore, Thane and Hannah stopped for a dinner break.

She had decided to reorganize the store, starting with moving the Fiction section so that it would be near the back of the store, since that's where the majority of her clientele gravitated. She got the idea after noticing how grocery stores put their most frequently purchased staples at the back of the store, in the hope that customers would grab additional items on their way to get milk.

The bag of tacos came from the El Flamin Taco food truck near Echo Park. As hard as Thane tried not thinking about his time in prison, he couldn't help remembering that El Flamin's al pastor tacos were on his shortlist of possible last meals in case his death sentence was ever carried out. Back then, he assumed that would be the only way he would ever savor one again, but he much preferred this setting: sitting on the floor, back against a shelf of books, next to his wife.

Hannah took the lids off their plastic cups of margaritas and handed him one. Thane wiped the sweat from his forehead with his shirt sleeve, then pulled a hefty taco out of the bag and unwrapped it.

"I'm guessing you'd be hard-pressed to hire anyone else to move all these books for a bag of tacos." He took a large bite, like a shark biting into a mackerel.

"They're darn good tacos, though."

"They are at that," he said, relishing the mouthful of heaven.

"Although I've been wanting to start eating healthier, so you're sort of a bad influence here, but I'll try not to hold it against you."

"If you'd like, I can eat your tacos for you." He held out his hand, but she turned to shield her dinner from him. "How much longer you think we have to go tonight?"

"Probably a couple more hours at most, if that's okay." She reached for her margarita and held it against her cheek in an effort to cool off. "I appreciate your help."

"Happy to. Besides, we've been talking about how we needed another impromptu date night, so here we are."

"You romantic, you." She lifted her taco to her mouth, but didn't take a bite. She held it there for a couple of seconds, then put it back down on her plate. "I've decided to apply for the position at the Shelter. That's one of the reasons I'm making some changes to the store; in case I decide to sell it."

"It will be a great fit for you."

"It will if I get the job. I'm sure there will be other applicants, but I feel like I at least have a chance, especially with Evie's support."

Thane hadn't wanted to talk with Hannah about his situation at work until they were home and the time was right. Or maybe that was just an excuse to put off telling her, but he knew he had to say something sooner than later.

"I hope I don't mess things up for you," he finally said, immediately wishing he had waited after all.

She looked at him curiously.

"You remember I was telling you about the guy I spoke to? The suspect in Joseph's murder?"

Hannah put down her plate. "You mean the guy you shouldn't have reached out to in the first place and who you in absolutely no way should represent because of everything that might bring with it?" she said, with no amusement in her voice. "I do seem to recall something about that."

"I get the feeling you have a sense of where this is heading."

"Thane, no. Please tell me you didn't agree to represent him."

"He hasn't been charged, so technically I'm not actually representing him. But I am trying to help him out."

"And if he does end up getting charged?"

Thane hesitated, although he was sure she already knew the answer. "Then I said I'd represent him."

Hannah slid her taco to the side and focused exclusively on her margarita. "Have you not had enough publicity lately? Is that it? Are you feeling ignored now that we can actually walk down the street and not have people stare at us?"

"It's likely he won't be charged. I don't think anything will come of this, Hannah."

"Yes, because your track record has certainly shown that things you get involved with usually stay under the radar."

Thane slid closer so that their shoulders touched.

He never tired of having a physical connection with her, even if it was just touching her hand, stroking her hair, or leaning against her.

"I don't want the wrong guy to go to jail for Joseph's murder."

"And I don't either. But if it does go to court, you'll once again be a major topic of conversation in this city. I really feel like these last few months, we've made some progress getting back to whatever normal is for us."

Thane felt the same way. The adjustment from death row was much harder than he had expected.

"I'm sorry," he said. "I hope it won't come to that."

"I'll be honest," she said, "I feel like I'm in a difficult position here, and it makes me mad. I know I was also adamant against you taking on Skunk's case. I'm ashamed when I think about when I told you that you had to choose between us and taking on Stone in court. But you were right, and you were vindicated, and everything is so much better than I ever imagined it could be. And now I'm here once again telling you I don't think you should take on a case, and even though I'm convinced I'm right, I don't feel like I can say that to you."

"I'm sorry I've made you feel like that. I know it's not fair, and just because it worked out last time doesn't mean you're not right this time. And I swear to you, I'm not trying to take on cases that might make things difficult for us."

"I know that. It's just, I feel like things are finally starting to get back to normal. The old normal, not the new normal. Can't we just live quietly for a while? Haven't we earned that?"

Thane wanted nothing more than to live quietly with

Hannah. He recognized the irony of telling everyone he wanted the right man to go to jail for Joseph's murder, when in fact, that was the last thing he wanted.

"Hopefully the Shelter will offer you the position before any of this hits the news. And if, by chance, it does become public and it moves forward, I hope the people making the decision at the Shelter will understand this has nothing to do with you."

"It's not the job I'm worried about. I like to think they would appreciate your desire to make sure the right person went to prison for the death of our friend. I'm more concerned about stepping back into a damn firestorm." She finished off her margarita. "Is there anything else about the case I should know before the storm hits?"

Thane hesitated, then finished off his drink before saying quickly, "You mean besides the fact he ran with an Arian gang in prison? And that he once tried to kill me?"

Hannah started to laugh, then stopped when she realized Thane wasn't kidding.

"Wait. What?!"

"Yeah. You know those scars on my chest? Well, uh…"

She stared at him, dumbstruck, until finally mustering up the closest she could find to the right words.

"I'm going to need another margarita."

15

Gideon leaned against Jamie's apartment building. He had redirected his Uber driver after Pearl had found and texted him the kid's address.

He held an open 24-ounce Budweiser can by his waist, having stopped by a convenience store, but he wasn't taking any swigs from it. He waited for someone to go in or out of the building so he could get through the locked front door.

He had already been standing there for over twenty minutes, wondering whether anyone actually lived in the building, but after having spent many years in a prison cell, he had the ability to stay in one place doing absolutely nothing for an extended period of time without getting restless.

Finally, a skinny teenager in a Kia screeched to a stop and double-parked in front of the apartment complex. The pizza delivery sign on the roof of his car lit up like a tiny billboard. He hopped out wearing a Pizza Parlor shirt and carrying a hot box, walked up to the steps, and pressed the buzzer with Jamie's apartment number next to it. When the kid was buzzed in, Gideon walked over.

"I got it. I'm on my way up to Jamie's anyway."

The kid glanced at the name on the order, then looked

at Gideon nervously, uncertain what to do. "That's okay. I'm sort of supposed to deliver it myself."

Gideon took out two twenties and handed them to the kid with one hand, while taking the pizza with the other. "That's okay. I'm sort of telling you I'll take it."

The delivery boy looked at Gideon, then looked at the bills. He took the money and turned to leave. "Enjoy your pizza."

"I always do."

As Gideon stood in the lobby waiting for the elevator, he opened the box and took a couple of dinosaur-sized bites from one of the pieces before tossing it back in the box. He got on the elevator, and once he reached the fourth floor, knocked on the door of Apartment 4B.

"You're fucking late, dude," came a nasally voice.

Jamie opened the door, his scowl quickly replaced by wide eyes when he noticed the large Black man standing in the hallway with his pizza. "But that's okay. Traffic can be a bitch this time of night."

"That mean I ain't getting a tip?" Gideon asked.

"Oh. Well, I don't usually tip. Just my personal philosophy. But thanks for the pizza."

He reached for the pizza box, but Gideon walked into the apartment, forcing Jamie to hop to the side to avoid getting bowled over.

"But sure, I'm guessing I've got a couple of bucks for a tip. Gotta support the working man, am I right?"

Gideon stood in the middle of the living room, checking out the place. It was upscale in terms of furnishings and decor, at least for a kid his age. It was the sort of place a kid with affluent parents would live, but it also looked like a fraternity house after an end-of-semester blow out party. Clothes strewn everywhere, dirty plates and glasses piled high on the coffee table and on the arm of the leather sofa, the smell of rotting food wafting from the kitchen.

"Hey, what up, bro?" Jamie said, his voice cracking.

"*What up, bro?* Seriously?" Gideon continued looking around, trying to see if anyone else was in the apartment. "I'm guessing it's safe to say you ain't got a girlfriend."

"I'm between ladies right now."

"Yeah, I'll bet."

"I had a girlfriend, but I lost her to the Big C."

That stopped Gideon. He wasn't overly empathetic, but it surprised him, given the kid's age. "No shit? Christ, how old was she?"

Jamie looked at him, a puzzled expression on his face. "Nineteen?"

"Damn, man. And she had cancer?"

"Cancer? She didn't have cancer."

"You just said you lost her to the Big C."

Jamie nodded. "Yeah. Big C. Carl Stronsky. They call him the Big C because the guy's like three hundred pounds. What's all this about, bro?"

"First thing's first: you call me 'bro' again, I'm going to shove this pizza up your ass and—spoiler alert—it's still hot. Second, I'm Goose's—Gus's—uncle. I'm also sort of like his lawyer, and you and me are going to have a little talk."

Jamie's normally pasty complexion somehow managed to turn an even lighter shade of white. Gideon thought if the kid turned any more pale, he'd become transparent. "I'm not supposed to talk to anyone from Gus's family."

"Then I'll talk, and you listen." He looked at Jamie,

who was now starting to sweat. Gideon lifted up his Budweiser can as he spoke. "You look like you could use something to drink, dude. Let's go get you a glass of something."

Gideon put a firm hand on Jamie's forearm and guided him to the kitchen, taking the opportunity to continue scoping out the apartment as they walked. Gideon found a large, dirty glass next to the sink and filled it with water, then set it on the counter next to Jamie.

"I've been around enough to know a set-up when I see it," Gideon said. "Here's what I think is going down here. You're a rich white kid who figures you can do pretty much anything you want, but then you're busted with drugs and learn that that's actually frowned upon by the police. You're then given the option of setting up your friend Andre or going to jail. You could probably get out of this with a high-priced lawyer, but you don't want your parents to know. So, you agree to do it, but instead, Gus takes the bag, so now he's the one being pressured to turn on Andre because he's from a family that doesn't have much money."

"Look, br—sir. Sir. Look, I understand why you want to help out your nephew. I know Gus and his family are good people, but this isn't the sort of world you want to be a part of. There's some tough people involved and, no offense, it's probably not safe for you to be messing around in this."

"You best understand one thing right now, boy. I'm not like the rest of Gus's family. They're good folk. But me? I'm not that good."

Jamie gave a feeble attempt at laughing. "You telling me you're the black sheep of the family?"

Gideon's chest inflated as he loomed over Jamie. "Oh I'm Black, but I ain't no damn sheep."

Jamie stepped back, his right eye starting to twitch. "Look, man, the cop wants Andre. I don't know if you know who his brother is, but that dude is bad shit. I can either testify that Gus is the dealer so that the cops can pressure him into testifying against Andre, or I can testify that Andre is the guy who gave Gus the bag, but then I'd be a dead man. Or I can go to jail. So given those options, with all due respect, *sir*, you're at the bottom of my radar. No offense, man. But I don't want to go to prison, and you don't know what Stick would do."

"I'm pretty sure I do know what Stick would do. The problem is, you don't know what I would do."

Jamie started sweating even more profusely as Gideon glared at him, then turned to run, but Gideon grabbed his arm and pulled him over to the counter.

"You need to understand something, *bro*. I'm not here to negotiate". Gideon tipped his Budweiser can, soaking one of the sleeves of Jamie's hoodie. "Whoops, looks like I spilled some."

"Man, if you think you're going to change my mind by pouring beer on me, then you're smoking something."

"It's not beer." Gideon pulled a lighter from his pocket and flicked on a flame. "It's gas. And I'm not going to be the one smoking."

Jamie's eyes widened as Gideon pressed the lighter onto Jamie's arm, causing the sleeve to go up in flames. Gideon placed his hand over Jamie's mouth before he could scream.

"If you believe nothing else I say tonight, boy, you need to believe this: you do not want to make me mad. I will hurt you bad, and after I hurt you bad, I'll hurt you even worse."

He gripped Jamie's wrist like a vice as he watched the kid's eyes watering in fear. Finally he grabbed the glass of water and doused out the flame. He released Jamie, who ripped off the jacket and threw it in the sink.

"Are you fuckin' crazy, man?"

"No, I'm Gus's uncle, and if you think Stick is trouble, then you don't know what trouble is."

"I—"

"Now here's what you're going to do. You're going to tell whatever detective is pressuring you that Gus didn't know there was drugs in the bag. And you're going to tell him you've never known Gus to have anything to do with drugs. Then you need to tell Mommy and Daddy to call their lawyer, and if you don't want to do that then I know a real good lawyer who will help you out for free. But that's what you're going to do. You don't need to say Andre is involved in any of this, so that should keep you clear from Stick. But if your options are to deal with Stick, or deal with me, or go to court as a rich, young white dude with a lawyer, well, hopefully you ain't *that* dumb."

Gideon took hold of Jamie's shirt collar and held him in place as he poured the rest of the fluid from the beer can over the kid's head, then lit his lighter once again. Jamie's eyes grew to the size of lemons.

"'Cause if you say Gus had anything to do with them drugs, next time you see me you'll end up burning for hours like a damn Duraflame log. I might even roast marshmallows over you. You best believe me on that, boy."

Gideon put away the lighter as Jamie spat the taste of

gas from his mouth. On the way through the living room, Gideon opened the pizza box and took a couple of pieces.

"And you need to start tipping the delivery staff, you cheap fuck."

Gideon walked out of the apartment, newly energized. He felt he'd gotten his message across loud and clear, and while he didn't rule out hurting Jamie if the punk continued to testify against Gus, he knew he wouldn't actually light the kid on fire.

For one thing, he didn't even like marshmallows.

16

Thane looked up from some paperwork when Letitia knocked on his open door. She stood there smiling as she looked down at Cricket, the granddaughter of Thane's former neighbor. The young girl was more dressed up than when he first met her, the jumpsuit likely the result of her grandmother's insistence.

"Your 9:00 AM appointment is here," Letitia announced.

"Thanks, Letitia. Come on in, Cricket."

Cricket started into the office, then turned and shook Letitia's hand. "Thank you for your assistance." She then walked on into Thane's office, shutting the door behind her. She hopped up on a cushioned chair positioned in front of Thane's desk. "So, what have you got for me, Thor?" She tried unsuccessfully to keep a grin from crossing her face.

Thane looked at her and shook his head, smiling. "How come you treat Letitia with so much respect, but you give me a hard time?"

"Because she's a sister stuck doing the scut work for the high-priced mouthpiece. I'm just trying to keep you humble."

"Given that I'm representing you for free, I don't

know that you can call me high-priced."

"Still want to keep you humble. So what's new in my case? You threaten to sue them yet?"

Thane picked up her file and looked it over.

"So here's the deal. Apparently, you didn't just splice into a neighbor's cable or something like that…"

Cricket sighed and rolled her eyes as Thane just called into question her professionalism. "Yeah. And?"

"You were actually able to hack into their system and bypass security points they said were next to impossible to get past."

"The operative words being 'next to impossible.' But obviously not impossible."

"Which is why the cable company is taking it seriously. But I've talked with them, and they're willing to drop all charges against you in exchange for you telling them precisely—and I mean precisely—how it is you did what you did. That is far more valuable to them than prosecuting a ten-year-old girl. I wasn't, however, able to get them to toss in a DVD set of *Chip and Chad's Home Makeover*."

Cricket looked down at the floor and furrowed her eyebrows as she carefully weighed the pros and cons of this offer. Thane assumed she would be happy at this option, but apparently that wasn't the case.

"You think we should hold out for the series? I mean, if my knowledge of their system is that important to them—"

"I think you should take the offer."

"Maybe they'd be willing to toss in some cash as well, you know, as sort of a good faith gesture?"

"I think whatever good faith ever existed was lost

when you hacked into their system."

Cricket crossed her arms across her chest and sighed, not looking nearly as happy as Thane thought she would.

"Man, I thought you were going to fight for me. Isn't that what a good lawyer does?"

"A good lawyer keeps their client out of jail. They also keep their client's grandmother from having to part with large sums of money she doesn't have."

"Fine. I'll take the offer. But just so you know, nobody buys DVDs anymore. I only wanted to download the series onto my MacBook." She suddenly looked up toward the ceiling, deep in thought. Thane could see her already figuring out another way to make that happen.

"No," Thane said. "You're not going to find a way to download it for free before giving them the information they want. I tell you what: you write up the step-by-step process on how you hacked into their system, and if it's what they're looking for, I'll buy you the series."

She brightened and nodded, finally ready to accept the offer. "I sort of like having my own lawyer."

"And I sort of get the feeling you're going to be needing one as you go through life."

"You going to keep representing me?"

"I don't know that I liked your grandmother *that* much. But yeah, for now, if you find yourself getting into trouble again, feel free to reach out. But another strategy might be to stop getting into trouble. Just a thought."

Cricket hopped up out of her chair and nodded. "I'll give that some serious consideration. When do you need this instruction manual?"

"Can you get me something in a couple of weeks?"

"I can do anything I put my mind to," she replied

confidently.

"Yeah, that's what worries me."

Thane walked her out to the reception area where Gideon was leaning against the front desk, wrapping up a call on his cell phone. He looked up to see Cricket staring at him.

"Dang, man, that's one of the first iPhones! You get that back in nineteen fifty-eight or something?" She offered him a big smile as Letitia let loose a giggle.

Gideon looked at Thane. "I'm still getting used to being on the outside. Is this where I'm supposed to say 'cute kid'? Or am I mistaken that it's now frowned upon to swat a child?" He scowled at her with a look that could boil water.

"Ah, I know your type," she said. "You act tough on the outside, but on the inside you're just a big old softie." She glanced back at Thane for confirmation, but Thane ever-so-slightly shook his head. Cricket's smile disappeared as she looked at her watch and headed toward the door, steering clear of Gideon as she passed the front desk.

"Thanks for your help, Thor. I'll get you something soon as I can."

She left the office, glancing back over her shoulder cautiously at the big guy as she closed the door.

"I want to adopt her," Letitia said.

"If you do, you better go to your bank and set up a bail fund account," Thane responded.

As Thane turned to go back into his office, the door to Kristin's office flew open and she stormed into the reception area, shouting at Gideon with her fury turned up to eleven. "What did you do?!"

"I just got here. I ain't had time to do nothin' yet, but

it's still early."

"I'm not talking about this morning; I'm talking about last night. Care to tell us how you spent your evening?"

Gideon stared at her, betraying no expression, and not saying a word.

"I just called the kid who Gus said gave him the bag of drugs," Kristin said, her anger not abating, "to see if I could meet with him. He told me that Gus's uncle—his uncle *the lawyer!*—came to visit him last night and he's now willing to say whatever it is we want him to say."

"That's good, isn't it?" Gideon asked. "I sort of thought that was the objective."

"Not if you intimidated or threatened him to get him to say it."

"Excuse me," Letitia said. "Are you accusing him of violence because to you he's just an angry black man?"

Kristin looked at Letitia like she was talking crazy. "He IS an angry black man! Have you honestly not spent any time with him at all?"

Gideon grinned, then turned back toward Letitia and nodded in agreement.

"When the only tool you have is a sledgehammer, everything looks like an egg," Kristin yelled.

"I'm not sure that's how the saying goes," Thane offered.

"It is for Gideon!" she shouted at Thane. "We can't be intimidating witnesses. We'll not only lose the case if it gets discovered, but we could also be disbarred. We have to play by the rules and trust the legal system."

At this, both Letitia and Gideon let out a laugh.

"Right. The legal system," Letitia said. "Did you notice how the kid who actually gave Gus the bag of drugs is free and not even being charged? Any chance that's because he's white and can afford a high-priced lawyer?" "Look, I expect you to be on Gideon's side on this," Kristin said.

"Because he and I are Black? I know we haven't worked together for long, and you don't know me all that well, but don't assume I'm going to always agree with Gideon just because we're both Black, same as I'm not going to always agree with you just because we're both women, or that I'm always going to agree with Thane because…" She looked over at him, but couldn't come up with a reason. "Anyway, the point is, I think for myself."

Kristin shifted her focus back to Gideon. "Did you beat him up?"

"No, I didn't beat him up."

"You didn't?"

"Not technically."

"What does that mean, not technically? What did you do to him?"

"Nothin'."

"What did you do to him?"

"I didn't do nothin' to—"

"What did you do to him?!"

"I lit his hoodie sleeve on fire."

"You what?!" Kristin cried.

"You what?!" Thane echoed.

"It wasn't gas. I just told him it was. It was just an itty bit of kerosine. It burns bright but it doesn't really burn like gas does. It's like those fancy flaming drinks you probably get at your hipster bars. It wasn't going to hurt him."

"Are you out of your mind?"

"I got him to agree to tell the truth. That's a good thing. He gave Gus the drugs and that's what he's going to testify."

"He's going to testify however the last person who threatens him tells him to testify. And he'll likely tell the DA what you did, so who knows what will come of that?"

"He ain't gonna tell anybody. He just ain't."

Kristin looked over at Thane. "You've got to talk to him."

"If he has to talk to me," Gideon said, "he can talk to me in his office." Gideon walked into Thane's office. Kristin and Letitia started to follow but Thane held up his hand, stopping them.

"Let me talk to him alone."

Thane went into his office and shut the door. Gideon slumped down in the chair where Cricket had been sitting.

"Seriously? You set him on fire?"

"You all say that like I burned him. The kerosine probably didn't even hurt his punk-ass hoodie. He can probably keep wearing it if he wants."

Thane leaned back, unsure of exactly what to say, mainly because he knew Gideon wouldn't want to hear it.

"Kristin's right, Gideon. We can't be threatening witnesses. All that's going to do is hurt Gus's case. I know at Forsman the ends usually justified the means, but that's not how it plays out on this side of the prison walls. Kristin's got this. She'll do a good job."

"I'm not looking for someone to just do a good job. I want someone who's going to win the case. You should be taking the lead on this. You understand that sometimes you need to do whatever it takes in order to get the result you want. Did you play by the rules with Skunk's case? You telling me you didn't go with the ends justifying the means?"

Thane didn't respond. It had never even occurred to him that Gideon may have figured out that there was more than met the eye during their previous case. If Thane was willing to admit it to anyone, he'd feel most comfortable telling Gideon, but he didn't see anything good that would come from it.

"This is family, man," Gideon said. "You should be doing whatever it is you need to do to get him out. Don't get me wrong, I like little Miss Typhoon Kristin. More than that, I respect her, and that's saying something, coming from me. I think she's going to be a damn good lawyer one day, but she's still a little naive when it comes to playing by the rules."

"I'm keeping an eye on this case, Gideon. And if I ever feel like she's going down a bad path, I'll insert myself. She and I talk about it a lot and so far, she's doing exactly what I would be doing."

"And what if you come to the conclusion that you need to go down a path she'd object to in order to win? Because that's what I'm looking for. Someone who's going to do whatever it takes to make things right."

"We're going to get your nephew out of there. We'll win this thing. I promise. Just don't make it harder for us. You should have let Kristin talk with this Jamie guy first."

"She wouldn't be able to do anything with a punk like that."

"But she needs to have the chance. If we come to a dead end, then maybe we talk about other options. And I totally get where you're coming from. That's the whole reason I started this firm, to help people who are getting screwed by the system, but if we go vigilante for everyone we try to help, we'll be shut down before we do our clients any good."

"Gus isn't a client. He's family." Gideon stood. "I think you did whatever you thought you needed to do to get justice for yourself. You took everything I taught you at Forsman and you used it to right the wrong that was done to you. Well, I'm going to do the same thing for my nephew if I have to." He started for the door.

"Gideon, look…"

"Don't worry. I'm not going to go beat anyone else up right now. But I'm holding you to your promise about getting Gus freed." Gideon opened the office door, then muttered to himself, "Christ, it was just a little kerosine."

As Gideon shut the door, Letitia's voice came over Thane's telephone intercom speaker. "Detective Struthers is on line one. Said it's important."

Thane took another deep breath, then picked up the call.

"Detective. What can I do for you?"

"Do you have a minute to talk, Mr. Banning?"

"Please, call me Thane."

"No."

"I have whatever time you need," Thane sighed.

"I understand you are representing Mr. Miller. Or perhaps advising is the right term, since he hasn't been arrested yet. Either way, I have to admit, I was a little surprised to learn you had inserted yourself into this case. Given your history with the man—and your friendship with the murder victim—you are the last lawyer I would have expected would be willing to help Mr. Miller."

"I'm not helping Mr. Miller. I don't like Mr. Miller. But you're right that the man who was murdered was my friend, and I want to make sure the right person gets arrested."

"Perhaps you should leave the murder investigation to us."

"And I will. But if the person you arrest is found to be innocent, then all I'm doing is helping keep the investigation going."

"Because you're all about making sure the right person is held accountable."

Thane couldn't tell if Struthers was expressing his skepticism or hinting his suspicions.

"As I'm sure you are," Thane responded.

"Oh, you can count on that. But I'm not going to dwell on the past, so let's simply look forward. I'd like you to bring your client to the station later this afternoon. We have some questions we'd like to ask him."

17

Thane called Kilo at his second job to tell him about his call from Struthers. Kilo asked if he was being brought to the station to be charged with the murder. Thane didn't know, but they both felt it was likely Kilo wouldn't be going home that evening.

Thane said he'd meet Kilo at his home and that he would drive him to the police station. He was surprised to learn that Kilo lived in Boyle Heights, an area that was more than ninety-percent Hispanic. It was a low-income neighborhood, so it made sense for Kilo, but Thane had figured that a self-proclaimed white supremacist would have looked for housing in a more Caucasian neighborhood.

Thane pulled up in front of a square, one-story home that had the architectural design of a Lego block. The place likely wasn't bigger than a thousand square feet in size, but it was neatly kept and stood on a quiet side street. The shrubs bordering the front porch were immaculately trimmed, and the small front lawn was green and lush. The place looked like it had been painted recently, a deep blue that almost looked purple in the late afternoon sun.

Thane sat in his car for a couple minutes to see if Kilo would come out, but when the door opened, it wasn't

Kilo who appeared. As surprised as Thane had been to learn that Kilo lived in Boyle Heights, he was even more surprised to see a pregnant Hispanic woman in her early thirties stepping out onto the porch and motioning for him to come into the house before she disappeared back inside.

As Thane approached the front door, he heard a small boy inside shouting that he wanted Cheerios, not Rice Krispies. Thane leaned in the front door and saw the woman in the kitchen, again waving him into the house as she tried getting a three-year-old girl to sit in a highchair and eat something from a spoon, while the boy, who appeared to be around five, was pulling on his mother's dress.

"Come on in and get out of the heat," she said. "Kyle's running a few minutes late."

Thane looked around the house, which was as neat and well-kept as a house could be that housed two small children. In one corner of the living room was a small, round table acting as a Mexican altar, likely set up in advance for the upcoming Día de los Muertos celebration.

"Please, come join me. I'm getting ready to release the hounds, so the noise level should be dropping significantly." The woman handed the young boy a bowl of dry cereal and lifted the girl from the highchair. Thane couldn't hear what she whispered to them, but both children left the room, the boy shyly glancing up at Thane as he passed, the little girl giggling as she scampered behind her brother.

Thane went into the kitchen where the woman was pouring two glasses of water. She set them down at the kitchen table and wiped her hands on her apron before extending one of them to Thane. Her expression was one of exhaustion.

"I'm Ana. Kyle's wife."

Thane smiled and said it was nice to meet her, but apparently, he hadn't been able to hide the surprise from his face. Ana laughed boisterously.

"I can always tell when I'm meeting someone Kyle knew in prison. They're expecting to see some white chick wearing a confederate flag t-shirt, with a hayseed in her teeth, but no, I'm one of those minorities he was likely ranting about in prison."

"How long have you two been married?"

"Nine years this December. We dated three or four years before that. Please, have a seat. I'm sorry I can't offer you anything stronger, but we don't keep alcohol in the house. That doesn't mean Kyle doesn't sneak out for the occasional beer. It's not like it's a problem for him or anything; it's just not something I want around our kids."

Thane sat and accepted the glass of water as Ana sat down with him, emitting a weary sigh.

"Thank you for what you're doing for Kyle. I can't tell you how happy I was when he told me he'd reached out to you and that you'd agreed to help. I was afraid he'd be too stubborn, but he stepped up and did the right thing."

"I hope I can help."

"If you can't, then probably nobody can." She took a long drink of the cool water, then held it up to her forehead before setting it back down in front of her. "Kyle told me you and he didn't hang in the same circles at Forsman."

"No, we didn't."

"That's good, because there's no place in my home for any racist redneck espousing that sort of crap."

Thane looked at her curiously. Ana let out another laugh.

"There's that face again!"

Thane smiled as he felt himself turning red. "It's just—well…" Thane stopped when he heard a rough-running engine pull up in the driveway. Ana smiled at him.

"I wish we had more time to talk. There's so much I'd like to tell you, but before Kyle gets in here, let me tell you this: he's a good man. He really is. He's working two jobs trying to support us so that we can start saving for our children's education, and he's been trying to nail down a third part-time job. He's not who you probably think he is."

She rose from the table and glanced out the window as Kyle was getting out of a beat-up pickup.

"Kyle's father abandoned him when he was four, so he never really had a good male role model. He told me not long ago that he doesn't really know how to be a father, but I can assure you he's doing everything and more to try to make up for the mistakes he's made in the past. But the main thing to know is that when Kyle looks like he has an anger issue, it's not anger he's wrestling with—it's fear. He'll try to come off as a tough guy, but that's mostly just a front. He's a good man, and I hope you can help him."

Thane nodded, then thanked her for the water as Kilo walked into the kitchen. He stopped when he saw the two of them talking, then walked over and took a drink of Ana's water before leaning down and kissing her on the top of her head.

He then looked over at Thane.

"Sorry I'm late. We better get going."

Thane thanked Ana again, then walked into the living room to give Kilo and his wife a moment alone. Through the reflection of the living room window he could see them embracing in the kitchen, Ana's head pressed tight against Kilo's shoulder.

"If I don't come home this evening—" Thane heard Kilo tell his wife.

"Don't say that," she said.

"If I don't come home this evening," he repeated, saying each word slowly, "I'll have him give you a call and he'll tell you what's happening. But we'll get this straightened out." He kissed her and started toward the living room, then stopped and turned back toward his wife. "You know I didn't—"

"Of course I know. I know you better than you know yourself."

"Yeah, and I've always found that a little scary."

"Do you want to say something to the kids before you go?" she asked.

Kilo appeared to think about it, then shook his head. "I don't know what I'd say."

Ana nodded. "In that case, you can come on home and tell them goodnight. I'll even cook you a thick steak."

"Do we have steak?" Kilo laughed.

"If you call and tell me you're on the way home, I'll go get you one."

The car was quiet as Thane pulled out of the driveway.

155

Kilo looked back at his house where Ana stood on the front porch. She wasn't waving, probably because that might feel too much like goodbye, but apparently, she also didn't want to let him simply drive away without watching him, perhaps afraid it would be the last time she'd see him on the outside again.

Thane wished he'd had music on, to make the silence less oppressive, but for whatever reason he now felt that turning it on would be acknowledging the awkwardness. Thane tried to think of something to say, but Kilo beat him to it.

"I don't understand what's going on."

"My sense is we'll have a better idea after we meet with Detective Struthers."

Kilo just nodded. After a couple of minutes, he spoke again.

"I'm trying to do what you're supposed to do on the outside. I was able to get a couple of jobs—nothing fancy, but they pay enough to keep everyone fed and taken care of. I'm not doing drugs, not drinking myself drunk, not looking for trouble. I'm doing everything they told me to do."

"I can tell. But you know as well as I do that this whole concept of 'you paid your dues' and 'start over with a clean slate' is a fantasy. You're always going to be in someone's sights, even when you haven't done anything wrong. That's why it can be so hard adjusting to being on the outside."

"I'm guessing it's probably easier when the city gives you a check for millions of dollars as an apology." Kilo gave Thane the closest thing he'd come to a smile since their paths had crossed.

"That does, indeed, make things easier, but it still doesn't make them easy. I still don't feel as though my feet are on solid ground. I want to go back to who I was previously, but I'm not that person anymore. I'd like to be, but I'm not."

Kilo looked out the passenger window. "It's the opposite for me. It was at Forsman that I felt I had to act like someone I wasn't."

"A skinhead?"

"But that's not who I am, as you might have guessed from my little family. But I thought I needed to be part of a group in order to have protection, and that group of assholes was the only one who welcomed me. I played the part so I'd fit in."

There was a long pause as Kilo tried to speak a couple of times, but each time the words seemed to break before they came out. He finally continued his thoughts.

"I couldn't even let Ana come visit me because someone would see. You have any idea how painful that was, not just to me, but to her? But once I signed up with the Aryan Crew, I didn't think I could just say I'd changed my mind. They would have killed me. Trust me, I despised myself for keeping her away."

Thane knew informal rules inside a prison were rigid, although he felt Kilo was acting like more of a victim than he needed to. People always had choices. Just the same, Thane remembered when he no longer would see Hannah because he wanted her to move on with her life. That almost killed him.

"I know that saying I'm sorry for what went down between us doesn't mean much," Kilo continued, "but I *am* sorry." He took a deep breath. "I'm very, very sorry,

Banning."

Thane kept his eyes on the road. He wanted to pursue this further, but also wanted to leave it in his rearview mirror.

"When you told me to stop hanging around Gideon, did you really care about that, or were you just doing what your gang was telling you?"

"It didn't matter to me who you were friends with, but those wingnuts I hung out with didn't like it, and they put it on me to stop it. I think it was more of a test to see how committed I was to their group and to see if they could trust me."

"So that's why you stabbed me."

Kilo nodded. "That's why I stabbed you, and I have to tell you, I hated you when you kept on hanging out with him."

"Why'd that make you hate me?"

"Because you had the damn backbone to do what you wanted to do, and you weren't scared off by a group of guys threatening you. It was like you held a mirror up to my cowardice and it pissed me the hell off. I didn't realize people could do what they thought was right."

Thane was caught off-guard by Kilo's honesty. He wanted to say something, to let Kilo know how much he hurt him, not just physically, but emotionally. But he realized there was likely nothing he could say that would make Kilo hate himself more than he already did.

"But once I got out," Kilo continued, "I decided to be who I was. First thing I did was make an appointment to tattoo over that stupid swastika symbol they gave me. Then I broke with the other Crew members that were on the outside. They didn't like it, to say the least. Accused me of being part of their gang when I needed protection in jail, then ditching them once I was back on the outside. And they weren't wrong. Before, I would have caved into their threats and would probably be back in jail or dead right now, but seeing what you did, I told them I was out."

"That probably wasn't easy."

"No, it wasn't. It's also another reason why I can't go back to Forsman, or pretty much any other prison in the area. If I get convicted of this murder, it won't matter if I get the death sentence or not, I'll be dead within a month. The Aryan Crew members who are still there will kill me, and it's not like I can join any other prison group, since most of them hated the Crew."

"Well then, I guess we'll have to make sure you don't get convicted. But let's not get too far down the road just yet. They haven't even charged you with anything."

"You think that will still be the case after we're done today?"

Thane didn't answer.

18

Kristin stood outside Andre's apartment and knocked a second time, this time harder. The young man had finally agreed to meet with her, after much cajoling on her part and even more resistance on his, but now he wasn't answering the door. Maybe he'd just told her he'd talk to her to get her off the phone. She was starting to think he'd even given her a fake address, in which case it was probably best no one was answering.

After one more hard knock, she walked back toward the elevator when the apartment door finally opened. Andre leaned out and caught Kristin's eye as he popped his Air Pods from his ears.

"Hey. Sorry about that. I was in the bathroom and forgot to take these out. I didn't realize it was this late. Come on in."

Kristin hesitated before entering the small and neat apartment. The furniture wasn't fancy, but it was nicer than she expected from a kid in his late teens living on his own. The only artwork in the living room was a large poster of Chadwick Boseman as *Black Panther*, and an even larger poster of Flo Milli sporting a waist-length bright red wig and fingering her microphone suggestively.

Kristin couldn't help but smile.

"Hey, sue me. I'm eighteen," he said, noticing her checking out Flo. "What posters do you have at your place? The Jonas Brothers? Who was your fave? Bet it was Joe. *So* brooding," he said, melodramatically.

"You seem to know a lot about them."

"I'm thinking of majoring in ancient history in college."

"Ouch. I'm used to being the butt of age jokes, but not ones where I'm the old person."

"You're not old. Just old-er. Besides, I like older women. The things they know, right?" He raised one eyebrow suggestively at her, then burst out laughing. "I'm just messin' with ya. Sit down."

He motioned to a cushioned chair next to a reading light. An SAT Exam study guide sat on the side table next to the chair.

"I gotta tell you," Andre said, "you don't look like any lawyer I've ever seen. What are you, fifteen?"

"Oh great, first I'm part of ancient history, and now I'm fifteen."

Andre offered up another genuine laugh. "I just mean I was expecting you to be some old, humorless crone who spends all her nights studying the law."

"Give me a couple more years."

"I doubt that. But listen, like I told you on the phone, I'm not sure I can help you out. I want to, but testifying would be—difficult—for me."

"Then let me ask you a couple of quick questions. Is Gus one of your best friends?"

Andre sighed, already seeing where this was heading. "Yeah, he's my boy."

"And did you know that the detective who arrested

him is trying to get 'your boy' to say you're the one who gave him the drugs, otherwise he's threatening Gus with decades in prison?"

Andre looked down and shook his head. "I didn't know that, but it doesn't surprise me. If they arrest me, they'll be doing the same thing to me to get to my brother."

"And did you know Gus is refusing to tell them what they want to hear, because it's not true? Did you know he's standing firm for you?"

Andre flopped back on the sofa. "That doesn't surprise me neither."

"All I'm asking is that if his case goes to court, you testify about what happened. Testify that Jamie was trying to get you to take the bag with the drugs in it, but that Gus said he'd take it, and that you have no doubt Gus didn't know what was in the bag. That neither of you knew. All of that's true, isn't it?"

"Yeah, all that's true."

"So what makes it difficult?"

Andre sat there and started shaking his head, like he was having some internal debate with himself. Kristin could tell he was struggling, but her sense of the kid was that he was going to do the right thing.

"Andre? Where's the complication?"

He hid his face in his hands for a moment, then looked back up at her. "The complication is Jamie. He's not near as good of a friend as Gus, but I've known him for years. If I testify, there would be serious consequences for him."

"Okay, but if there are going to be consequences, shouldn't it be for the guy who tried to get you to deliver a bag of drugs, rather than the guy refusing to roll on you? So what's the right thing for you to do here? I don't know what Jamie's record is, if he even has one, but if he hasn't been busted before with drugs, he likely won't spend much time in jail, if any."

"It wouldn't be a little time in jail. It'd be life."

"What? No way. He'll get himself a good lawyer and they'll get this pleaded down to—"

Andre waved her away. "Man, where'd you grow up? Candyland? I testify that Jamie tried to get me to take a bag of drugs to a place that was staked out? That's a life sentence for him."

Kristin didn't understand what he was saying. "So you're going to let Gus go to jail for years for something he didn't do, all because he was trying to help you out. And Jamie might be testifying that Gus knew about the drugs and is a big-time dealer in order to get out of doing time himself. And even with all this, you're standing by Jamie?"

Andre leaned forward and put his elbows on his knees and cupped his face in his hands. He then looked up at the poster of *Black Panther*, eyes beseeching the hero for advice.

"Aw hell, you already know who I'm going to stand by. Goddamn, Jamie. I don't know what the hell he was thinking. I'll do right by Gus. Tell me what you want me to do."

Kristin put her arm around Andre. She knew he was in a tough position. She didn't know a lot about his brother and his dealings, but she understood the situation was far more complicated than it should have been.

"Let me talk with my colleagues and I'll get back

with you. I'm assuming the easiest thing would be for you to talk with the detective and tell him what you know." Kristin saw Andre wince at the thought of meeting with a narcotics detective, so she quickly backtracked. "Or it may be that we just let them know what you're willing to testify to, then wait and see if it even goes to trial. But if we do that, the police will still likely want to talk with you."

"If they do, you willing to be my lawyer, too?"

"I'll help you however I can. But with you and Gus both telling the same story, and given that neither of you have had any issues with the law before, I don't think you'll need any help."

"I will if they start shaking my family tree. I'm not turning on my family. So if they're gunning for my brother, I'll need a lot of help. You just likely won't be able to provide it."

Kristin exited Andre's apartment building as the sun was starting to set. She felt optimistic but she also knew Andre was a guy in his late teens; it wouldn't surprise her if he changed his mind before she got home.

While still angry at Gideon for what he did to Jamie, if the kid who started all this really was willing to testify that Gus didn't know what was in the bag, then she felt she'd be able to get Gus released soon. But she didn't have the same level of confidence in Jamie that she had with Andre. For one thing, Andre seemed to have character.

When she reached her car, she paused before unlocking it. She glanced behind her, but didn't see anything out of the ordinary. But as a woman who sometimes traveled rough neighborhoods, she strove to always be aware of her surroundings and had developed a surprisingly accurate sense of when someone was watching her.

But even though her internal alarms were going off, she didn't see anyone nearby who appeared to have her in their scope.

Just the same, she jumped into her car and hurriedly locked the door before driving away from whoever—or whatever—it was that might have been watching her.

19

Kilo's interview with Struthers was going about as well as could be expected. So, not well at all.

Thane and Kilo sat on one side of a small table across from Struthers, whose laid back, easy-going style belied what Thane knew would be a well-thought-out plan of questioning.

So far, Struthers had established that Kilo was now working two jobs and was trying to nail down a third. The detective also brought up the fact that Kilo used to associate with the major drug dealer Stick, which Thane felt wasn't relevant to this discussion.

"I object," he said, when Struthers first asked about Stick.

Struthers looked up at Thane, surprised, then tried unsuccessfully to restrain a smile from crossing his lips.

"We're not in court, Mr. Banning. You can feel free to tell your client not to answer, but I'm going to ask what I want to ask."

Thane held up his hand, acknowledging he knew the process. He hoped he hadn't turned as red as he felt. After spending most of his career in real estate law, he was still relatively new to criminal law.

"I'm just wondering what my client's past associations

have to do with the case at hand."

"I understand. And you can continue wondering, but the question stands."

"It's a matter of public record," Kilo said. "So if it saves time, then yeah, I associated with him from time to time, but those days are over."

"Thank you," Struthers responded, as he wrote something in his notebook. "On the night of the murder of Mr. Crowell, were you at a neighborhood bar called Gulliver's?"

"I don't remember as far as that specific date goes. It was quite a while ago. I've been there more than once, but I can't say which exact days."

"That's okay. We have the confirmation we need that you were there."

"May I ask what that confirmation is?" Thane asked.

"Bar security camera. We have Mr. Miller at the bar on the night of the murder."

"What time was he there?"

Struthers shook his head, ready to move on. "You can try the case in court, but the video shows him there shortly before the murder." He referred back to his notebook. "Mr. Miller, do you ever recall seeing a 2022 dark olive Lexus LC 500 a couple of blocks from Sullivan's?"

"I don't know cars that well. I couldn't tell you."

"Let me ask it a different way. Did you notice an incredibly fancy, sleek-as-shit, obscenely expensive olive-green luxury car that would have caught any person's eye, regardless of whether they knew cars or not?"

Kilo looked over at Thane, who shook his head by way of instructing him not to answer. He knew Struthers was referring to Joseph's car, and while he didn't know for sure what the downside was to answering, he still wanted to see where this was going.

Kilo didn't answer.

"That's fine," Struthers said. "We do have a partial print found on the car handle that is a match for yours."

"What? But how—" exclaimed Kilo. "The answer to your question is no. I don't remember seeing a car like you described."

"Partial prints aren't admissible in court," Thane jumped in. "Just because it *may* be a match for my client's prints, that doesn't establish they are his."

"Actually they are admissible, but you're right that they aren't definitive. But in the detective business, we do find them to be relevant."

"What made you look at the video for an image of my client? What made you compare his fingerprints to that of the partial print?"

"The police received an anonymous tip that your client was responsible for Mr. Crowell's murder. We get a lot of tips like this that usually don't pan out—and perhaps this one won't either—but as we look further into Mr. Miller, we keep finding smoke, so I'm checking to see if there's also a fire."

Thane felt the police didn't have enough to hold Kilo, and probably didn't even have enough to charge him. The partial print and the video tape maybe made it understandable as to why they would be looking at him, given the tip. The partial print was concerning to Thane, but again, he knew it wasn't the same as a full fingerprint. That would be another story altogether.

Struthers closed his notebook and leaned back in his chair, appearing to be wrapping up his questioning for the day. Thane assumed he would soon be driving Kilo back home to his promised steak dinner, until Struthers added one more thing.

"There was also a witness. I need you to participate in a line-up, Mr. Miller."

And there it was. The reason why they were called to the station. Thane didn't understand how there could be a witness against Kilo.

But if there was, he had the sinking feeling there wouldn't be a steak dinner for Kilo tonight after all.

Thane stood behind a one-way mirror, preparing for the line-up. He had the right to be present, to ensure the witness wasn't coached or that the line-up wasn't rigged against his client.

Struthers signaled for the witness to be brought in.

A skinny hipster guy strolled into the room, looking hyper and bored at the same time. His tight-fitting black and white checkered pants with cuffs ending a foot above his sock-less ankles were paired with an unbuttoned red and black plaid flannel shirt with a black t-shirt underneath it. Blue suspenders pulled the whole ensemble together, although not in a positive way. The scent from the young man's spicy mustache wax was strong. The curlicue-twists at the ends of his mustache made him look like a bartender in a bad B-movie western.

As he looked for a place to safely set his diamond crown fedora hat, the young man looked up and noticed

Thane. At first, he appeared to look through Thane—just another 'suit'—then his eyes lit up in recognition.

"Oh my god, you're the lawyer guy! The guy who stuck it to the man!" He glanced at the detectives, then looked back at Thane. "Dude, you've gotta come on my podcast. I'm serious."

"Mr. Reynolds," Struthers said, trying to get on with the matter at hand.

"Like I said before, call me Rabbit."

Thane looked at Struthers and smiled.

"Dude," Rabbit said to Thane, "you've only given like one interview since you got out of prison and nailed the DA. Your story needs to be told!"

"Why?" Thane asked, matter-of-factly.

The question appeared to stump Rabbit, as if simply being on a podcast should be reason enough.

"Mr. Reynolds, please," Struthers said, more firmly. "We need to move on to the line-up. You told me you had a job you had to get to."

Rabbit looked at Thane and nodded, then extended both hands out flat, palms down, and started moving them in circles. "I'm also a DJ. That's my main calling in life."

Thane watched as the man mimed scrubbing two records. "You're obviously very good."

"Thanks, bro! You should come on down to The Zombie sometime and watch me work. My music is faster than Usain Bolt."

"Thus the name 'Rabbit'," Thane guessed.

Struthers walked over to the intercom and requested the line-up. He then directed Rabbit to the window as six men walked into a well-lit room and stood facing the mirror. Kilo was second from the left but carried the same expression as the other five men. He didn't look nervous—or guilty—which Thane was glad to see. He was confident this wasn't Kilo's first line-up.

But while none of the men in the line-up looked uncomfortable, the same couldn't be said about the witness.

"They can't see me, right?" Rabbit asked.

"That's correct. They're just staring at their own reflection. Now, I want you to take your time on this." Struthers directed the men over the intercom to turn to the right.

"You don't need to do that. I already know which man it was I saw."

"If you'll allow me, I want to make sure we do this by the book." Struthers glanced over at Thane, before telling the men to turn to the left, and then to once again face forward.

"Can you identify the man you saw dragging a body the night of Mr. Crowell's murder?" Struthers asked.

"Seriously, dude? I just said I could." Rabbit looked over at Thane and subtly tipped his head. "Number two is the guy."

"Are you positive? Any uncertainty at all?"

"No, that's the guy. But I just thought he was helping a friend who was passed out drunk, not moving a dead body." He shivered at the thought, then refocused on himself, which appeared to be his favorite subject. "Can I go now? I gotta get set up for tonight." He looked once again at Thane. "Seriously, dude, you should come by. At a minimum, let me give you my phone number and we can talk more about my podcast. You'd love it. It's called *Rabbit Food for Thought.*"

He dug out a money clip from his front pocket and

took out a business card, extending it to Thane.

"I don't think that would be appropriate, given the circumstances."

"Circumstances change, man. If there's one thing I've learned in life, it's that circumstances change." He slipped the card into Thane's jacket pocket when he realized Thane wasn't going to take it.

"Okay, it's been a pleasure, gentlemen, but this rabbit has to hippity-hop." He placed his hat atop his head and ran one hand down his beard, making sure it still ended in a sharp point. One of the policemen escorted him out of the room.

"Any concerns with the way this line-up was handled, Mr. Banning?" Struthers asked.

Thane definitely had concerns with the line-up, but nothing about how it was conducted. His sole concern was that his client had been ID'd by an eyewitness. Thane tried his best to appear unbothered by the afternoon's event.

He shook his head, then took Rabbit's card out of his pocket and handed it to Struthers. "You should check out his show. I hear his music is fast. And don't forget to call him Rabbit."

Struthers took the card and threw it in the trash can.

"You never know," Thane said. "If there's one thing he's learned in life, it's that circumstances change."

"I'm betting that's about the only thing he's learned," Struthers said, then hardened his eyes. "I'm assuming you already know this, Mr. Banning: we will be charging your client."

Thane was given an hour to meet with Kilo before he was charged with the murder of Joseph Crowell.

During the first couple of minutes, neither man said much. Thane couldn't tell if Kilo was in shock at being arrested for a murder he didn't commit, or if his quietness simply reflected his belief that it didn't really matter what he did or didn't do in life. Either way, he was going to end up in jail.

Thane imagined, though, that most of Kilo's thoughts were centered on his wife and family. When he had been falsely accused of murdering Lauren McCoy, Thane remembered thinking more about Hannah and what she was going through than about what he was facing.

"So what was the witness like?" Kilo finally asked. "Was he—or she—credible?"

"He looked like the newest douchebag boyfriend of one of the Kardashians," Thane shrugged. "But he also sounded convinced of what he saw. It didn't take him but a second for him to point you out as the guy."

Kilo shook his head, but his confusion couldn't have been greater than Thane's, who was almost positive Russell McCoy hadn't used anyone else to help him kill Joseph.

Was it possible McCoy didn't think he had it in him to kill another man and, therefore, had hired someone to actually pull the trigger? Thane didn't think so. Although McCoy was a man who followed God's commandments, Thane was certain he was willing to make an exception in this situation. Besides, McCoy had already shot and killed Gruber, the ex-cop Joseph had hired to kill Lauren, so there was no reason to believe he didn't dispense the same justice toward Joseph.

"Did you ever know a guy by the name of Russell McCoy?" Thane finally asked, reluctantly.

"McCoy? Not that I know of. Was he in Forsman with us?"

Thane decided he wanted to get away from the topic of McCoy as quickly as possible.

"Yeah, but it's not important. The witness just reminded me a little of him is all. Squirrelly and sort of full of himself."

Kilo nodded his head quietly, as if what Thane was saying made sense. As if any of this made sense. Finally he spoke without looking up from the floor.

"You still my lawyer?"

"What?" Thane said, surprised. "Yeah, I'm still your lawyer. Why wouldn't I be?"

"Because apparently I was near the area the night of the murder, a partial print matching mine was supposedly found on the car door, and there's an eyewitness saying he saw me do it."

"That doesn't mean you did it. And the witness isn't saying he saw you shoot Joseph; he's saying he saw you dragging a body."

"Oh, well, that should make all the difference to the jury."

"I'm not saying it's a big difference, but it's a difference. There was also an eyewitness against Skunk in his case, but that turned out to be mistaken identity. I didn't give up on him just because a lot of evidence pointed to his guilt."

"Yeah, but you knew Skunk and you didn't think he could kill anyone. You also liked him. I'm someone who tried to kill you, so my willingness to try to murder someone has been established. And the person who was murdered was your friend. So I'm not sure why you're sticking with me."

"I've already told you—"

"Yeah, I know, you want the right guy to be arrested for your friend's murder, but here's the thing I haven't been able to figure out: why don't you think I'm the right guy? Everything points to me, especially now. And yet I don't think you've ever asked me a question to even try to gauge whether it's at all possible I might be the guy who did it."

"I've seen what you're doing now, and I met your family and I see someone who's an entirely different person than I thought he was. So for whatever reason, I don't think you did it. I don't know what else to tell you."

Kilo studied him hard.

"You can tell me you're not setting me up. That you aren't going to pretend to represent me but then just go through the motions and see me sent to death row. Hell, I wouldn't blame you. I'd probably do the same thing if I were you."

"No, you wouldn't," Thane said matter-of-factly.

Kilo appeared caught off-guard by that, and seemed to give the scenario some further thought. He finally nodded his head slightly and looked back down at the floor. "No, you're right. I don't think I would."

"Can you think of anyone who might want to set you up?" Thane asked. "Besides me, I mean." He offered a smile.

"Sure. I did a number of guys wrong at Forsman. I also wasn't exactly a choir boy before I went to prison, either. At least not when I was younger."

"How about the gang you used to hang with? You said you broke away from them and there were hard feelings."

"Hard feelings is an understatement, but they would be more likely to bash my head in with a metal bar or shoot me in the face. Setting me up for a murder seems far beyond their intelligence level. Plus, someone would need to know I was at the bar that night. And why wait so long to call in the tip?"

That bothered Thane as well. He wasn't sure why it took this long after the murder before Kilo's name surfaced in the investigation.

"Would you mind calling my wife for me and letting her know what's going on?" Kilo asked. "I don't think I can handle telling her myself."

Thane wasn't sure he could handle telling Kilo's wife either. An innocent man was being kept from his family because of something he had set up, although that wasn't totally true.

He hadn't set up Kilo. But it was on him to figure out who did.

20

The rapid, staccato knock on the door to Kristin's condominium sounded like a woodpecker was trying to get in.

She had a couple of friends who sometimes dropped by unannounced, but that didn't happen as much lately, once she asked them to text first. Plus, it was 9:00 PM on a weeknight, which made the visit even more puzzling.

She put down her cup of tea on the kitchen table where she'd been looking through Gus's case file, and walked through the living room toward her front door. Her place was immaculate, with Scandinavian-style furniture; she had purchased the condo not long after accepting the job with Thane and had run up considerable credit card debt in order to furnish it the way she wanted.

She looked through the front door's peep hole and saw a young woman who appeared to be in her early twenties. She couldn't have been much taller than five-two and probably didn't even weigh ninety pounds. She wore a cropped, black Lycra top, the sort of thing Kristin wore when she went to yoga.

The young woman knocked on the door again while Kristin was looking at her, apparently not having noticed the light from the peep hole had disappeared. Kristin put the chain on the door, unbolted it, and opened it part way.

"Yes?" Kristin said.

"Are you Ms. Peterson?"

At first, Kristin assumed the young woman had the wrong condo number, or was handing out religious material, but when she heard the woman say her name, she realized that wasn't the case.

"Yes, but it's sort of late to be stopping by a stranger's home, isn't it?"

"I gotta talk to you. It's important. It's about Andre. He told me you wanted him to help you out, and I just wanted to tell you that you don't know the whole story."

"And who are you?"

"Name's Boo. I'm a friend of Dre's and I'm scared if he tells you everything that really went down, it won't just hurt him, but it'll put Gus in an even worse situation. Please, can I talk to you for just a few minutes? It's important."

Kristin hesitated, though the young woman looked harmless. "Like I said, it's getting late. How about you come by my office tomorrow, and we can talk then."

The young woman sighed, then waved off Kristin. "Never mind," she said as she started to turn. "I got a job during the day. I'm just trying to help, but whatever. Forget it. Sorry I bothered you."

Boo started walking down the hall toward the elevator. Kristin's curiosity was piqued; she didn't want to ignore any relevant information. She quickly unchained the door and stepped out into the hall as the woman pressed the elevator button.

"Wait a minute. Let's talk."

An enormous Black man who had been standing to

the side of the hallway opposite the elevator suddenly put his hand across Kristin's mouth and picked her up with his free arm like she was a bag of groceries.

"Afraid Boo has to go. But I'll talk to you."

As she was carried back into her condo, Kristin saw the young woman look at her and shrug as she stepped onto the elevator. The man carried her inside, kicked her front door shut, and spun her around to look at him.

He was huge—bigger even than the WWE wrestler she saw recently on a bad first date. He wore a black leather vest over a dirty blue t-shirt, faded blue jeans, and black bovver boots. He set Kristin back on the floor and kept her mouth covered, then reached into his vest pocket and flipped open a switchblade, placing the business end under her eye.

"I ain't here to hurt you, you understand? I just want to talk a sec, but if you scream, the first thing I'm going to do is cut out your tongue so you can't scream no more. You got me?"

Kristin could only stare at the man with the knife, frozen with fear.

"I said, do you understand?"

Kristin nodded. The man slowly took his hand away from her mouth. Her throat felt so parched, she wasn't sure she could scream if she wanted, but she could also tell he was serious about cutting her. There was something missing in his eyes that made her think he could do anything at all and not feel any remorse.

"Who are you?" she panted. "What do you want?"

"I'm Stick. Andre told me you want him to testify for you, and I stopped by to tell you that ain't gonna happen. Not—gonna—happen. Nuh-uh." Stick shook his head slowly to emphasize his point.

"Andre said he was willing to testify because his friend Gus is being loyal to him. He understands it's—"

Stick raised his hand as though he was getting ready to backhand Kristin, and she flinched.

"You under the impression we're having a conversation here? Because we ain't having a conversation. I'm here to tell how things are going to be, and that's how they're going to be. As for Gus being loyal, he sure as shit better be loyal, otherwise his whole family is going to say night-night."

"But—"

"Listen to me real close, blondie. My brother, he's not like me. He's going to go to college and get a good job and do good things in the world. You get him messed up in this, and the cops are going to pressure him to come after me."

Kristin started to speak, then stopped, still worried what would happen if she spoke. But after Stick glared at her, he nodded for her to say what she was going to say.

"The cops are already trying to use him. His friend Jamie was trying to get your brother to take the drugs. The only reason Gus is in prison is because he was trying to help out Andre. I just need him to tell the court—"

"He's not telling the court nothing. But you saying that punk Jamie was trying to give the bag to Andre? He didn't tell me that."

As Stick's anger appeared to build, Kristin realized she had said too much. Stick looked at her for longer than was comfortable, then broke out into a grin.

"You look just like them Barbie dolls my sister had when we was kids. I used to love playing with them dolls growing up. That surprise you?"

Kristin could only nod, assuming that was the right answer.

"Yeah, I loved them little bitches. Each time she'd bring home a new Barbie, I'd get out the power drill and I'd drill a hole up that little doll's ass. Plastic chips flying everywhere, and when my sister started screaming at me, I imagined it was Barbie, just screaming and screaming. Then when the drill bit was as deep as it could go—and Barbie was starting to get on my nerves with all that screaming—I'd snap her fucking head off like she was a little bird."

Stick laughed at the memory. He then looked at Kristin and licked his lips.

"You look just like those fucking dolls."

Kristin wanted to run, but Stick stood between her and the front door, and she had no doubt he'd catch her even if she tried to get past him. She had a can of mace in her purse, but even if she could reach it, she had the feeling it would simply piss him off. He looked like he who wore mace as cologne. He scared the hell out of her, making her feel like she was dealing with an animal, not a human being.

A feral, predatory animal.

Stick stepped closer to Kristin, causing her to back into the kitchen until she found herself up against the kitchen table. His breath smelled rancid.

"I'm going to give you a choice here," he finally said, eyes hard. "I can either hurt you a little bit now—well, more than a little bit—or I can not hurt you at all, but if you ever approach my brother again…"

He grabbed her, spun her around, and bent her over

181

her kitchen table. He placed his hand across her mouth again then stepped forward until he was pressing himself hard against her backside.

"I'll drill you so far up the ass you'll be screaming for me to snap your head off." Stick once again pulled out his switchblade and pressed it against her neck. "Which is what I'll do, but only after I'm sure you're about to pass out, because I'd want you to feel the blade going into your throat. And I won't be needing no power drill, neither. I'll be my own power drill."

He thrust himself against her hard one last time, then spun her back around.

"Now, you may think this is a trick question, about whether I should hurt you a little bit now or hurt you a hell of a lot more later, but it's not. What I've come to learn is that some people need to understand I mean business, and so a broken nose or a couple of black eyes the first time is enough for them people to know better than to go against me. It's like if they don't get hit the first time, they feel maybe I'm not serious, then they start crying it's not fair when the next time around I rain holy hell down on them. Other people, though, seem to get it right up front that I'm not fucking around. They don't need to be convinced the first time."

Stick looked at Kristin, who wanted nothing more than to awaken from what was the most terrifying nightmare she'd ever had. Her eyes started to well up with tears.

"But most of the people who need to be smacked around first are usually braindead losers who are always going to be losers. You, on the other hand, strike me as being a bright young thing. But you tell me: do you want me to convince you I'm not fucking around here, or are you willing to take me at my word?"

All Kristin could do was nod.

He grabbed her hair and pulled her head back so that she was looking straight up at him, feeling as though her neck might just snap.

"You need to say it out loud, baby bird. Do you believe me?"

Kristin again nodded, then gasped, "Yes. I believe you."

Stick released her hair and stepped a little closer to her so that he was peering down at her from his great height.

"And you're going to leave my brother alone?"

She wanted nothing more than to tell him she couldn't be intimidated. She wanted to tell him he couldn't just come into her place and bully her and threaten her, but she knew none of that was correct. That was exactly what he was able to do.

"Yes," she said.

"Yes what?"

"Yes, I'm going to leave Andre alone."

He raised his hand quickly again, which again made her flinch, but he simply patted her on the head.

"Good girl. That shows you how much I like my brother, because it's been a long time since I drilled one of those dolls and I'm sort of jonesing to do it again. I miss the screaming. And trust me, baby bird, you bother my brother again—or if you even think about calling the police—I'll be hearing those screams again big time. For a long time."

He then stepped back from her.

"Don't you cross me, girl, or I'll snap your bones until you're nothing but a bag of broken parts. Or better yet, you have any idea how much I could sell you for? I ain't kidding, a sweet-smelling babe like you, I'd have buyers calling me nonstop. After a couple of weeks of being someone's property, you'd wish I'd killed you." He turned and started toward the front door. "And stop opening your door to strangers. That shit ain't safe." He walked out the front door and left it open.

Kristin stood in the kitchen, still frozen, staring across the living room at the open door. She finally ran over and slammed it shut, turned the deadbolt, then clicked the button on the doorknob, although she was certain none of it would stop Stick if he wanted to get back in.

She power-walked around her living room, pacing in a circle, wanting to scream, wanting to cry, wanting to collapse, but she told herself to keep moving. Tears started to fall as she walked into the kitchen and then back out into the living room and then back to the kitchen again. She felt like if she stopped walking, she would fall to pieces, but then she realized she'd already fallen apart.

She didn't know how long she would be able to keep walking.

She didn't want to think about what would happen if she stopped.

21

Thane grabbed lunch from a small cafe in L.A.'s Little Tokyo district and ate it at the Grand Park dog park. He always had a dog growing up, and he and Hannah had talked about perhaps getting one now that they were settling in.

He was far more comfortable with that conversation than one about children.

He watched some dogs racing around, barking, and playing with the pack, while others stuck close to their owners as if they, too, were just there to watch. He smiled as he noticed a chihuahua terrorizing a Great Dane, chasing it across the grass. It reminded him of something he learned in prison: it wasn't always the size of the dog in the fight that made the difference.

Across the street from the dog park and to his right was City Hall, and across the street directly in front of him was the office of Angela Day, the new Los Angeles District Attorney. She had called him earlier that morning, asking if he could stop by after lunch to talk about something that had come up.

It was, she said, something she preferred discussing face-to-face.

Thane's first reaction, as always, was concern that the

investigation into Joseph's murder had gone in a direction he didn't want it to go, but he told himself that if that were the case, it would have been Struthers calling. Or, more likely, Struthers wouldn't have called; he'd have simply shown up, accompanied by a couple of police officers.

When it was time for his appointment, he approached the reception desk, staffed by a harried woman who appeared to be juggling twelve things at once. She didn't look at him when she asked if she could help him, but once Thane gave his name, her head immediately shot up.

"Oh," she said. When she didn't say anything else, but continued staring at him with a stunned expression on her face, he told her he had an appointment with Ms. Day.

Thane sat in the waiting room for less than a minute before a young, efficient-looking administrative assistant appeared and escorted him down a long hallway and past an open area with numerous cubicles. A couple of people walking toward him in the hall were laughing until one of them looked up and saw Thane, which quickly silenced him and his colleague.

At the same time, he noticed an older woman standing at a copy machine, giving Thane a similar look as the receptionist. It wasn't one of support or disdain as much as one of curiosity. When they made eye contact, she looked down at the floor, appearing embarrassed—or possibly even ashamed—by what had happened to Thane at the hands of that office.

Thane also received a stern glare by a suited man who sat in his office behind an important looking desk. It reminded him of the encounter he had at Hannah's charity event with Barry Warlick. Thane would be fine not running into Warlick again on his way to Day's office.

He was led into the District Attorney's office where he was greeted with a smile and a warm handshake. Day directed him to sit in one of four padded chairs that made up a conversation circle on one end of her impressively expansive office.

"I appreciate you coming down here on such short notice. I felt this was a conversation best had in person."

"It's not a problem. I didn't really think much about where I was until I started walking down the hall to your office. I think my presence caught some people by surprise."

"I hope everyone treated you professionally."

"Nobody threw anything at me, if that's what you mean."

"Yes, that's where I've set the bar," she said, laughing. "But seriously, while I know there are a few people who, for whatever reason, blame you for what happened to Brad Stone, a whole lot more were furious about what he did, and more than a few are embarrassed by it. I would be comfortable wagering you have far more supporters in this office than you have detractors."

"Good to know."

"But speaking of detractors, I do want you to know that Barry Warlick has been assigned the prosecution of the case against your client, Kyle Miller. He was in line to take on the next case like this, and I didn't have a good enough reason to pull him off it. I had a long talk with him, though, and he convinced me he didn't even know you were representing Mr. Miller. And in fact, I think that caused him to rethink taking on the case, given his interaction with you the other night, but he told me he was planning to apologize to you."

"Is that what you wanted to tell me in person?"

"No, I just wanted to mention that before I forgot."

"Then before we begin, I was wondering if I could ask you a question. It might be a little personal, in which case feel free to say, 'no comment'."

"Ask away."

"I'm also representing a young man named Gus Cleveland. Young Black man, eighteen years old. He's being charged with cocaine distribution."

Angela nodded politely, although Thane was doubtful she'd be involved in a case that minor.

"I am certain," Thane continued, "that he's being pressured to give false testimony in exchange for having his charges dropped. Obviously, no one has come right out and said it, but the message is clear. Now, I understand a lot of big cases come from having lower-level people make a plea agreement in exchange for cooperation, but that's not what's happening here."

He paused to see if she had any reaction to his story so far, but again she simply nodded for him to continue.

"I don't think the tactics being used on my client would be as effective on a white person with resources. So as a Black woman running an office that isn't without its blemishes in terms of racial and economic injustice, how do you balance doing your job versus trying to fix decades of systemic abuse?"

"Damn, I was sort of hoping your question pertained to something like World History. I was always good at that subject in school." Angela seemed to think about it for a moment. "First of all, I believe addressing that sort of racism *is* a part of my job. But instead of only giving you the political answer, I'll be as honest with you as I can.

"I am, as you have already noticed, Black and I am a

188

woman. That is who I am, and I'm proud to be both of those. But inside this office, I am the District Attorney. I will fight for justice, regardless of the race of the perpetrator, and if I feel any prosecution is racially motivated, then I will address that."

Thane smiled. "No offense, but that sounds like the political answer."

"That's because it was, although it's also one hundred percent true. The rest of the answer is that this is an elected position. I need to be re-elected in order to continue working toward the things I hope to accomplish here. So, while I can nip and tuck at the system where I feel it is falling short, if I tried implementing all of the significant changes I feel need to be made here all at once, I wouldn't be long for this job. It's frustrating, but it's also the reality of this position."

"That was the argument Brad Stone used to frame my last client, Scotty Burns," Thane responded. "He believed that if this office had come out and said they were wrong about their prosecution, then Stone wouldn't be re-elected and all the good work he'd been doing would come to an end. They used re-election as their reason for doing what they did."

Day's expression slowly shifted from one of understanding to one of sternness. "But what he did was a violation of every ethical and legal code of conduct there is. I am not saying I will do whatever I can to stay in office, whether it's legal or not. I'm simply saying that I can't address all the inequities in the system as quickly as I would like, but that won't stop me from trying to move the ball forward."

Thane respected the position she was in, and even

though he didn't know her well at all, he trusted her.

"I'm sorry. I didn't mean to imply I thought you were in any way like Brad Stone. I just get uncomfortable sometimes hearing that one must be judicious when trying to do the right thing. That sometimes you have to wait before you can do the right thing."

"Oh, please tell me you're about to quote Martin Luther King to me. There are so very few things I enjoy as much as having a white man quote MLK to me."

Thane laughed. "Again, my apologies. But I'm sure you didn't ask me to come here to discuss Gus Cleveland's case."

"As a matter of fact, I did."

That surprised Thane. He didn't understand how Gus's case could have made it onto her radar unless, perhaps, it was simply because he was associated with it. Was it possible the District Attorney's office was so consumed with Thane and his actions that they were going to closely follow every one of his cases, regardless of how minor?

"I believe one of the people you work with is someone you also served time with. Gideon Spence." She studied Thane closely. "What can you tell me about him?"

Thane immediately didn't like where this was heading. Had the police already learned of his visit to Gus's friend, Jamie? If that was the case, he was certain he would be hearing about that from Struthers first.

"Would you mind first telling me what this is about?"

District Attorney Day reached over and picked up a file that had been sitting on a side table.

"Something's come up," she said. "Something serious."

Thane had hoped to wrap up their team meeting before 4:00, but he still had a couple of things to cover, and one topic he wished he could avoid. He decided to save it for the end.

He updated everyone on the status of Kilo's case. Even though most everyone had been against Thane taking him on as a client, everyone but Kristin asked at least a couple of questions as he gave a summary of where things stood. Even Gideon asked about Thane's sense of the witness, even though during these meetings he usually stayed mute.

Kristin, on the other hand, hadn't said more than a few words, which was unusual. She could always be counted on to pepper Thane on any topic he brought up, however mundane, much to the amusement of her colleagues. But today she looked like her mind was in a galaxy far, far away.

She also looked like she hadn't slept at all.

"As for Gus's case, I know you all are working hard on it, but before we get an update on how that's going," Thane nodded at Gideon and Letitia, "I'm going to have to ask the two of you to do something to help me with Kilo's case. And I know you probably don't want to."

He noticed the nonverbal negative response from Letitia. Thane was sure Gideon felt the same way, but he'd been conditioned to hide most external reactions.

"Gideon, regarding the witness who claims he saw Kilo dragging a body out of that bar, his last name is Reynolds. I don't know his first name, but he's a DJ and goes by the name Rabbit."

"'Course he does," Gideon grumbled. "Was Squirrel already taken?"

"I'm interested in finding out whether anyone on the street is familiar with him. If he had any possible drug problems or other issues that might have compromised him with the police. And Letitia, check police records to see if you can learn whether he was recently charged with a crime. I'm skeptical about this guy."

"Why's that?" Letitia asked.

"If you meet him, you'll see. So that's all I have about that case. Anything new with Gus's situation?"

Everyone turned and looked at Kristin, but she simply stared at her notes and shook her head. Thane noticed Gideon watching her with concern. He was usually the first to give her a hard time about anything, but he was giving her some space this afternoon.

"I've got one thing," Letitia offered. "The guy in the house who Gus passed the bag of drugs to is out on bail. He didn't even spend the night locked up, so that's telling."

"Why do you suppose that is?" Thane asked, already able to guess at the answer.

"Because he's white," Letitia said.

"Because he was part of the set-up to begin with," Gideon countered. "Not that yours isn't also a good answer."

Thane nodded. "That's what I'm betting, too. I think he knew the cops were set up outside his house to make this bust. They probably arrested him to make it look more convincing."

When no one else had any other updates, Thane finally

had no choice but to give his final bit of information.

"I have one more piece of news about the case, and I'm sorry to have to report this, but the kid who gave Gus the drugs—Jamie—was found dead last night."

Letitia clapped a hand to her mouth while Gideon didn't betray any emotion, but Thane knew that didn't mean anything. Kristin, on the other hand, had blanched. He had wanted to give her a heads-up before the meeting, but she was out when Thane got back from the District Attorney's office. She had also shown up a couple of minutes late to the team update, which was another sign that something was amiss.

"He was found outside his apartment building, lying in the middle of the street with a broken neck."

"Hit and run?" Gideon asked.

"No, police say the neck was broken by someone who then dragged him out into the street and left him there."

"Well don't look at me," Gideon said defensively. "I didn't do it. He said he'd tell the truth, so there was no reason for me to kill him. Not that I would have killed him if he'd gone back on his word, but you know what I'm saying. I'm innocent."

"But you know that being innocent isn't always enough," Thane said, "and unfortunately, you're on the cop's radar. A pizza guy said he saw you there the night before. He recognized you from the publicity on Skunk's case. I talked with DA Day this afternoon and told her you didn't have anything to do with it."

"And of course she believed you because you guys are good pals now."

"She said the cops suspect it was Stick."

"It *was* Stick," Kristin said. "Jamie's dead because of

me."

She looked like she wanted to run from the room. Thane gave her a moment, then asked her what she meant.

"Stick came to my apartment last night."

Even though Gideon didn't respond, Thane could see his muscles tighten as if he was getting ready to break something.

"I told him about Jamie trying to give the bag to Andre. I wasn't thinking. I figured his brother had already told him what happened. Andre told me testifying against Jamie would mean life for his friend. I thought he meant life in prison, and I told him it wouldn't be that long, but he just rolled his eyes, and now I understand why. He knew what his brother would do. It's because of me. I'm the one who told—"

Kristin looked down at the table, then rapped it hard with her knuckles before sighing.

"Do we have a real name on this asshole? I feel stupid calling him Stick."

Everyone looked at each other but no one had an answer.

"I'm guessing even his mama calls him Stick," Gideon said.

"I'll get you his real name," Letitia chimed in. The dynamics between the two women had sometimes felt a little tense, but Letitia now looked as though her main goal was to take care of Kristin.

"What did he want when he talked to you?" Thane asked.

Somehow Kristin managed to speak calmy as she said, "He said he wanted to break my neck."

She then told them about the switchblade and the promise of cutting off her head. She told them that Stick wasn't going to allow Andre to testify.

Thane could tell she was holding back some of the things Stick must have said or done to have shaken her that badly. He glanced over at Gideon, who looked like he was ready to snap off his side of the table with his bare hands. Thane had seen that expression on Gideon's face more than once during their time together in prison, and each time, someone ended up getting hurt, and badly.

"It's not your fault, Kristin," Letitia said. "Stick would have found out what happened when Jamie testified."

"But maybe charges wouldn't have been brought once the DA's office learned what Jamie would be saying."

"Listen to me," Thane said. "Stick killed Jamie. Not you. You can't start taking responsibility for the actions of a sociopath."

He could tell Kristin wanted nothing more than for the meeting to be over, so he ended it there. Letitia rose slowly and looked as though she wanted to put her arm around Kristin, but likely sensed she didn't need that right now. Gideon also looked like he wanted to wrap his arms around her too.

When Gideon and Letitia quietly left the office, Thane continued sitting at the table with Kristin, who hadn't made a move to leave.

After a long moment of silence, Kristin finally looked up.

"I am so scared. And angry. So damn angry. Angry that he could terrify me and intimidate me like he did. I would have said anything he wanted just to make it all stop."

She paused, then took a deep breath.

"I used to think of myself as being strong, someone who could take on anything without fear, but I didn't. I hated feeling like he could have done anything he wanted to, and I wouldn't have been able to do a damn thing about it. I've never thought of myself as a helpless woman, but he made me feel that way."

"You're one of the strongest women—one of the strongest people—I know. You only feel helpless because you are out of your element in that world."

Thane could sense her skepticism.

"Look, when I was first sent to Forsman, I was terrified. *Terrified.* Every morning when I woke up, until every night when I finally went to sleep. I wanted to curl up in a ball on my cot and never leave my cell. I wanted to scream. I was surrounded by a level of violence and evil I had never experienced before. So, I know how you feel, because I also felt totally helpless."

She looked at him for more, but he felt uncomfortable revisiting those first few days at Forsman.

"Would someone like Stick still scare you as much today?" she asked.

"No, although that's not to my credit. I was in prison for five years. Five years is a long time. I fear different things now."

Kristin studied him for a long moment, but instead of asking him more questions about his time in prison, she finally stood, so Thane did the same.

He watched her go into her office, then saw Letitia rise and go in behind her and shut the door. She sat on the other side of Kristin's desk and neither one appeared to be speaking, but Thane was glad to see the two young women sitting together. Letitia could talk to Kristin in a way neither Thane nor Gideon could.

Thane walked into Gideon's office. The big man was standing, looking out his window at nothing in particular.

"Don't take matters into your own hands when it comes to Stick," Thane said.

"I won't," Gideon responded, emotionless.

"Don't take matters into your own hands."

"I said I won't."

"Don't do it."

Gideon whirled around and glared at Thane. "You tell me a fourth time, I might have to hurt you."

"If I thought telling you a fourth time would do any good, I'd be willing to take that chance."

22

Kilo sat waiting in one of the interview rooms at the Twin Towers jail. He didn't know why he had been taken there, but once you were in the system, it was usually best to simply go where you were told to go. He'd never found any real upside to arguing or asking questions.

He had just spent his first night behind bars in months, and had gone from believing everything would be straightened out to feeling resigned to the fact that he would likely be going back to Forsman, this time for good. He still didn't have a handle on his lawyer and what his true intentions might be.

It was possible Thane was being straight with him regarding wanting to find the right person who killed his friend. If that were true, then maybe he had actually had a chance.

The door opened and Narcotics Detective Mahone entered the room, wearing faded jeans, a 'Straight Outta Compton' t-shirt, and a pair of white Converse sneakers. If he didn't know the detective worked undercover, Kilo would have thought he had come in on his day off.

Mahone walked over and sat down like he owned the place. "And so, here we are," he said with a smile.

Kilo watched Mahone stare at him, and was not

interested in playing games. The detective wanted to meet with him, so eventually he would tell him why. But if the man wanted to just stare at Kilo to get him to speak first, then Mahone was going to be disappointed.

Finally, Mahone leaned back on his chair so that the front two chair legs were a good eight inches off the floor. Kilo would have given good money to see the chair tip over, but he knew people like Mahone—and their chairs—never tipped over.

"I understand you've gotten yourself into a bit of trouble."

"You understand wrong."

"Seriously?" Mahone said, his smile now one of curiosity.

"I haven't done anything to get into trouble. But that doesn't mean trouble won't find you."

"Ah yes, the old 'I didn't do nothing' defense. That's fine. Let me rephrase it: so, I understand trouble has found you yet again."

Kilo stared at him, emotionless.

"As we've discussed before, you used to work with Stick." Mahone again looked at Kilo, but since that wasn't a question, Kilo didn't see the need to answer it. "I just so happen to still want to take Stick off the street. Want to help?"

"I haven't worked with him for several years, and I'm not working with him now."

"But you know how he operates. I'm putting together a case against him, and your testimony could be helpful."

Kilo continued staring at him, blank-faced.

"In exchange for your cooperation, I can get the charges against you reduced. Most likely significantly reduced."

Kilo couldn't help but shake his head. "So all I need to do is help you out, and you'll be able to get the District Attorney to reduce charges on a high-profile murder that was front page news? Color me skeptical."

"And if I'm not mistaken, your favorite color is white." Mahone laughed at himself. "I understand your skepticism, but I'm not asking you to trust me because I have a pretty face. I would give you assurances—in writing—so you'd know I could deliver on my promise. But first, I need to know if you're interested in pursuing this relationship further."

Kilo was more than skeptical, but one upside to having done a lot of time in prison was that cops knew he wasn't some gullible rube. "So all I'd need to do is testify?"

"Provide me with answers to some questions I have, and then testify, yes. It's that easy."

Kilo nodded slowly. "That does sound easy. Well, if you don't count the near certainty of Stick killing my wife and kids before coming after me. That probably makes the equation *slightly* less easy, but I appreciate your optimism."

"We can protect your family."

"No you can't. Not from Stick."

Kilo thought about the possibility of a reduced sentence and protection for his family. But whether he was being conned or not, working with the cops against Stick wasn't a good long-term strategy.

Mahone appeared to have sensed him coming to that conclusion, because he continued, "The alternative, of course, is to be sentenced to life in prison, and most likely the death penalty. And word on the street might be that you offered to help me with Stick anyway, so that would be even more of a problem. But, of course, I don't want to go there."

"But, of course, you just did." Kilo stared at Mahone, his ambivalence starting to morph into anger, his tone becoming dark. "Let me give you a word of advice, detective: if you want me to work with you, then don't threaten me, and don't *ever* threaten my family. That's the absolute worst way to get me to help you. But you also left out a third option: beat the murder charges, and then I won't need your help."

Mahone shook his head as if he was talking to a naive child. "I suppose that's another option, but I want to add a couple of thoughts to that. First, if you decide to take your chances in court, then the deal's off the table. That's all good and fine if you're found not guilty, but you and I both know the odds are against you. Once the trial starts, we're done."

Kilo watched him closely.

"And second, your lawyer is also representing a young dealer who I'm also wanting to get to testify against Stick. He's also holding out. Now you gotta ask yourself, why is it that Thane Banning is representing people who all seem to have a connection to Stick? You don't suppose he's actually working for King Psychopath, do you? He takes on cases he can deliberately lose to make life easier for Stick?"

Kilo wondered if that was the angle he'd been missing, but it didn't make sense.

"Thane offered to represent me because I was charged with the murder of his friend. He didn't know you'd be coming in here to ask me to testify against Stick. I doubt he even knew at one time I'd worked with him. So no, I don't believe he took my case because he's working with Stick, but I am starting to get a whiff of desperation on your part."

Mahone laughed. "Dude, I am so far away from desperation here, it's not even funny. After I get done filling out some paperwork this afternoon, I'm knocking off a little early. I'll probably stop by a neighborhood sports bar I like and have a beer or two, then head home where my wife will have made me an incredible dinner, then I'll turn on the game. So no, if you're smelling any desperation, it's not from me. My life is great. You're the one looking at life in prison. Maybe you shouldn't sit downwind from yourself."

Mahone looked at his watch, then rose.

"Gotta go. If you change your mind, give me a call. Otherwise, get ready for your wife and family to never see you wearing anything but an orange jumpsuit." The detective walked out of the room, the door clicking loudly behind him.

Kilo sat quietly, waiting for the guard who would be escorting him back to his cell. He needed to talk with Thane to let him know what the detective was offering. It was obvious Mahone preferred to approach him directly rather than involve a lawyer in the conversation.

Kilo knew that if he agreed to work with Mahone against Stick, it would only be a matter of days—possibly hours—before Stick heard about it. Kilo didn't care how confidential something was, there were too many ears in the department for anything to stay secret for long. He also had no doubt Stick would come after him, but probably not before threatening his family first.

But if he could somehow get released—even temporarily, perhaps on bail—by agreeing to help Mahone, then he could go after Stick himself. If he did end up going to jail for killing someone, it would be for protecting his family.

He'd also feel at least a little better doing time for a murder he actually committed.

23

Thane got out of his car and leaned against the hood. After having spent the last hour sitting behind the wheel, looking up at Gideon's apartment, he needed to stretch his legs.

When he'd left his house, he was vague when Hannah asked him where he was going. All he could say was he had to make sure Gideon wasn't going to do something stupid.

As it closed in on 8:00 PM, Thane felt like it was getting close to the time when his friend might make his move. It was possible he had misjudged Gideon's ability to practice restraint, but it was also possible he would win that night's Power Ball lottery. He wasn't sure which was more likely, even taking into consideration the fact he didn't play the lottery.

When the light in Gideon's apartment clicked off, Thane knew he had guessed correctly.

Gideon lumbered out of his apartment building and stopped when he saw Thane, shooting him a glare harsh enough to give Thane a sunburn. Gideon approached him, then walked past. Thane pushed himself off his car and followed.

"Looks like I needed to tell you a fourth time after

all," Thane said.

"Yeah, I'm sure that woulda done it," Gideon responded. "You need to go on home. Ain't nothing good going to come out of this for you."

"I don't know about that. Maybe I can keep you from going back to prison. Consider it just another employee benefit the firm offers."

Gideon took another couple of steps, stopped, wheeled around, and stomped back to Thane.

"That son-of-a-bitch broke into our girl's home and threatened her. He scared her to death. I didn't think nothing could scare her. I can't let that stand."

"Then let's not let it stand, but that doesn't mean going in, throwing punches, and somebody getting killed while somebody else gets locked up."

"So what you suggest we do? Go in and ask him real nice? Hey there, Mr. Stick, I was wondering if you'd be nice enough to stop threatenin' to rip the head off one of my associates. Golly gee willikers, I sure would appreciate it."

"Well, I'm not sure about the 'Golly gee willikers' part. Where'd you even learn that?"

"From *Leave it to Beaver*. I'm trying to learn how to communicate better with white folk." Gideon shook his head and waved Thane away. "Go home."

"Not happening. We're going together. I'm assuming you've already been asking around to find out where he hangs, so I'll drive us there."

"You'll just slow me down."

"Yeah, that's sort of the idea." Thane reached out and put his hand on Gideon's shoulder. "Look, I'm going with you. I'm just as angry about this as you are, but we can get the message across without throwing punches and smashing in faces."

"But you're always saying in team meetings that we need to learn to play to our strengths."

"Come on. I'm driving. You already know I'm coming with you, so let's stop wasting time and get this done."

"You better not get in my way once we're there."

"And you better not do anything that will land you back in Forsman. Kristin would be pissed as hell at you."

Gideon turned and followed Thane back to his car.

"That girl didn't deserve what Stick did to her," Gideon muttered. "He needs to pay."

Thane pulled up in front of the Star Bright Bar, a small neighborhood joint that looked like it had been condemned at least a decade ago. It was 8:45 on a Tuesday night and the place appeared fairly empty. Gideon had learned this was where Stick and his crew usually hung out during business hours, which for them probably started around that time of night.

Gideon started getting out of the car, but Thane held out his arm to stop him. "Wait a second. I have to make a quick call."

"The life of a married man."

Thane placed his call. "Hey, it's me. I'm running a little late, but I won't be long. I'll give you a call when I'm done. Talk to you soon."

"How about now?" Gideon asked, as Thane put away

his phone. "Can we go in now, or do we need a hall pass?"

They entered the bar and immediately felt eyes on them.

A mangy old man about a hundred years old sat on a stool behind the bar watching a small TV hanging over the bottles of liquor. His wispy, gray ponytail must have been much more robust when he was younger; now it looked like an ancient feather duster that had been used for far too long. He didn't look like someone who could break up any fights, but Thane had little doubt there was a pistol or, more likely, a shotgun, under the bar.

A couple of derelicts who looked like they spent so much time there they might have been paying rent sat huddled over their shot glasses. Thane noticed a couple of young men in their late teens who were in the middle of a game of pool. Both wore baby blue shirts and eyed Thane and Gideon for a long moment.

Or, more accurately, they eyed Gideon.

Another man leaned against the wall near the table, watching as Thane and Gideon approached. A tall, slim man, he wore an ankle-length trench coat, despite the heat and despite the fact he was inside.

On the other side of the pool table, with his back to Thane and Gideon, Stick sat on a tall stool, watching the pool table and the game that was underway. He didn't lift an eye toward them, but Thane had no doubt Stick knew they were there.

The young men glanced at Stick knowingly, then resumed their game. One of the kids grabbed the bottle of talcum powder off the side of the table and put some on his hands, rubbing the powder up and down the cue stick to make it slide smoother. He made an impressive bank shot on the 8-ball, ending the game. He stood at attention and laid his cue on the table as Thane and Gideon approached.

"This table is occupied."

"That's okay," Thane said. "We're not here to play."

"Then get the hell out. You don't belong here." He looked defiant talking to Thane, but was less convincing when he tried the same glare on Gideon.

"Is that cause we ain't wearing baby blue?" Gideon asked. "I think it's so cute you all have a favorite color. Sort of like a club, ain't it? Do y'all have a favorite animal, too? I'll bet it's a unicorn! A unicorn sitting on a rainbow eating a cupcake. How cute is that?"

Gideon walked up to the pool table, took the cue ball, and rolled it into one of the side pockets. Thane stood at one end of the pool table, closest to Stick.

"We need a minute of your time," Thane said.

"My time is valuable," Stick replied, finally making eye contact with him. "What you willing to pay me to listen to whatever bullshit it is you got to say?"

"You didn't play nice with a colleague of mine."

"Ah, lemme guess, you're Barbie's boss. Well, I don't play nice with nobody, so you've got five seconds to turn and leave, otherwise I won't play nice with you either."

Gideon glanced at Thane, but Thane didn't break eye contact with Stick.

"Not until we say what we came here to say."

Stick nodded at the guy in the trench coat. The man walked over to Thane. "Leave," he barked.

"Not yet," Thane said.

The man clamped down hard on Thane's shoulder and spun him around while cocking his free hand to throw a punch. Thane grabbed the bottle of talcum from the edge of the table, crushing the bottle and shooting powder into his attacker's eyes. He then spun out of the man's grip and rammed the man's face onto the side of the pool table. The guy's nose cracked like a rack of billiard balls.

The two young men started toward Thane, each pulling a switchblade from their pockets. Gideon grabbed the pool cue from the table and stood between them and Thane. The two punks flanked him so that Gideon had one on each side of him.

Gideon held the cue in both hands, ready to do battle.

Each kid made a jabbing motion toward Gideon, knowing he couldn't protect himself on both sides with one pool cue, but Gideon didn't flinch. He stood holding the cut, then held it out in front of him and broke it like a breadstick. He took half of the cue in each hand, now more than able to defend himself from each side. The two teens looked at each other nervously.

"Look, Stick, we're not here to cause trouble," Thane said.

Stick couldn't help but smile. "Glad to hear that, but just out of curiosity, what would you be doing if you *were* looking for trouble? 'Cause it seems to me this is a pretty good start."

"All I'm asking is for you to hear us out, but if your boys feel like they need to strut their stuff first, then we're going to have to swat them on the nose." Thane looked at the tall man on the floor, clutching his bloody and broken nose. "And we swat hard."

Stick thought about it for a moment, then signaled for the two kids to step back.

"Best keep your big dog on a leash," he told Thane.

"There's not a leash that exists that could hold him back," Thane responded. "It's only as a personal favor to me that he hasn't already shoved the jagged edge of that pool cue up your ass."

Stick sat up straighter. "Careful, lawyer boy."

"So you know who I am, which means you know I'm trying to help out a kid who is being loyal to your brother."

"I don't give a damn about—"

"Yeah, well I do," Thane said. "We got his weasel friend Jamie to agree to testify, which meant your brother wouldn't need to. We were handling things, but then you screwed it all up."

"I handle things my own way."

"Your way is stupid," Gideon said. Stick turned toward him but didn't appear to want to include him in the conversation, so he turned back to Thane.

"Why'd you have to kill him before he could testify?" Thane asked. "We're all working for the same thing. Detective Mahone is after you. He's also after a client of ours."

"I don't give a damn. Far as I'm concerned, the enemy of my enemy is *still* my fucking enemy."

"Listen up, Twig," Gideon said. "You even breathe the same air as that girl you threatened, I'll take you apart, piece by piece, 'til you look like a box of Legos."

Stick looked at him, dead-eyed.

"You sit over there like you're some sort of damn kingpin," Gideon continued. "You're nothing but a punk-ass bitch. I used to deal with posers like you every day at Forsman. Guys like you show up there start acting all hot shit, but after a couple of hours they'd be curled up in the fetal position under their bunk all weepy. The thing is, you're all talk. I am a man of few words, though, 'cause words don't make blood pour out your skull."

"Ask Jamie if I just talk tough. Oh, wait, you can't ask him. He's dead."

"A girl scout could have taken Jamie down."

"Listen," Thane said, trying to keep things from escalating. "We're not here trying to pretend like we're your friends."

"That's good, because I don't have friends."

"Have you considered showering?" Gideon quipped. "That might help."

"We're just here to tell you to stay away from our colleague. I'm serious, Stick. I'm trying to do you a favor here. If she even thinks she sees you on the street, that won't be good for you."

Stick laughed. "Good one, counselor. You're a funny man, you know that? But you seem a little tense. How about I get you a girl? How young you like 'em? I just got me a fresh 14-year-old who ain't even broken in yet. You want to do the breakin'? I can give you a good deal."

"You bother my colleague again, you're the only one I'll be looking to break."

"That case, all I can say is I hope you have your will made out, seeing as how L.A. gave you a shitload of money."

"As a matter of fact, I just updated it yesterday. All of my money, minus a quarter million, goes to my wife."

"And where's the quarter mil go?"

"To a bounty, if anything happens to my colleague, to my friend here, or to me."

Stick thought about it, then laughed.

"See? Like I said, you're a funny man. But I'm a little insulted. Only a quarter mil? Don't you think a million would make more of a statement?"

"You know as well as I do that around here, I could probably get someone to kill for fifty bucks and a ham sandwich. But I want to be sure I get somebody good."

"And you put that in your will, huh?"

"Of course not, but you think I don't know people after spending five years in Forsman who are more than capable of setting something like this up? Just stay away from my friends and me. It's not worth it, Stick. Trust me."

"Man, you have any idea how many people have tried to come at me? You go ahead and put your bounty out on me, lawyer boy, I don't give a damn. I can take care of myself."

"The bounty's not on you. It's on your brother."

Stick stopped laughing. Even the young men glanced at each other.

"If you did that, then you're a dead man."

"Then so's your brother." Thane could see Stick trying to guess if he was bluffing. "Give him a call."

Stick and Gideon both looked at Thane, puzzled.

"The guy I'm working with is with him now, in case you didn't take me seriously. It's all friendly, for the time being. I just wanted you to know I'm not playing."

Stick stared at Thane, then pulled out his cell phone.

"Hey, it's me," Stick said. "Just checking in." There was a long pause, then Stick looked at Thane as though he might fly across the room and bite him. "Yeah, that's okay. You can tell him everything's fine. Didn't mean to bother you."

Stick hung up the phone, then stared at Thane.

"Listen, I'm simply trying to tell you two things," Thane said. "First, all I'm asking is that you stay away from my colleagues. Seriously, that doesn't seem like too much to ask, does it? And the second thing you need to understand is that if you decide your ego won't allow you to play nice, then your brother is going to be shot in the head and my friend here will rip your heart out through your throat and use it for batting practice."

Gideon took one of the pool cue pieces and did a slow-motion swing.

"You do not want to fuck with me, Stick. Trust me."

Gideon walked over and stood directly in front of Stick, their faces less than a foot apart.

"Do I look like I'm scared of you?" He placed the jagged end of the broken pool cue hard against Stick's throat. "The only reason I'm not jamming this through your windpipe right now is because I don't want to make my friend here an accessory to murder. But trust me when I tell you that if you bother that girl again, I'll tear you apart. I don't care how many members of the YMCA you have hanging with you."

Stick didn't flinch. The two men stared at each other until it was obvious neither was going to back down. Gideon finally dropped the pool cue to the floor and turned and walked away. Thane felt they had been heard.

As they walked toward the exit, Stick hollered out to him. "Hey!"

Thane turned, expecting to see Stick pointing a gun at them, but instead he was just looking at him.

"You open to new clients? You're the kind of mouthpiece I need to have representing me."

Thane saw the man was serious.

"Let's get through this case first. Right now, it'd be a conflict of interest, seeing as how I might have to kill you."

Thane kept an eye on the rear-view mirror to make sure nobody ran outside with a shotgun, but no movement came from the bar. He was surprised his heart rate had hardly raised at all during their encounter with Stick & Company. Prior to Forsman, his pulse would have been firing off like a pinball machine.

Gideon looked over at Thane.

"Just for the record, you was the first one to get all vigilante, smashing that guy's face into the pool table. I was just being friendly."

"I don't like people grabbing my shoulder," Thane said. "You think Stick will make a move? Maybe to save face?"

"I don't. I also don't think his brain is wired right, so I can't say for certain. But I think he's more interested in keeping his face on his skull. Guys like that understand force, and I think that came through. Besides, I'm pretty sure his younger brother is his kryptonite; he doesn't want nothin' to happen to him, and that's why he threatened Kristin. There's no upside for him to keep this going."

Thane hoped Gideon was right about the retaliation, but if Kristin did feel threatened again, he was ready to ramp things up, although he didn't want to think too much about what that might mean.

"I wish there was a way to keep from worrying about you ending up back in Forsman," Thane said. "You know it doesn't have to be a necessity that you live behind bars."

Gideon nodded. "I know. Used to be, I figured it was just the way things were going to go, but I know I've been given a real chance here. I've never had a real apartment and a real salary and a real job before, and I'm not looking to blow it. Trust me, I'm trying. Don't get me wrong, I'm not saying the odds are heavy in my favor for staying out of trouble, but I feel at least I have a fighting chance." He shook his head as he turned toward Thane. "But he shouldn't have done what he done to Kristin. There are limits to my easy-going nature."

"I hear you."

"And maybe you should be spending a bit more of your attention on yourself. I take it that wasn't your wife you were calling before we went into the bar. That was a pretty gangster move, that whole bounty line. Who'd you have over there with Andre?"

"Benny Benson."

"The forger? That guy wouldn't hurt a fly."

"Stick didn't know that. I got Benny to tell Andre his brother had sent him over to keep him safe for a couple of hours. I figured Stick had done that in the past."

As they drove on, Thane thought once again about something that had been bothering him.

"When I told the team I was taking on Kilo's case, Kristin and Letitia both understandably expressed their concerns about having someone like that for a client. You, on the other hand, know Kilo better than any of us, but you haven't said anything against me helping him. Why's that?"

"I think I know why you took the case, and it makes sense to me. I'm okay with it."

"Why do you think I took the case?"

"Because the dude tried to kill you, and now you got yourself a chance to have him go back to prison, and as a bonus, you don't need to be looking over your shoulder."

"Why would I be looking over my shoulder?"

Gideon looked like he wanted to spit on the floor of the car. "Ah man, don't do that with me. I don't even want to be having this conversation, but you seem to want to, so here we go...

"I'm just saying that when you were always sticking up for Skunk, and saying how you couldn't believe he killed that detective, I thought you was unbelievably naive, especially after having spent five years at Forsman. It was stupid to keep thinking he was innocent, after all that evidence kept popping up. I figured maybe it was simply one of those things I didn't understand about people who are truly good at heart. That maybe they had a faith in the goodness of others that someone like me wouldn't ever understand. But I don't think it was that."

Gideon looked at Thane.

"I started thinking you might have been naive when you entered Forsman, but you were an ocean away from that when you got yourself sprung. So maybe there was another reason you were so sure Skunk didn't do it.

"Then I saw how things played out with Stone and him saying what it was he done, and then your boss ends up getting killed. If you tell me all that was a coincidence, then fine, it's all a coincidence. Conversation over. All's I know is, if you had a hand in any of that—and now you have someone who tried to kill you charged with one of those murders—then I'd be taking that case, too. And when ol' Kilo gets sent off to death row, I'd be putting on my best frowny face and saying how sorry I was that I couldn't win the case."

Thane didn't want to keep talking about this. He should have known, though, that if anyone figured out what had really gone down during their last case together, it would be someone like Gideon. Or at least he hoped that it wasn't as obvious to anyone else, especially someone like Detective Struthers.

"I am going to try to help Kilo. You can believe me or not, but I am trying to help him."

"Then maybe that's just another one of those things I don't understand about good people." After they drove on for another moment, Gideon added, "Or you're just stupid."

24

Thane sat in the Twin Towers Correctional Facilities waiting for Kilo, who had called earlier and said he needed to talk as soon as possible. He wouldn't give any more information over the phone.

The door to the interview room opened and Kilo was escorted in, wearing his frayed, orange jump suit. He didn't look tired or overly worried; you could tell who was new in the system versus those who had done time before—the latter slipped back into the day-to-day routine of prison life as easily as changing shirts. That didn't mean Kilo was happy to be there, but he wasn't suffering from panic attacks.

"So what's up?" Thane asked after the guard left them.

"That cop Mahone came and talked to me. He said if I helped him get Stick, he could get me a dramatically reduced sentence. But he said I had to decide before the trial started."

"So he's saying if you help him get the guy he's been after, then suddenly he can get your sentence reduced if you're convicted of a high-profile murder?"

"I'm not sitting here saying I believe it," Kilo said.

"Good, because no prosecutor is going to agree to

a reduced sentence just to help some narcotics detective make a bust. That isn't going to happen."

"In that case, I wanted to ask you if the prosecutor has offered any sort of plea deal."

"It's too early for that. Why would you want to talk about that now?"

"Because Mahone hinted he might let Stick know I was cooperating with him, which would put my family at risk while I'm behind bars. I can't have that happen."

"You think he'd do that?"

"I don't think so, but that's the problem: I don't *think* he would. I don't know it for sure. And if I plea this out, Stick will know I'm not working with Mahone."

"And you'll end up in prison where you said there were people who wanted to kill you."

"But my family would be safe."

Thane was feeling backed into a corner. He needed more time to figure out what the hell was going on. He couldn't let Kilo go back to Forsman.

"I'll push to have the trial take place as quickly as possible. I'll make sure the press reports we've turned down any offers to plea this out—even though there haven't been any deals made—and I'll get word to Stick that you're leaving him out of this. If the DA's office is feeling confident in their case, they'll be happy to push for a speedy trial as well. They'll want to tackle this while it's fresh in the public's mind."

"Then do that," Kilo said. "I talked with Ana yesterday and she said someone from her church made an anonymous donation to help her with expenses while all this takes place. Not sure who in the hell would do that, or why, but what's she going to do? Say no? I don't know how long this donation thing is going to last, so I want to get all this put on the fast track, you know what I mean?"

Thane understood Kilo wanted to help his wife and family have a better life. He remembered the disappointment he felt when he was released from Forsman and saw where Hannah had to live once Thane could no longer help her financially.

The least Thane could do was help Ana and her family with support.

The thought of financial support made him wonder what would happen if he had to confess his role in Joseph's murder. Would the money the city gave him be taken away from him—from Hannah—perhaps as the result of a civil suit? Would he end up back in Forsman and Hannah once again reduced to living in subsidized housing, especially if she lost her job because of him?

"I'll see what I can do to move things along. But I wouldn't mind having our legal strategy in place before jumping too quickly into trial."

"You think we're going to have a strategy?" Kilo asked, sounding somewhat surprised. "I mean beyond luck and prayers?"

Unfortunately, so far, luck and prayers was the only strategy Thane had been able to come up with.

25

The deposition of Rabbit Reynolds was being held in Thane's conference room. Assistant District Attorney Barry Warlick had agreed to Thane's offer to host so he could see where the money the city gave Thane was going. He wasn't much friendlier to Thane than the night he approached him at Hannah's fundraiser, but he also wasn't hostile, maybe because this time there wasn't alcohol at play.

Warlick sat alone on one side of the conference table, having apparently chosen to do the deposition without assistance from anyone else in the DA's office. Thane sat on the opposite side of the table next to Kristin. Off to one side of the room was the court stenographer, a woman in her late fifties who wore the same sort of neutral—if not bored—look that court stenographers always seemed to display in court.

Letitia knocked on the door, then escorted Robbie "Rabbit" Reynolds in. Rabbit was once again dressed like he'd just come from a photo shoot for Hipster Monthly, although this time he also wore large, round, plastic horn-rimmed glasses, the lens only slightly smaller than the coaster holding Thane's bottle of water.

Rabbit turned and tipped his fedora hat toward

Letitia. She looked at Thane like she was getting ready to ask for a raise, then shut the door in Rabbit's face.

Seeing Thane, Rabbit's eyes lit up.

"Dude! You never called me about my podcast."

"Mr. Reynolds," Warlick said, "if we can go ahead and get the deposition started, that would be appreciated."

Rabbit turned toward the Assistant DA. "Man, I've told you like a million times, call me Rabbit. All my friends do."

"Well, if we ever become friends," Warlick said, "I'm sure I will. Until then, Mr. Reynolds, please have a seat."

Rabbit looked at Thane, then plopped down in the seat at the head of the table, shaking his head and offering up a 'what can you do' shrug.

After Rabbit was sworn in, the questioning was kept basic, at least at first. Thane wanted to get a better sense of the man before delving too deep into what he saw the night of the murder. The thing Thane liked best about a deposition was that it wasn't as formal as an actual trial. He could ask much broader questions and even ask for the witness's opinions without fear of the question being objected to. Warlick could argue a question wasn't relevant, but so far, he'd been willing to let Thane go where he wanted. The Assistant DA, of course, knew some of Thane's questions wouldn't be admissible in court.

"Mr. Reynolds—" Thane started, before the inevitable interruption.

"Please… it's Rabbit."

Warlick inserted himself into the conversation. "Mr. Reynolds, during this deposition, you will be referred to as Mr. Reynolds, or The Witness. If you and the defense attorney want to go out clubbing after this deposition, you're more than welcome to do so, but the record has already established that you'd like to be called Rabbit, and the record will also show that we're not going to do that. So, let's move on, shall we?"

Rabbit looked as if he'd just had his sock garters snapped.

"You said that you are a DJ," Thane continued. "Is that your main occupation?"

"That's my main source of income, but I consider myself a professional blogger, podcaster, and video curator."

"What is a video curator?"

"I take videos and post them on my site. Last week I came across a potato in the grocery store that looked like Kim Kardashian. I got almost fifty views on that alone, and that was just a potato. Then last month I saw a kitten trying to play with a pit bull. Bro, so cute. I got over a hundred views. 'Course, I had to edit the video at the point where the pit bull turned on the kitten. Trust me, that wasn't cute at all." He winced, then washed the memory down with a large drink of water.

Thane looked at Warlick and felt if they had nothing else in common, they likely shared a similar opinion about the prosecution's star witness. Warlick looked like he'd be willing to pay twenty dollars to anyone who had an Advil to sell.

"And you said you were in the neighborhood the night of the murder, trying to line up future DJ gigs, is that right?"

"Yeah. I wasn't real optimistic about finding something in that part of town, but you know, sometimes when things get tough you need to get out and beat the bushes."

"Have you been encountering lean times lately?"

"I do fine, thanks, but a guy would have to be cray to pass up some extra guap."

Thane glanced at a notepad that Kristin had been jotting words on. She had angled it so that he could easily see what she'd written: **cray=crazy** and **guap=money**. Thane grinned at her and turned back to the witness.

"But you didn't find any new gigs in the area, right?"

"No, like I said, that area isn't exactly DJ-friendly, so I decided to head on over to the Hills and check around."

"And it was on the way back to your car that you say you saw someone who appeared to be helping a drunk friend down the sidewalk."

"Yeah. Your client." Rabbit paused, then looked at Thane sadly, as though they were buds and he had just let him down. "Sorry, dude."

"Those are some impressively thick lenses," Thane said.

"I got the idea from a rapper I saw at The Novo. I think he got the idea from those cartoon Minions. I thought they were totally deck."

Thane again glanced at Kristin's notepad as she wrote down **deck=cool**. He also noticed the Assistant District Attorney trying to read Kristin's interpreting efforts, albeit upside down.

"Were you wearing your glasses the night you say you saw my client?"

"You kidding me? You have any idea how many people in that neighborhood would want to steal these?"

"I'm going to guess none, but that's not relevant.

Were you wearing other glasses that night?"

"No."

"Contacts?"

"No, but I don't need those things. I see fine without them. My eyesight is sharp as—well, a rabbit." He lit up at that description, as if just realizing its cleverness, then took off the glasses and handed them to Thane. "These are just for stylin'."

Thane looked through the lenses and saw they were plain glass. He handed them back to Rabbit and tried not to look disappointed.

"So you say my client looked like he was trying to help out a drunk friend."

"Yeah, the guy looked like he was out cold. Dead drunk." Rabbit paused, then grinned at his choice of terms. "Guess I was half right, huh?" He laughed and raised his palm to high five Thane, but apparently thought better of it and lowered his hand.

"And you have absolutely no doubt the man you saw was Kyle Miller."

"If that's the guy I identified in the police line-up, then yeah, I have absolutely no doubt. Why don't you believe me?" Rabbit looked like he truly wanted to know.

"I'm only trying to make sure I clearly understand what you're saying," Thane said. "That's all. It's not a question of believing you or not believing you."

"Well, you can believe what I'm saying, the same as you can believe me when I tell you that if you'd do a podcast with me, it would be the break I need. Come on, bro. Help a Rabbit out. You and I could really spill some tea."

Thane and Warlick both looked over at Kristin, but

she just shrugged.

26

Thane paused upon reaching Rita McCoy's front door.

He wasn't even sure what to ask the woman whose husband had actually killed Joseph Crowell. But she had been pleasant enough on the phone when he asked if he could stop by and talk with her. Or maybe 'pleasant' wasn't exactly the right word, but she had said he could come over.

Rita McCoy was a small woman in her late fifties. She was dressed nicer than she probably normally would have been in the middle of a weekday; Thane assumed she had changed to be more presentable for his visit.

She stared at Thane for a moment longer than was comfortable, then opened the door and invited him in. He thanked her for agreeing to see him, and she nodded politely before telling him to have a seat on the sofa. She sat across the room in a small wingback chair with a side table next to it that held a pair of reading glasses and an open book, turned upside down to save its place.

The house somehow seemed gloomy. Maybe it was because most of the curtains were closed, despite it being a sunny day. Her husband, Russell, had died only a couple of months ago, so she likely had not yet come through the other side of that loss. Or maybe the house had looked like that ever since her daughter was murdered almost six years ago.

"Can I get you anything?" Rita asked. "Coffee, tea, water? Anything?"

"No, thank you, Mrs. McCoy. I don't want to take up much of your time."

Thane paused, still trying to figure out what it was he thought he could learn from her. He had felt certain that talking with her might be helpful, but now that he was there, he wasn't sure what that help might be.

"Again, I appreciate you seeing me. I obviously saw you in the courtroom, but I'm glad to finally have the opportunity to speak with you in person."

She nodded then looked away, wringing her hands slightly as they sat on her lap. She finally looked back up at him.

"I apologize if I seem nervous," she said. "I hope you understand that for five years, you were pretty much the devil incarnate in this house, back when my husband and I thought you killed Lauren. I think back to the things I said to you before your sentencing, and it shames me to know I was saying those things to an innocent man."

"You didn't know I was innocent, Mrs. McCoy. I don't blame you for the things you said."

"But I'm surprised I still feel a little nervous, so I'm sorry about that. Intellectually, I know you were found to be innocent—and I have no doubt you are innocent—but emotionally I was trained to despise you."

Thane slid forward on the sofa. "I can leave if you'd like. I certainly don't mean to make you uncomfortable."

"No, no," she said and motioned for him to stay. "To be honest, I'm glad to have the chance to speak with you.

You also suffered as a result of Lauren's murder, so in that regard we share a common bond. But what was it you wanted to talk to me about?"

"I was wondering how your husband reacted to the fact that DA Stone allowed the wrong man to go to prison for the murder of his daughter."

Rita thought about it for a long minute. She started to answer a couple of times, but paused each time as the words were starting to leave her lips. Finally, she shook her head.

"Russ felt tremendous anger toward you when he thought you were the one who took Lauren from us. He wanted justice, and when you got out of prison, it ate him up. But after it was revealed you didn't kill Lauren, Russ didn't seem to shift his anger to Stone, or even to Detective Gruber. Maybe it was because Detective Gruber was dead. Maybe it's because someone already..."

She paused and gave Thane a long look, like she wanted to ask him something but at the same time, didn't want to know the answer. Like she seemed to sense something wasn't quite right.

"Some of Russ's anger seemed to dissipate a little, even before you were found to be innocent. Instead, he acted regretful. He was quieter after your trial, like something was bothering him. Although, it might have been that the anger kept him going, and once that was gone, he had nothing to do but mourn Lauren's death. It wasn't but a few months after that that I lost him to a stroke. I believe all those years of wrestling with his anger took its toll."

She grabbed a Kleenex from the box next to her chair and wiped her eyes. She stared down at the carpet, then finally sighed and turned her attention back to Thane.

"Did my husband ever threaten you after the trial, or act like you were in any way involved in Lauren's death?"

"No, he didn't. Do you think he might have still held me responsible in some way?"

Again she hesitated to answer. "I don't think so. He seemed to feel bad about saying the things he did to you and trying to hurt you that time outside the courthouse. It's just…"

She stopped and shook her head.

"It's just what, Mrs. McCoy? Something is obviously on your mind."

She studied him, then her face became set as she opened up more directly.

"Russ was away from the house the night your friend was killed, and when he came back, he was vague about where he had been. And when I saw your friend had been killed outside your office, a very small part of me wondered if he still had a vendetta against you. If maybe he had shot and killed your friend by accident, thinking it was you. I don't really think he could have done that, but you have to understand, the anger he felt—"

"I'm sure he knew I was innocent. In fact, he reached out to me after the trial and apologized to me, like you did today."

This wasn't true, but that's only because they had resolved the issue of Lauren's death some time earlier. And Joseph had paid the price.

"I didn't know that," Rita said, surprised. "He didn't tell me, but then again, he probably wouldn't have. I'm glad to hear it, though. And don't get me wrong, I didn't really think he had anything to do with your friend's death. It's just…"

She lowered her head and again wiped her eyes.

"I, um… I sort of wondered if that's why you wanted to talk with me. I read you're representing the man who has been charged with your friend's murder, and I thought maybe you believed the same thing, that Russ had somehow been involved."

Thane shook his head. He wondered if by chance the police had questioned her about Joseph's murder, although he thought that was highly unlikely. But then again, maybe McCoy and Thane had left a clue somewhere that led the police to suspect McCoy.

Or him.

"What don't I know, Mr. Banning?" she asked. "Something happened, and I don't know what it was. Maybe Russ was simply finally able to truly mourn the loss of Lauren without the hate that had consumed him all that time. But I also feel like he did something that weighed on him. Weighed on him as a Christian man, and I don't know what it could have been."

"If there was something," Thane said, "would it change anything? I don't know what it could have been that should keep you from moving on."

"I'm not looking to *move on*. I hate that term. I'm not leaving my husband and Lauren behind. I'm staying with them. I'm not *moving on* anywhere."

Thane nodded, wishing there was something he could say that might lessen her concern.

"So if you aren't here to talk about your friend's murder, Mr. Banning, what is it you wanted to talk with me about?"

Thane wanted to ask if her husband had ever talked about a Kyle Miller. He wanted to ask if he could look at her husband's computer, to see if there was anything he might have written or looked up that might be incriminating, but he couldn't ask either of those. He had come wanting to know whether Russell McCoy's wife was privy to what it was her husband had done, but it was obvious she wasn't, despite her suspicions.

"I just wanted to give you my condolences in person. For the loss of your daughter, and your husband. As I said, your husband reached out to me, and I like to think we were able to put all the animosity behind us. I would have felt the same way he did—the same way *you* did—if I believed someone had killed my child. And as for your daughter, she reached out to me the day of her murder, trying to do the right thing, and I believe that's what got her killed. She was a good person. She didn't deserve what happened to her."

"Nobody deserves that."

Thane didn't agree with her on that one. He felt that some people did, in fact, deserve to be killed, but it pained him that he no longer had the empathy and compassion that was so present in the woman who had lost her husband and daughter.

27

Gideon could tell jail was starting to overwhelm Gus.

He watched his nephew, the young man's eyes red but no tears making an appearance yet. He hoped Gus didn't cry when he was around others, although maybe that just meant the kid was better at being a human being than he was.

Not that he ever had any doubt about that.

Kristin once again told Gus they were doing everything they could to get him out on bail, but that it likely wasn't going to happen. It was to Mahone's benefit to have Gus locked up, because that would make him more likely to make a deal as the days passed.

"You need to think about giving Mahone what he wants," Gideon said, interrupting Kristin as she started into her third apology for Gus having to stay in jail.

Gus shook his head, but Gideon cut him off.

"Hear me out," he said. "This is how the system works. You're a young Black man and they got you by the balls. Give 'em what they want or spend twenty or thirty years in prison. Them's your options. They don't give a damn if you did it or not."

"But I didn't do it!" Gus exclaimed.

"Meaning what? Life ain't fair? Well boo-fucking-hoo. If you're just now figuring that out, then you've led a pretty sheltered life."

Gus turned to Kristin. "Are you sure Andre won't testify for me?"

"He called and said he'd changed his mind. Said he wanted to, but he just couldn't."

"So then why you protecting him?" Gideon asked Gus. "If he ain't loyal enough to stick by you, why you willing to go to jail rather than give the man what he wants?"

"Because he wants me to say the drugs were Andre's, and they weren't. And like I said before, I'm not just refusing because Andre's my friend. If I testify against him, his brother will come after me and my mom and dad. And you, Uncle Gid. The guy's a psychopath."

Gideon saw Kristin stiffen at the mention of Stick. He knew she didn't need any convincing about Stick's ability to instill fear in a person.

"The guy's a punk. I saw him last night. He may talk tough, but he don't scare me. I'll protect you and your family."

"What do you mean, you saw him?" Kristin asked Gideon. He knew he'd made a mistake, watching her flush with anger.

"I went and talked to him. Wasn't no big deal. Don't worry, I didn't light him on fire or nothing."

"You didn't what?" Gus asked, confused, but this was Kristin's time to ask questions.

"Didn't we talk about you taking matters into your own hands? Why'd you go talk to him?"

"Why'd I talk to him? Because he threatened you." When he saw Gus lean back in his chair, trying to put some space between them, he figured he'd now blown this as well. "All I did was tell him to keep away from you, and I'm pretty sure I made my point. That's all."

"Are you frigging kidding me?" Kristin yelled. "I didn't ask you to do that!"

"Why should you have to ask me? He scared you, trying to act like he's tough shit, and you want me to just let him get away with that? He needs to know you've got some muscle on your side. That's the only thing thugs like him understand."

"But I...you shouldn't...I can't believe..." Kristin struggled to get out what she wanted to say, probably because she didn't seem to know exactly what she wanted to say. "Damn it, you need to let me deal with this."

"What were you going to do? Report him? File a restraining order? Give me a break. I thought you'd be grateful."

"Grateful? I can't..." She took a deep breath, then slid her MacBook back into its sleeve and stood. "Gus, I'll talk with Thane and then get back with you. Just stay strong, okay?"

"Where you going?" Gideon asked.

"Back to the office."

"I ain't done talking with Gus yet."

"That's fine, because you need to find your own way back anyway." She turned and banged on the door to the interview room, signaling for the guard to let her out.

After she left, Gideon looked at Gus. "What the hell just happened there?"

But Gus just stared at the floor, shook his head, and looked like he had given up. Gideon gave him a couple of minutes to sit in silence.

Finally, Gus spoke again. "You really think I should give up Andre, even though he didn't do anything? Wouldn't that make me a punk?"

"No more of a punk than Andre not helping you out. Listen, it's good you're thinking the way you are. It shows you're a good person, but I hate to break it to you, being a good person don't count for much in the legal system."

"But it shouldn't be that way."

"So what? You're right, but if you want to change it, you ain't going to do it in Forsman. And as bad as you think things are here in county jail, they'll be about a hundred times worse for you in Forsman. That place wasn't built to house humans, it was built to cage animals, and that's how you'll be treated. All this bullshit about what's the right thing and being noble, none of that means nothing if you're in prison. You don't get an extra serving of pudding at lunch because you did the right thing."

Gus squirmed in his chair like it was starting to heat up. Gideon could tell his nephew wanted nothing more than to scream. He'd seen it more times than he could count with newbies on their first day in Forsman.

"You wouldn't be giving up Andre to be mean. You'd be doing it because that's how the system is set up. The system is asking you to lie. All you'd be doing is what the system is asking you to do. I'm not saying that makes it right, but it is what it is."

"So you're saying I should tell the detective that Andre gave me the drugs and that they're his, even though they're not."

"Listen," Gideon said. "I didn't have much of a father growing up, at least not the type you see on TV shows, so I'm not saying I'm any good at giving advice. And looking at my life, I sure as hell ain't no sort of role model, so to be honest, I'm not even sure why you'd listen to what I have to say at all. But I think you need to do whatever you can do to get out of jail. Right now, that's all that matters."

Gus watched Gideon closely and appeared to be regaining control of himself. He sat up straighter, and no longer looked like he was about to cry.

"You say you're not a role model, but mom said you took care of her. She's said on more than one occasion that she and her sisters are indebted to you, that they would never be able to repay you. So maybe you didn't need a father to emulate. Maybe you do fine by yourself."

"No, I don't do fine by myself. My record shows that loud and clear. But I'm going to do whatever I can to keep you and your parents safe."

Gus sighed.

"Look, maybe you could talk to Andre about testifying, and if he doesn't, then I'll do what you're suggesting. I'm not promising anything, but I'll probably do what you say."

"I know this ain't easy, Goose—uh, Gus."

Gus laughed. "That's okay, Uncle Gid. You can call me Goose if you want."

Gideon shook his head. "No, you were right. You ain't a kid anymore. You're a man. I'm fine calling you Gus, but there's no way I'm calling you August. That just ain't a name."

Gus smiled. "So if Dre testifies, it will be his and my word against Jamie's, if he doesn't step up."

Now it was Gideon's turn to shift around in his seat.

He wished Kristin was still here to take the lead on this, but she wasn't, so he decided to go with his gut.

"Jamie ain't around no more."

Gus's smile disappeared. "What do you mean he isn't around?

"Kristin thought it best we tell you about this later, but Jamie's neck got broke."

Gus started to tremble and tears once again started to well up. "It was Stick, wasn't it? It was Stick."

"That's what we're figuring."

Gus paused and appeared to have to think about something before he opened his mouth again.

"I'm not telling that detective that Andre was involved. If you can't get him to testify on his own, then I'm screwed."

Thane heard Kristin approaching as soon as she came through the firm's front entrance. She marched directly to his office, not stopping to leave her things at her desk. When she blew into his office like a dust devil, Thane could tell this wasn't going to be a quiet conversation.

"Gideon told me he went to see Andre's brother."

Thane started to answer, but Kristin didn't let him speak.

"He went and threatened that psychopath. I didn't ask him to do that. I didn't want him to do that. Why does he feel like everything can be solved with his fists?"

Thane started to answer, then sniffed the air. "Have

you been drinking?"

Kristin glared at him with bloodshot eyes. "I had two shots of whiskey. I thought it might calm me down before talking with you."

"How'd that work?"

"Maybe I should have had a third."

She dropped her briefcase and jacket on the floor like they were anvils she'd grown exhausted of carrying.

"Look," Thane said, softly, "Gideon was simply trying to watch out for you. When you told us what happened, I could tell what he was going to do, so I went with him to try to keep him—"

"Wait! What?! You were there too? Are you kidding me?" The force of her own voice sent her back an unstable step or two. Thane had assumed Kristin knew the whole story, but now he wished he could rewind their conversation a few seconds.

"He was going to confront Stick either way. I went along to keep him from ending up back in prison."

Kristin stomped her foot with indignation.

"When I told you what happened, I wasn't asking you to go fix it! I was upset and wanted to vent, but God forbid a man should just listen and then defer to what the woman wants to do."

"I'm sorry. You're right. But if it's any consolation, I'm confident we got our message across."

"No, that's not any consolation! I don't want to be someone who needs a man to fix things for me. I can take care of myself. I'm strong and independent, and..." She leaned over at the waist and faced the floor before letting out a primal growl of frustration, then clenched her fists and placed them on the side of her head.

Thane gave her a moment as she gathered herself. "I am sorry, Kristin. I really am. But what's really going on?"

She kept taking deep breaths, then loudly sighed. "I'm angry because I felt so helpless. That psychopath walked into my apartment like he could do anything he wanted with me, and he could have because there wasn't a damn thing I could have done to stop him. I'm mad because I don't feel like I can go to the police, and I don't feel like I can approach Andre again to get him to testify even though it would be in the best interest of our client. I'm having trouble sleeping, I'm not comfortable going out after dark, and I tense up anytime I hear someone coming up to me from behind. I don't want to be like that. That's not who I am."

She looked like she was starting to regain her composure when Thane heard Gideon's heavy footsteps crossing the reception area floor and his voice calling out to him, "Watch out. I think our girl's on the warpath."

Gideon stepped into Thane's office as Kristin started to redden. Thane wished he had a paperweight on his desk to throw at his friend's head. Gideon looked at Thane with an expression that said nothing but 'uh-oh', but at that point, 'uh-oh' summed it up perfectly.

"Yes, Gideon," Kristin said, "the *girl's* on the warpath. Silly little girl, all pouty and being a crybaby."

"Why you so mad? We was trying to help you."

"I don't need your help!"

"The hell you don't! A girl like you is out of her league with a nut job like Stick."

"Gideon," Thane said, trying to stop him from speaking. "Please..."

"Stop calling me a girl! And next time you think I

need the menfolk to get together and defend my honor, ask me first. I'm surprised you didn't get the night janitor to help, too. He's a guy. Why not include him, too?"

"Ernie? That guy wouldn't be no good in a situation like this."

Thane waved his hand at Gideon, trying to get him to stop talking, but Gideon was looking at Kristin, totally perplexed.

"Listen, I'm sorry you're pissed off, but we didn't go confront Stick because you're a girl—a lady—whatever. We went because you're part of our crew, and someone threatened you and where your boss and I come from, you don't just let that pass. If somebody thinks another person is alone, then they figure they can do whatever they want, but once they know they're part of a team, they'll think twice about doing anything. And trust me, Stick will think three or four times before crossing paths with you again."

Kristin began to open her mouth to shout at Gideon, then appeared to think about what he said. Thane knew better than anyone the importance of having people around who had your back if things got rough, and he hoped Kristin would view it as being something a gang might do, rather than something based on gender.

"If I got in trouble," Gideon continued, "because I did something stupid, wouldn't you help me? Even though I'm a guy?"

"You'd probably have gotten into trouble *because* you're a guy. You aren't the most evolved gender."

"But I could count on ya if I needed you, couldn't I?"

Kristin started to respond a couple of times, but didn't appear to know what to say. Finally she turned back to Thane and sighed.

"I just wish you'd talked with me first. Please don't act as though I'm some helpless *girl*," she said, looking back over her shoulder at Gideon as she spit out the word. She looked back at Thane. "I'm not helpless. I'm not."

She turned and walked out of the office, looking exhausted.

Thane saw Letitia get up and once again go into Kristin's office with her. When they shut the door, Gideon sniffed the air.

"She been drinking?"

Thane nodded. "Yeah. Hanging around you will do that to a person."

"Ain't the first time I've heard that. How can I make things better?"

"Probably not calling her 'girl' would be a good first step."

"Yeah, I sort of picked up on that." Gideon looked out across the lobby at Kristin's closed office door. "She going to be alright?"

"Yeah, she's going to be alright," Thane said. "You remember how I was those first few days after I got to Forsman. How'd I turn out?"

Gideon looked at him closely, also interested in the answer to that question.

"I don't know. How did you turn out?"

"I'm still trying to figure that out."

Gideon nodded, then turned to leave. "Just so you know, Gus asked me to talk to Andre. I promise to play nice and not bring any matches, but he needs to know he's gotta step up."

"I already tried reaching out to him. I figured I was probably the right person to talk to him."

"Any luck?"

Thane sighed.

"He's disappeared."

28

The past two months had been spent preparing for this day—Kilo's trial had begun.

As Thane predicted, Warlick was more than happy to accommodate the defense's request for an expedited trial. No more had been said about a possible plea deal, as the DA's office felt confident they had what they needed so the trial date was fast-tracked.

Thane felt he had a good chance to get his client acquitted, but his certainty came from knowledge he had to keep secret to protect himself.

In the packed courtroom, Thane sat at one end of the defense table, while Kristin sat at the other end looking through paperwork, with Kilo sitting between them. Kristin wasn't nearly as involved in this case as she had been with Thane's previous high-profile case, but he still wanted her to be a part of this because he had a great deal of respect for her insight.

Gideon sat in the gallery directly behind Thane, similar to where he sat during Skunk's trial. He saw no need to be at the defense table, and still hadn't grown comfortable even being in the courtroom. He'd been there on too many other occasions, always sitting where Kilo was currently positioned.

Kilo was dressed in a dark sports coat and dress pants that Thane had brought him. He squirmed in his seat as if not used to wearing a jacket indoors, but all in all he looked respectable.

Kilo's wife Ana had given her husband a thumbs up and a forced smile when he was escorted into the courtroom. It looked like she hadn't slept in a year.

"What do you know about the judge?" Kilo asked Thane, even though he'd already asked that same question two other times previously.

"Sarah Kaelin. I don't know a lot about her, but from what I've heard, she runs a professional courtroom and isn't as biased toward the prosecution as a lot of judges."

"Which doesn't mean she's completely neutral," Kilo noted.

"No, but not having the deck completely stacked against us is at least something."

Assistant District Attorney Barry Warlick entered the side door of the courtroom, accompanied by his stern-looking associate, Netty Meyers. He wasn't sure if the woman was naturally humorless, or if she'd been coached to look that way whenever she was within eyesight of the jury. But Thane supposed that if he had to work closely with Barry Warlick, he probably wouldn't smile much either.

Warlick looked over and acknowledged Thane's presence with a professional nod, which was more than Thane expected. This was their third encounter, and the score was now two checkmarks under the professional column and one under the alcohol-induced tirade column.

After Judge Kaelin entered the courtroom, thanked the jurors, and instructed the gallery to be quiet and respectful, the charges against Kilo were read, and it was time for Warlick to give the prosecution's opening remarks. Thane quickly learned that one didn't achieve a high-level career in the DA's office without exuding power and confidence in court. Warlick definitely looked the part as he stood and addressed the jury.

"Ladies and gentlemen of the jury, we are here today to seek justice for a man who was brutally murdered. A man who is no longer able to speak for himself. A man who needs you to speak for him."

Warlick paused, then stepped from behind the prosecution's table and walked over to the jury box.

"I don't know if any of you have ever been caught in a flash flood. That's something that happened to me several years ago while vacationing in Oregon, and I can assure you, it's quite frightening. What started out as a light rain turned heavier, and in less than two hours, a river had formed that literally swept away a pick-up truck a couple hundred feet from us. That night I marveled at how rain is simply made up of individual drops of water, each one small and unable to do much in and of itself, but together, able to wash away a five-thousand pound pick-up."

Warlick paused. Thane could tell the jury had no idea where this was going, but they were intrigued.

"The case I will be presenting to you over the next several days is a little like that rainstorm. I will be establishing the defendant's proximity to the crime the night of the murder. I will offer you evidence that connects the defendant to the murder victim's car, a tip from the police hotline tying the defendant to the crime, and other facts pointing to the defendant as the killer of

Joseph Crowell.

"I will be the first to admit that each piece of evidence in and of themselves might not be enough to convict, but taken together—much like the drops of rain and the rivers they create—will be enough to show, beyond a reasonable doubt, that Mr. Kyle Miller is guilty of first degree murder."

Warlick started back toward his seat, then paused, as if he had just remembered something.

"Oh, yes. And a witness. We also have a witness, just in case all those smaller pieces of evidence just aren't enough."

Warlick glanced up at Thane as he returned to his table. The look of disdain on his face made this seem very personal.

After Warlick sat down, it was time for Thane to offer opening comments for the defense. He had worked on his opening for quite some time, and had bounced it off Kristin, but both of them knew it wasn't going to make a big impression on the jurors.

Still, Thane had to try to evoke confidence and certainty, neither of which he felt.

"Ladies and gentlemen of the jury," he began, "I want to echo Judge Kaelin's appreciation for your service today. To serve on a jury is an important role under any circumstance, but to be put in a position of deciding whether to lock up another human being for the rest of his life—perhaps even put him to death—is a weight that is almost unfair to ask of anyone, and yet that's how our system works."

Thane noticed how much more comfortable he was speaking in front of the judge and jury than he had been during Skunk's trial. He also noticed how different it felt to not be looked upon by the jury as a man who had gotten away with murder. Instead, he was now being watched with eyes that were almost sympathetic. He was now looked upon as a source of interest and curiosity, rather than viewed with disdain.

"I have to say, I thought it was telling that Assistant DA Warlick himself commented on the weakness of their various pieces of evidence. If you've been around courtrooms very much, you know that prosecuting attorneys like to play up the evidence they're going to present, not admit right at the beginning that it's a little shaky. I mean, let's face it: most of the time when you're dealing with rain, you simply end up getting all wet."

Several members of the jury chuckled.

Thane smiled at Warlick, who looked like he already wanted to stand and object.

"But even when the prosecution does say they have evidence that will show beyond a reasonable doubt that an individual is guilty, a lot of times that doesn't turn out to be the case. I, myself, have been involved in cases where the prosecution said that a case was so open-and-shut that it was going to be easy to convict, but it turned out not to be open-and-shut, and it definitely didn't turn out to be easy. It also didn't turn out that the prosecutor was correct."

Thane saw more than one juror fight to restrain a smile, with one of them failing that fight. Most of them knew he was talking about his recent duel with Bradford Stone: how the District Attorney had promised one thing to the jury, and delivered something surprisingly different.

"So what I'm going to ask of you today, and in the days to come, is to truly think about what the prosecution lays in front of you, and ask yourself, if you were in the defendant's position, would you feel like you were being treated fairly, or would you demand that actual, concrete evidence be offered before asking a group of twelve individuals to pass judgement on you.

"Now I understand the prosecution's desire for a conviction. The Assistant DA would like to secure a conviction and a resolution to this case more than almost anyone. I say *almost* anyone, because as much as he wants to see the guilty man go to jail for the murder of Joseph Crowell, he doesn't want to see it more than I do.

"There is no one in this room who would celebrate the arrest and conviction of the man who murdered Mr. Crowell more than I would, but unfortunately, the person who committed that crime is not sitting in this courtroom today and for that reason, I will fight like hell to make sure the search continues. Mr. Crowell deserves better than having someone arrested because they sort of look like they could be found guilty."

Thane thanked the jurors and sat back down next to Kilo. If any of the jurors kept up to date with local news, they would know the murdered man was Thane's friend, and those who didn't know it soon would when the jurors got together outside the courtroom.

He wanted the jury to understand that this case was personal.

He only hoped they would never learn just how personal.

After opening statements, the prosecution began its case by calling Detective Vince Struthers to the stand, which didn't surprise Thane. Best to start off strong, and nobody conveyed confidence and competency like Struthers. His smooth presentation of facts was like sitting around a campfire, listening to a master storyteller.

Struthers testified that he had received an anonymous tip saying Mr. Kyle Miller was involved in Joseph's death. The tip came in about four months after the murder. Struthers talked with colleagues from the narcotics division, and learned Miller was a repeat offender who at one time had been associated with a ruthless drug dealer.

"And how did you go about investigating the tip?" Assistant DA Warlick asked.

"We were told Mr. Miller was at a nearby bar a couple of blocks from the murder site, right before the shooting took place. So we went to the bar and were able to secure footage from their security camera showing that Mr. Miller was, in fact, at the bar."

Warlick turned toward a video monitor placed so that the jury could see the screen, as could most of the gallery.

"The following footage is from Gulliver's, the bar in question," he told the jury.

He pushed the remote and the video began. The footage had a date and time stamp in the bottom corner of the screen. Thane was familiar with video time stamps, as that had been the downfall of DA Stone in his previous case. He watched along with everyone else as the camera showed footage of people sitting at the bar.

People walked back and forth in front of the camera. Three rough-looking men sitting at the bar looked like they had come straight from filming a Harley Davidson advertisement, with their bandanas, tattoos, and leather vests.

"Please note based on the time shown on the video that we are now a little more than twenty minutes before the murder took place," Warlick said. He waited another few seconds until Kilo appeared in the frame, walking up to the bar and ordering a drink.

"And there is the defendant, Mr. Miller."

In the video, Kilo paid for his bottle of beer and walked back out of the frame, apparently to sit somewhere outside the camera's viewfinder. Warlick turned off the video and returned his attention to Struthers.

"Detective, after establishing that the defendant had, in fact, been at the bar immediately before the murder—a bar that was only two blocks from where the murder took place—what did you do then?"

"I gave more weight to the tip that had been called in. Obviously, this didn't prove Mr. Miller was involved in the murder of Mr. Crowell, but it gave weight to the possibility of his involvement."

"So you felt the tip you had received was credible."

"Yes, I did, so my next step was to compare Mr. Miller's prints to a partial print taken from the side of Mr. Crowell's car, and it was a match."

"The prints were the same," Warlick confirmed.

"Yes. Now, it was only a partial print, so the jury shouldn't think that's the same as matching fingerprints. It's not as conclusive as that, but it is a strong piece of corroborating evidence."

Thane admired the way Struthers tackled in advance what he had to know was going to be Thane's line of attack. Just put it out there to the jury, be upfront, and the jury was likely going to give it more weight than it deserved.

"I understand," Warlick said. "But you had to feel like you had your man."

"As a detective, you always want more, but yes, I felt confident we were going in the right direction. And then once we found an eyewitness, the pieces came together."

"Thank you, Detective. That's all I have for you, other than a quick acknowledgement of a job well done working this case."

Struthers seemed to frown at the courtroom theatrics, the 'job well done' sort of statements that played to the jury. Thane could tell Struthers was a straight-forward man who likely felt the facts should speak for themselves, and that all the antics and attempted manipulation of the jury took away from his solid police work.

Thane stood as Warlick took his seat, then approached the witness stand.

Detective, based on your review of the video footage, where did Mr. Miller sit after he walked away from the bar?"

"I can't answer that."

"Did he quickly drink his beer and then leave?"

"I can't answer that."

"Do you not have security footage covering other areas of the bar?"

"No, there is just the one camera, located above the cash register. The assumption is that if there were to be a hold-up, the robber would be standing there."

"So you don't know anything about what Mr. Miller

did, or did not do, after he walked away from the bar?

"Not with certainty, no."

"No?"

Thane paused. He even glanced over at the jury, as if perhaps they might have the same question. He finally shook his head and moved on with the questioning.

"You mentioned the partial print found on the passenger side of Mr. Crowell's car. Did you come up with Mr. Miller's name after running the print through your data base? After all, Mr. Miller's prints are on file in the L.A. database."

"No, his name wouldn't have come up. Partial prints are just that: partial. The database can't compare them to other prints and come up with a direct match."

"But you could have run them through the database, though, correct? It's something you could do if you chose to."

"I suppose you could, but that's not something we would do."

"Because you would have had too many hits to make it a practical way of finding someone. Is it likely there are potentially hundreds of matches? Even thousands?"

Struthers paused, doing the math in his head. "I can't give you a figure, but there would be a lot of matches."

"If there was a complete fingerprint match, then the odds of it being the defendant's would be almost one hundred percent. But it was only a partial match. What would you say the odds are that there is someone else in this room—anyone else in this room—even the Judge, whose fingerprints would also match that partial print?"

Struthers slightly shook his head. "I don't know the odds, Mr. Banning."

"But it's possible, correct? And I don't just mean theoretically possible, or possible in a 'I suppose there's an extremely remote chance' sort of way. But is it safe to say it wouldn't surprise you at all if someone else in this courtroom also matched?"

"That's correct, Mr. Banning. It might have even been yours."

Thane froze.

"And that's why I said earlier," Struthers continued, "that partial prints are not definitive proof. They are simply one piece of the puzzle."

Thane nodded, feeling he had overstayed his welcome with that line of questioning.

"Do you know what type of car Mr. Crowell drove that night?"

"It was a 2022 Lexus LC 500."

"That's an exceptionally fancy car."

Struthers didn't respond.

"This particular Lexus, which is a beautiful dark olive color, sells for over a hundred thousand dollars. It's more than a car: it's a piece of art."

"Your Honor," Warlick rose again. "Is there a question somewhere in all of this?"

The Judge looked to Thane for an answer, so he obliged.

"For the sake of argument," Thane continued, "let's say my client did touch that car. Let's say a man walking through what is safe to say, at best, a lower-middle class area, a man who lives paycheck to paycheck, walks past a car like that. Is it unreasonable to think he might have walked over to check it out? Detective Struthers, have you ever walked up to a car that impressed the hell out of you, just to look inside and see what it was like?"

Struthers nodded. "Yes, I've done that before."

"Did you happen to notice any other policemen who were on the scene of the crime also walk up to the car or make comments about it?"

"I believe I did."

"Any chance we would find partial prints of any of the officers on the car from that evening?"

Struthers appeared to be tiring of Thane. "I don't know, but if someone had told me they were involved in the murder, and if they had a history of violence, and if other evidence pointed at them, then I would have investigated those leads as well. But as it was, Mr. Miller was the person who was checking all the boxes."

"I understand. It just feels like so far, all of this is incredibly circumstantial. No further questions."

Thane returned to his seat. He felt like he had scored a few points, but he also knew that even Struthers had said initially that these first few pieces of evidence weren't definitive. And like Struthers said, there was more to come, which was evidence Thane didn't know how to rebut.

Once court was adjourned for the day, Thane turned to Kilo.

"Nothing they presented today is going to sway the jury to find you guilty."

"Even the print?"

"We can bring in a fingerprint expert to make sure everyone understands a partial print is not conclusive at all. And even if it convinces a couple of people, the majority of the jury aren't going to think it's enough."

"But the witness will make them think that."

Thane didn't respond at first, although he also knew

he didn't need to. They both understood the weight an eyewitness would have.

"There was an eyewitness in my last case that turned out to be false. And there was also an eyewitness at my murder trial."

"And you ended up doing five years for a murder you didn't commit."

Kilo stood and put his hands behind his back so the guard could put his handcuffs back on. Now that the jury was out of the room, he looked over his shoulder at Thane.

"Talk to Mahone." Thane shook his head, but Kilo continued, "I know you don't think we need to do it now—and I'm not saying I'll decide to do it—but I want you to at least hear what it is he's offering, if anything. When that cop Struthers was testifying, I could see a couple of those jury members look over at me like they'd already decided I was guilty. You and I both know Mahone saying the deal was off the table once the trial started is just a tactic cops use. I'd like you to at least hear him out before the witness testifies."

"I'll reach out to him." Thane felt they were jumping the gun by expressing any interest in what Mahone had to say, but he agreed he would be in a better position to give a recommendation if he understood what Mahone was supposedly offering.

As Kilo was escorted out of the courtroom, Kristin slid over into the chair next to Thane, and Gideon walked up to the rail separating the gallery from the defense table.

"You gonna talk to Mahone?" he asked Thane.

Thane nodded as he closed his briefcase. "I owe Kilo that."

"Mahone's an asshole," Kristin said.

"Yeah, but he's an asshole with power," Gideon responded.

"Fine, as long as we all at least agree he's an asshole," she said, then snapped her briefcase shut.

29

Thane sat in one of the interrogation rooms in the LAPD's Central Bureau station, located in L.A.'s Skid Row. He assumed Mahone preferred meeting with lawyers in the small room, viewing it as a comfortable, home field advantage. Or maybe the detective felt this setting would make Thane uncomfortable, given his past experiences in an interrogation room.

If so, he assumed correctly.

Waiting for Mahone, Thane remembered sitting in a room similar to this for several hours, answering questions following the murder of Lauren McCoy. Interrogation rooms were bleak, interior rooms with harsh overhead lighting, a small table, and a couple of uncomfortable, hard plastic chairs. No decorations, no frills, no hope.

He hadn't met Mahone before, but was curious if he was as big of a jerk as Kristin portrayed him to be, or if she was simply frustrated because she hadn't been able to get Gus out on bail. Even with Thane's previous unique experience with a crooked cop, he believed the majority of those on the police force were good people trying to do an exceptionally challenging job. He'd found as a lawyer that if you treated them with respect, they understood you were simply doing your job, and would respond in kind.

Mahone finally blew into the room, holding a can of Red Bull and taking the seat across from Thane.

"Sorry for the wait. Busy day around here."

Mahone looked at Thane curiously, likely having seen him on TV or in the newspapers.

"It's good to meet you," Mahone said. "I couldn't help but laugh when I heard you were representing Kilo."

"What made you laugh?"

"When I heard the city was giving you all that money to start a law practice for people in need of good representation, I figured it would be poor schmucks like yourself who hadn't done anything wrong. I wasn't envisioning the typical Thane Banning client being a drug-dealing, white supremacist, three-time loser gang member who could be flushed down a toilet without anyone missing him."

"I'm pretty sure his wife and kids would miss him."

Mahone laughed and sat back in his chair. "Ah, so you're a sentimentalist. That's cute. So what'd you want to talk about? Let me know if I should grab myself a couple of Kleenexes first, though, in case you're gonna make me weepy."

"Mr. Miller—"

"Who?" Mahone asked, then laughed again. "Oh yeah, Kilo. Sorry. Go ahead."

"Actually it's Kyle. He said you had made him an offer in exchange for testimony against Stick Sturgess, and he asked me to learn more about it."

"Sure, we can do that. I just hope you're more practical than that blonde chick you've got working for you on that other case," he said while shaking his head. "In fact, maybe when we're done talking about ol' Kilo, we should spend a couple of minutes talking about the Black kid."

Thane wondered if Mahone deliberately tried getting under the skin of defense attorneys because he thought it gave him some sort of psychological edge, or if irritating other people simply came naturally to him.

"Kyle said you could get his sentence dramatically reduced if he cooperated with you regarding Stick."

"That's right. I can guarantee Kilo will get out of prison a hell of a lot sooner if he works with me than if he just relies on the kindness of the judge."

"You can guarantee it."

"Guaranteed."

"So this guarantee is corroborated by someone in the DA's office?"

"No. This is my personal guarantee."

"But you know the DA's office is where sentencing recommendations come from. If you think one thing, but they think another—"

"They won't."

"Then get us something in writing with specifics."

"Not possible. Not at this time." Mahone shrugged. "Look, I get it. You want something in writing that's signed, notarized, and sprinkled with holy water, but that's not something I can do for you. Not right now. You'll just have to trust me."

"I just have to trust you?"

"I know it's not what you want to hear, but it's better

259

than what you've got. He's definitely not going to get *more* prison time because he worked with me. And I'm telling you, I can have a major impact on his sentencing. I don't see the downside."

"I suppose one downside would be Stick going after his family as soon as he hears Kyle is helping you out. And you know Stick will hear about it."

"We can protect the family."

"And I should trust you on that, too."

"Is there a reason you wouldn't?"

Thane looked at Mahone, almost surprised the man would open himself up to a question like that.

"You have my other client, Gus Cleveland, locked up and being threatened to be charged as a major drug dealer if he doesn't lie about who gave him the drugs. You're wanting him to testify to something that's not true so that you can then go after the brother of a big-time drug dealer, probably to do the same thing to him. And you're asking me why I might not trust you?"

"I'm not telling the kid to lie."

"You're telling him that if he says Andre gave him the bag of drugs, then he'll be kicked free for cooperating, and that if he doesn't, you'll be going at him hard and heavy."

"But I'm not telling him to lie."

"You're putting him in a position where he feels like he has no choice but to lie in order to get out of jail. What difference does it make if you're not directly telling him to lie? He's already told you that's not how it went down, but you're still telling him that that's the deal. Don't insult me with the whole 'but I'm not *saying* he should lie' bullshit. We both know what you're doing. Why not own it?"

Mahone grinned at Thane. "I see now where the blonde chick gets it."

"Her name is Kristin."

"I don't care if her name is Queen Elizabeth. Look, my job is to get drugs off the street. How many young kids do you come across every day who are strung out or who are laying on a slab in the coroner's office? Because I come across a hell of a lot of them. And I'm not just talking kids seventeen or eighteen, I'm talking eight, nine years old, sometimes younger. Scum like Stick are responsible for families being torn apart by drugs, robberies taking place by junkies trying to get their next fix, people living under the freeway overpass because they've lost everything they had to addiction. So what I'm *trying* to do, Banning, is take people like Stick off the streets."

"And you're going to do that by having people say something that isn't the truth."

"What is truth?" Mahone asked.

"What is truth? Are you kidding me? What is this, freshman philosophy class now?"

"I'm serious. What is truth? I don't view it as making people lie. I know for an absolute fact that Stick deals drugs. You probably know he deals drugs. I know all sorts of things about him, so if I tell someone who's been busted to say something, it's because I know that that something is true, even if they don't. If it results in getting people like Stick behind bars, then it's not a lie. Stick deals drugs. That's the truth."

"But you know Gus isn't a drug dealer. You know it the same as you know Stick is, but you're still threatening him with a long jail sentence if he doesn't cooperate."

"No, that's not a threat, it's a fact. People on the street

need to understand that not cooperating with the police comes with ramifications."

"Doing time for a crime they didn't commit."

"Ahh, but you see, he did do it. He absolutely took a bag of drugs and delivered it to a low-level dealer. That's the truth you're so concerned about. I don't make the law; I only enforce it. He did exactly what he's being charged with doing."

"But you know he didn't realize what was in the bag."

"Because he said he didn't? Right. I've never heard that before from someone I busted. Look, I don't write the laws, and I don't write the sentencing guidelines. He won't be sentenced to anything beyond the sentencing guidelines."

"But you'll work to make sure he gets the maximum."

"Only if he doesn't help me."

"By not telling the truth."

Mahone sighed as he finished off his Red Bull with one last gulp. "I can see we're just going in circles here." He crushed the can against the top of the table and tossed it underhanded into a nearby trash can. "If Kilo or the Black kid decides to work with me, let me know, otherwise, I've got to get back to work. While you're trying to get a white supremacist back on the streets, I'm trying to prevent another set of parents from hearing they lost a child to a drug overdose."

Mahone sighed. He started toward the door when Thane called out to him.

"So what happens if you get Stick off the streets?"

Mahone stopped and turned around. "What do you mean, what happens? You mean to your clients?"

"No, what happens to the drug dealing? Are kids

suddenly going to discover they can't get their hands on any more drugs? Do drug deaths drop in the city? Does crime go down? Once Stick is off the streets, are all the other dealers going to shrug and say, 'Well, it was good while it lasted. Guess we might as well go get a job at McDonald's'?"

Mahone then marched back over to the table, his face reddening face with each step.

"You suggesting we don't make an effort because we're not going to stop all drug use in the city? Maybe we should also stop pulling over drunk drivers because there will still be drinking and driving, so what's the use?"

"No, I'm saying the benefit you get from arresting Stick isn't as great as the lives you ruin in the process. I know firsthand what happens when someone in authority feels that having an innocent person spend time in prison is sometimes for the greater good, so where does that stop? Sure, if somehow putting Stick away actually made a dent in the drug trade, maybe—and only maybe—your tactics could be more defensible. But it won't make a damn bit of difference, and you know it. You'll have your notch on your belt, but the morgue is still going to have some kid in it, and you'll have some other dealer that you suddenly have a hard-on for. The problem is, there will be a lot of other kids behind bars because they had the audacity not to lie for you."

"So just let Stick keep dealing?"

"Are those really the only two options? Strong-arm innocent people to lie, or let Stick continue operating? How about you just do your damn job and arrest him the right way?"

"Like how? Work with that Jamie kid who gave the

Black boy the drugs? Maybe I should do that now. Oh wait, I can't, because that kid had his neck broken. And who do you think killed him? You don't suppose it was the asshole who you're fine with leaving on the street, do you?"

"Who do I think killed Jamie? How about the person who coerced him into trying to get Andre to deliver a bag of drugs? Or do you not want to look that far back? Once again, how about just doing your job the right way?"

"My job is to take pieces of garbage like Stick off the street, so as long as I do that, I *am* doing my job. And I notice that Andre punk has gone AWOL the past couple of months."

"Because he knows you'd do to him what you're doing to Gus."

"Well, as soon as Gus tells me what I want to hear, I'll track the other boy down. They got family back East, so I'm betting he was sent there until all this blows over. Your client can either help out or spend a couple decades in prison. I can't imagine he's enjoying jail so far."

Mahone turned and stormed out of the interrogation room, slamming the door behind him. Thane sat the table for a moment longer, now certain Mahone's guarantee of getting Kilo a reduced sentence was nothing but another tactic. The detective was obviously comfortable saying whatever he needed to say to make an arrest. Whether it was true or not didn't seem to concern him.

Thane struggled to get one shelf level, and it was starting to piss him off.

He had spent the last two hours trying to build a new bookshelf for Hannah's store, and he felt like he should have been further along than he was. The shelf reminded him of the status of Kilo's case—off kilter, and not getting any better.

Thane still didn't know how he was going to free Kilo. It was hard to prove a negative, to prove Kilo didn't kill Joseph, at least not with the facts they had so far. Of course, in the legal system, one wasn't supposed to have to prove innocence: it was the job of the prosecution to prove guilt. But when the defendant was someone with Kilo's history and appearance, that was a nice theory, but the burden of proof was likely on him.

It seemed as though it should have been easy to get an acquittal for a client accused of a crime his lawyer orchestrated.

Thane had a fairly good sense of what had happened that evening, after he had simply left Joseph behind with McCoy. He had no doubt what the end result was going to be, but he didn't actually know the details of what happened during Joseph's final hour. That was to give Thane some deniability and, truth be told, give him at least the tiniest argument that he wasn't responsible for Joseph's death.

McCoy was the man who killed Joseph, not Thane.

Thane felt there were four possibilities at play here. The first was that the eyewitness mistook Russell McCoy for Kilo, but other than both of them being large men, they didn't really resemble each other. Plus, Rabbit's identification in the police line-up was definitive.

Another option was that Kilo was out on the street that night, perhaps had gotten in a fight with someone, or had helped a drunk down the sidewalk, and that's what Rabbit saw. But Kilo didn't remember a time when he didn't go straight from the bar to his home, and he was even more certain he'd never found himself helping someone down the street.

A third option was that McCoy had hired Kilo to help him take out Joseph. Thane didn't know how McCoy handled the murder, and maybe he felt he needed help with the body. But Thane thought Kilo was being honest when he said he didn't recognize McCoy's name. That wasn't to say, though, that McCoy used his real name. In fact, it was more likely he wouldn't have, assuming he'd reached out for help at all. So that was still a possibility.

The fourth option was that Kilo was being set up. There were apparently enough people who Kilo had angered. Hell, even Thane had at least entertained the notion of letting Kilo take the rap for Joseph's murder, and he was his lawyer. He also knew that the supremacist gang Kilo had been a part of wouldn't have taken Kilo's breaking away without feeling some need for retribution. And while Kilo was probably right that framing him for murder was pretty elaborate for them, calling in a tip and naming Kilo would have been easy enough. And once the police got the name of someone who fit the profile, sometimes it was easy to make the subsequent evidence fit that narrative.

But try as he might during these past two months, Thane hadn't been able to make any progress on any of these scenarios, and it frustrated the hell out of him.

Of course, Thane always had the wild card, and that

wild card was the truth. But while the truth would set Kilo free, it wouldn't do the same for Thane.

There was a small part of him that wanted to let the world know exactly what he had done and why he had done it, but it was a very small part. Just the same, he wondered what would happen to him if the truth came out. Given how he had been treated both by his former friend and by the legal system, would a sentencing judge understand why he did what he did and, therefore, be lenient in the punishment? After all, he didn't kill Joseph or Detective Gruber. And he didn't pay Russell McCoy to kill them.

Just the same, he recognized his hands were not clean by any stretch of the imagination.

He pried loose the small block of wood holding the shelf that wasn't level, and moved it down an inch or so before nailing it back into the wall. After placing the shelf on the brace, he got out the level and saw the shelf was now tilting too far in the other direction. He stared at the shelf, but this time, instead of once again removing the block of wood and adjusting it yet again, he took his hammer and started banging on the end of the shelf that was too high, as if pounding the hell out of it would somehow make it level.

Hannah dashed over from another part of the bookstore where she had been working to see what was going on. She reached Thane in time to see the shelf in question crack in half under the force of the hammer and his frustration. Thane put the hammer down and stared at the shelf, then sighed.

"Maybe this wasn't the best idea," Hannah said. "Working here when your case is underway."

Thane stared at the shelf, then turned and sat on the floor and rested against the wall. "It's not as though I'd be making any progress with that either."

"Maybe, but at least working on your defense, the most damage you could do would be to crumple up pieces of paper."

He looked at the broken board and then at the hammer on the floor, lying next to him like a murder weapon.

"Sorry about the board." He wiped his forehead with his shirt sleeve. "Sorry about all of this."

Hannah walked over and lowered herself down next to him. "You know, we don't have to do this tonight."

"I thought maybe it would help me get my mind off the case for a while."

"It does appear as though you've lost your mind, so maybe it worked?"

He smiled and nodded. He could tell Hannah was looking at him, most likely trying to see if she could better understand him.

"What's going on, Thane?"

"It's the case. The prosecution's witness is testifying tomorrow, and I'm not sure how I'm going to get the jury to not believe everything he's saying."

She didn't respond for a long while, then took his hand. "No. I'm asking what's really going on?"

He looked at her, not knowing how to answer. He waited her out, to hear what she was really asking.

"I know you're concerned about the case. I get that. But something else is going on with you, and I can't figure out what it is. You've been doing so much work here at the bookstore for me, and fixing things around the house.

You're acting like you're getting ready to go somewhere, and you're trying to get things lined up before you do."

Thane knew what she was talking about. In addition to doing a few odd jobs around the house that they'd put off doing since they moved in, he also had pulled together various financial documents and banking information into one notebook as a convenient resource for Hannah. If he ended up back in prison, he wanted to feel as though he had made things as easy as possible for her.

"We always used to be able to share everything," Hannah said. "But now I sense there's a part of you that is completely closed off, and it bothers me."

"I know, and I'm sorry. I built up a lot of walls when I was in prison, and it's taking me longer than I thought it would to bring them down."

"But I felt like some of the walls *had* been coming down these past few months. Recently, though, they seem to be going back up. I want to be supportive—I like to think that I *am* supportive—and I don't want to be the 'little woman' who is giving you a hard time about taking on this case or complaining that we don't talk anymore. I'm not saying we have to share all of our feelings and all of our secrets, but when it's something that could hurt our relationship, then that's something that needs to be out there."

Thane wanted nothing more than to be able to tell her what was actually going on, and in fact, there had been a couple of occasions when he had almost done that. He thought if he was completely open about what had happened, she might understand. The problem, though, was that she also might not.

Hannah reached over and put her hand around the

back of Thane's neck and stroked it lovingly.

"I'm sorry I was pressing you about what's bothering you. You have enough going on with this case to have to spend time talking about my feelings. But once this is over, we need to figure out what we have to do to get at least a little more on track, to see if we can't get a little closer to how things used to be."

"What if we can't get back to the way things used to be?" Thane asked.

Hannah paused for a long moment. "I understand things may never be exactly like they were. What happened to you—what happened to us—was traumatic, and we're always going to have to live with that. Maybe there are going to be some cracks. I just don't want the things that seep through those cracks to be things like trust and honesty. I need to be able to trust you. And I need you to be honest with me. I don't think we can make it without that, Thane. I really don't."

Thane felt if he was ever going to open up to Hannah and tell her what had really gone down with Joseph, it was now. And maybe he would still lose her. Maybe she would think she had already lost the man she used to know and love, but he would at least have been honest with her.

But if she could forgive him, and if she were to stay with him, then he felt it was more likely he could once again become the sort of man he, himself, could be proud of. He could be someone who once again played by the rules and was able to put the bitterness behind him.

He felt that now was the time.

But all he could do was to reach up and take her hand and hold it tight.

He wasn't ready to risk losing her for good.

30

Court resumed the next day with the main attraction being the prosecution's star witness, Robbie "Rabbit" Reynolds. If there was one label Rabbit had likely been longing for all his life, it was 'star,' and this day came with all the trappings of becoming one. Microphones, camera flashes, and shouted questions from the press. The gallery seemed to sense the day was going to be an important one.

Thane had no doubt the hipster-slash-DJ-slash-bon-vivant-about-town viewed this as his opportunity to propel himself into the public eye. Rabbit probably assumed if he played his cards right, he would make it into the VIP rooms of the most exclusive bars that had always shunned him before. Might possibly make it onto a talk show or two and even, if he were to reach total nirvana, be on *Dancing With The Stars*.

Kristin and Thane had worked together as they prepared for Rabbit's testimony, but never did come up with anything that could be called a strategy. The best they could do was try to get him to exaggerate his role in the whole thing, in the hopes of having him come across as being someone who was only in it for the publicity. Citizens of Los Angeles were more than familiar with that sort of attention-seeker.

When Barry Warlick called Robert Reynolds to the stand, Thane was disappointed to see the prosecution's witness dressed in a professional suit and tie. He guessed Warlick likely worked with him on watering down his hipster appearance.

Rabbit took the stand, trying to look distinguished by sitting up straight and summoning as much gravitas in his facial expressions as he could. Although occasionally, the start of a grin began to form before he could beat it back into submission.

All eyes were on him: it was a dream come true.

"Mr. Reynolds," Warlick began, "what is it you do for a living?"

"I do so many things, bro, but right now my main area of focus is being a leader in musical entertainment."

"You're a DJ, is that correct?"

"That's selling me a little short, bro, but I guess for the purposes of today's discussion, that's close enough."

"Excuse me," Judge Kaelin interjected, turning so she could look over at the witness. "Are you and Assistant District Attorney Warlick actually brothers?"

Thane couldn't help but smile. He'd take anything he could get during this testimony.

"No?" Rabbit answered, confused by the question.

"Then if you could refer to him as 'Mr. Warlick,' or 'sir,' or any other appropriate response, rather than 'bro,' that would be best."

Rabbit thought about it, then nodded to show he understood, even though Thane wasn't sure he understood at all.

Warlick continued with his questions, asking what Rabbit was doing earlier that night (just living life in his apartment), what time he was passing by when the murder took place (around 9:20), and what brought him to the site of the murder (trying to drum up new gigs because there were neighborhoods who had yet to experience the musical magic of Rabbit Reynolds).

Warlick then walked his witness up to what he had seen, which Rabbit described in great detail. When asked if the person he saw carrying the body was in the courtroom, Rabbit sat up even straighter and paused, as if waiting for dramatic music to swell up in the background, then pointed at Kilo with a certainty that looked as though he wanted to shout 'J'Accuse!' After Warlick had Rabbit tell the jury about the police lineup, and once again had the witness state how certain he was, Warlick said he had no further questions. As he walked back to the prosecution's table, Warlick looked as though he wanted to exhale a deep breath in relief that his witness hadn't gone full force flaky on him. Thane rose and walked toward the witness stand.

"Mr. Reynolds, in your deposition, you said you saw my client walking with another person, holding him up. Today you say you saw my client carrying a body. Those are two fairly different ways of describing it, wouldn't you say?"

"I said I thought that's what he was doing at the time: helping a friend who was so drunk he looked like he'd passed out. When I heard later what happened, I understood he was moving someone's body."

"You didn't call the police when you saw what you saw?"

"No. I didn't think it was any big deal."

"You didn't tell your friends or family later that night

or in the days to follow?"

"No. I just thought it was something funny to watch, that's why I noticed it, but I didn't tell anyone about it."

"What makes you think my client wasn't actually helping someone to their car? He was at a bar that night. He lives in the neighborhood. Maybe you saw exactly what you thought you saw."

Rabbit again paused, but Thane sensed this time he had just been asked a question that he wasn't sure how to answer. Finally he offered up a shrug.

"All I can say is what I saw. That's all. I'll leave it up to all of you to sort out what it all means."

Thane was disappointed that he hadn't been able to get Rabbit to answer the question in a less reasonable way.

"The following day," Thane continued, "when the murder was reported on TV and in all the newspapers, you didn't make the connection and immediately call the police to tell them what you saw?"

"I can't say I heard anything about the murder. I don't really keep up with the news. I'm more interested in making the news than reading it."

"Then is that why you're here today? To make news? To get publicity? To finally be seen?"

Rabbit winced a little at Thane's characterization of him. "Ouch. That was a little harsh, br... Mr. Banning." When he saw Thane wasn't going to apologize, he continued, "I'm here because a month or so after the murder, I read something about it, so I told the police what I saw."

Rabbit presented himself far better than Thane thought possible, and instead of self-aggrandizing, he came across as someone who was simply testifying to what he saw, and nothing else.

Thane stood looking at Rabbit, hoping the young man might offer more, but he had apparently been coached well by the DA's office.

"Mr. Banning," Judge Kaelin asked. "Do you have any more questions?"

"I don't, your Honor, but I would like to reserve the right to recall Mr. Reynolds during the presentation of our defense."

"So noted."

Thane said he didn't have any other questions, but that wasn't true. He had many questions. He wanted to give a description of Russell McCoy and ask if Rabbit saw him the night of the murder. He wanted to ask Rabbit how he could have seen his client carrying a body when that's not how Thane thought the murder went down. He wanted to ask how the hell his client could be on trial for a murder Thane knew for a fact he didn't do.

He couldn't ask those questions, but he sure as hell would like to have the answers.

Having presented its case, the prosecution rested. Due to a conflict with the judge's schedule, the case was adjourned for the day. As the courtroom began clearing, Thane told the guard he needed a few minutes with his client.

After being escorted to a small meeting space down the hall from the courtroom, Kilo told Thane he wanted to take a chance with whatever it was Mahone had to offer.

"I know you said you don't trust the guy," Kilo said, "and I don't either, but I don't have a lot of options."

"I'd just like you to give me a little bit more time. That's all."

"Look, you and I both know where this is headed," Kilo said. "The jury is going to believe that little twerp. Hell, you got sent to prison on the testimony of a two-bit loser, and you were a high-priced lawyer. A guy like me, you might as well put a big bow on my head and hand me over to the prosecution. What have we got for our defense? Me saying I didn't do it? Yeah, that'll be convincing."

Thane understood where Kilo was coming from, and with most any other case he'd agree. But this wasn't just any other case.

"Mahone said he could guarantee I'd get a dramatically reduced sentence if I help him out," Kilo said.

"And that sort of thing doesn't mean anything unless the prosecutor agrees to it."

"He said he'd guarantee it in writing."

"Is that what you need? Fine." Thane pulled a piece of paper out of his briefcase and wrote in large, printed letters, 'I guarantee you'll be found not guilty', then signed it and slid it over to Kilo.

"This doesn't mean anything," Kilo said.

"It means as much as Mahone's. Hopefully more." Kilo looked like he wanted to punch a wall, but after a minute, he appeared to once again resign himself to having no good options.

"Look," Thane continued. "If you think your family will be safe if you work with Mahone, then fine, maybe there's not a downside to seeing if he can do what he says he promises. But I'm guessing there's only so long they can stay hidden. You want your wife and kids to always be looking over their shoulders? This whole thing is predicated on the assumption that Stick will be convicted of something."

"What's 'predicated'?"

"It means based on. The safety of your family is based on the belief Stick will be arrested."

"Then just say that. I'll believe you're smart even if you don't use fancy words."

Thane nodded, not meaning to have offended him.

"You really think there's a chance in hell you can get me sprung?"

"I do. You just need to trust me."

"Okay," Kilo said, after a long pause. "I'll trust you for now, with that trust 'predicated' on the belief that you really do seem to be trying. But I sure as hell wish defense lawyers could use some of the same tactics the police use."

Thane stood and turned to leave, then paused and sat back down.

"Is there something else?" Kilo asked.

Thane continued thinking through an idea that had just sprung to his mind following Kilo's words. He wasn't confident it was a good idea, or even how it might play out, but right now it was the only thought that came to him.

"Do you know anyone at the jail who you really trust? Someone who would be willing to do you a favor—a big one—even if it ran the risk of getting them in trouble with the police?"

Kilo studied Thane, then smirked.

"I might, yeah. Why?"

31

When Thane got back to the office following court, Letitia said he'd just missed a call from Barry Warlick who had asked for a call back. He was able to reach the Assistant DA on the first try. Warlick told Thane he'd heard rumors that someone was suggesting Kilo could get a reduced sentence if he pled guilty, and he wanted Thane to know that that wasn't going to happen. Warlick knew he had a strong case, and he saw no need to negotiate.

After hanging up, Thane sat at his desk, not moving. He felt like he was soon going to be at the point where he would either need to confess his role in Joseph's murder, or let Kilo take the rap for it.

The whole purpose of his law firm was based on his strong conviction that he could help innocent people from going to prison. And it was this conviction that caused him to take on Kilo's case in the first place. But now, keeping Kilo out of jail might result in a different type of conviction—his own.

He didn't want to be separated from Hannah again. He also didn't want her to know what he had done. He feared she would quickly come to see that he was no longer the man she married: a man who tried to do the right thing and who played by the rules. He also saw the hypocrisy, though, of having her continue to think of him that way if he ended up letting another man be sentenced to death for something Thane had orchestrated. The red demerits on Thane's moral scorecard were starting to add up.

He slammed his fist down on his desk in frustration, right as Letitia appeared in his doorway. All he could do was stare back at her, uncertain how to explain his outburst.

"So," she finally said. "How's your day going?"

"I'm just sitting on a rainbow."

"Good to hear." She came on into his office and sat in the chair across from his desk. "But remind me to give you some space when things *aren't* going well. What does that entail? A chainsaw?"

"If you have one, it's probably best you keep it hidden for a while."

She nodded as she pretended to jot down a note on her pad of paper, saying the words aloud as her pen moved. "Keep...power...tools...away...from...boss."

She looked up from her pad of paper, but Thane wasn't paying attention.

"I take it your call with Warlick didn't go well?"

"He wanted to make sure I understood there wouldn't be a plea agreement. Apparently, word got back to him that Mahone was making promises he couldn't keep."

"You didn't really believe that dick-tective anyway, did you?"

"No," Thane said. "He's just looking to get what he wants. There's no way he could get Kilo's sentence reduced."

"That's what I'd figured, but—" Letitia began. She appeared to be thinking about something for a moment. "You know, I just want to state for the record that I'm not looking to make it a habit of trying to help white supremacist assholes—"

"I don't think that's who he really is anymore."

Letitia waved him off. "Yeah, sure, whatever. He's probably just misunderstood. Anyway, I was thinking last night, what if this narc Mahone actually *was* able to help cut a deal for our client?"

"And how could he do that?"

"Maybe he knows something we don't." When Thane didn't respond, she added,

"Maybe he knows something Warlick doesn't."

"Like what?"

"Not sure, but when your buddy the Klansman was here the first time, didn't he say that when his neighbor returned a bag of tools to him, he was suddenly surrounded by cops?"

Thane thought about it, and understood what Letitia was suggesting.

"You never cease to impress me, Letitia."

"If you think that's impressive, wait until you hear what I learned about your twerpy friend Rabbit."

The next morning, Thane entered the East Los Angeles Courthouse, where the L.A. Public Defender's office was also located. He had an appointment with Sheri Basten, a public defender for the past fifteen years who told him over the phone she could give him ten minutes at most, as her backlog of cases was starting to stretch beyond the point of no return.

Through a Google search, Thane had been able to identify several other cases where Mahone had been the arresting officer. Thane hoped to find individuals whose circumstances fit the detective's M.O. of coercion, in an effort to establish a pattern. He was confident Gus wasn't the first person to be threatened with jail time for not cooperating.

While scanning the list, one man's case jumped out at him.

Basten met him at the reception area and escorted him back to a cramped office half the size of a McDonald's restroom. Her desk held an impressively tall and unsteady stack of folders. He wondered if she'd developed the skill to pull a file from the center of the stack without it tumbling down.

Basten appeared to be in her late 30s, her blonde hair tied back into a bun in a way that made it look like she was trying to hide just how attractive she was. Thane wondered how many of her clients hit on her each day. She also appeared exhausted, although Thane guessed that was simply the result of a normal day in the Public Defender's office. Although obviously tired, she still didn't look like someone he would want to take on in court.

"I appreciate you seeing me on short notice," Thane said.

"Sorry I can't give you more time, but I'm due in court in half an hour. There was no way, though, I was going to pass up the chance to meet the cover-boy of Public Defender Monthly."

Her hazel eyes sparkled as she offered up an impish grin. Thane wasn't sure if she was kidding, or if there was any resentment toward what he was doing. It occurred to him he probably should have reached out to the head of the Public Defender's office, given that they had over seven hundred lawyers representing people who couldn't afford their own representation. He wasn't sure if he would be seen as part of the good fight, or someone who was cherry-picking the cases he wanted. He figured this was an opportunity to at least gauge the temperature from one of its attorneys.

"So just out of curiosity, how am I seen around here?"

She smiled at his directness. "The reviews are mixed in some areas. I mean, my colleagues and I are ninety-nine percent in empathy for what happened to you, and just as unanimous in toasting you after you toasted Brad Stone, so there's no dissension there."

"Good to know. Where are my poll numbers lower?"

She shrugged. "Don't get me wrong: people support the idea of what you're trying to do. Taking on cases of people who you feel aren't being given a fair shake by the system, but that's also what we do every day as well. I know some of my colleagues feel that the money the city gave you to start what appears to basically be a boutique-type office could have been put to better use by giving it to our office. We'd likely help out a hell of a lot more people with that amount of money than you will."

"And is that how you feel?"

She shook her head as she checked the time on her watch. "No. We wouldn't have been given that money anyway, so it might as well go to someone who can take at least a few cases off our hands. But unless you're thinking of running for office—and god, please don't tell me you're running for office—I'm guessing you didn't come here to check your poll numbers amongst the public defenders."

"No, as I mentioned on the phone, I'm interested in learning more about someone you represented a few years ago, a Lawrence Woods."

Basten lifted a file off the top of the stack and glanced through it.

"I got it ready for you. Are you now representing him on something? Maybe trying to get him released? God, that would be so great."

"Why do you say that?"

"Because he's a good guy who shouldn't be in prison. We deal with a lot of clients who deserve to be locked up, but Lawrence is one of those people whose conviction sickened me. The system really screwed him."

"I'm afraid I'm not working with him, but I checked the court records and saw where Detective David Mahone testified against him.

"That son-of-a-bitch. He was trying to get Lawrence to testify against a friend of his who had nothing to do with drugs, but Mahone thought the guy could help him with a case he was working on. He didn't care that my client only had a gram or two of coke on him. He said if he didn't help him, he'd paint him out to be some sort of drug kingpin and send him away for years, and that's exactly what he did."

"I'm dealing with Mahone on a similar case. Sounds like his M.O. hasn't changed."

"No, I'm certain Mahone's not someone who evolves. All I can tell you is he'll do what he threatens to do. Lawrence decided to do the stand-up thing and not lie about his friend. All I can say is, I wish I had friends that loyal. He's now doing ten to fifteen years. Maybe after this case that you're working on, you can see if you can throw him a bit of your expertise. He's a good guy who had a good future ahead of him, but ended up getting royally screwed."

"I'm scheduled to talk with him this afternoon, but I wanted to talk with you first. Would you have any problem with me getting a copy of the court transcript?"

"Sure, I'll have Tony at the front desk make you a copy. If it helps get your client out from under Mahone's thumb, I'll even waive the copying charge, although I suppose you are pretty flush with cash."

She followed that up with a beautiful smile, then checked her watch one more time as she rose and started sliding a couple of files into her briefcase.

"Sorry, I've gotta go. Do me a favor, though, would you? Next time you see Mahone, kick him in the balls for me."

32

When Thane got back to the office, Cricket was sitting low in one of the reception area chairs, clicking away on her phone at a speed that sounded like a Geiger counter hitting a uranium motherlode. She stopped what she was doing and looked up at Thane as he entered, throwing a scowl his way.

"I thought we had a three o'clock."

Thane looked at the wall clock opposite the reception desk. It was 3:07.

"Sorry. My last meeting ran a little longer than I expected."

"Not my problem. I've got things to do." Thane heard Letitia unsuccessfully try to stifle a laugh.

"You're ten," Thane said.

"That's ageist. Don't make me sue you."

She hopped up and headed toward Thane's office, not waiting for him. He glanced over at Letitia who was still having trouble restraining a smile. Thane sighed and followed Cricket into his office. She was already sitting in the chair across from his desk, so Thane took his desk chair and rolled it to the side of his desk.

Cricket handed him a manila envelope, then dramatically cracked her knuckles as if she was now officially done with that task.

"Don't know why you didn't just let me email you this. You do know you can send documents over the internet now, don't you? It's a thing."

"Yes, I read something about that."

"Good. I wasn't sure how much technology changed while you were locked up, but printing out this sort of thing is kind of 1928. Besides, think of the trees." Cricket put her hand over her heart.

"But if you'd emailed it to me, I wouldn't have had the pleasure of your company."

Cricket looked at him, then grinned. "Yeah. I get that a lot."

Thane opened the envelope and pulled out the document. He was impressed by the degree of detail Cricket had provided explaining how it was she was able to hack into a cable system that was supposedly hack-proof. The diagrams and sketches interspersed between the written descriptions looked like something from an MIT thesis paper.

"Think that's going to satisfy The Man?"

Thane continued looking it over. He stared at the first page for a long moment, although he might as well have been trying to read a page of Latin. "If it helps them come up with a fix so others can't do the same thing, then yes." He skimmed over the other pages quickly.

"No need to pretend you understand what it says," the young girl said. "Someone in their IT department should be bright enough to figure it out. Maybe. If not, perhaps they can hire me to explain it to them."

"I'm guessing this should give them what they need."

"Someone else will find another way to do what I

did."

"Maybe, but as long as that someone else isn't you, we're good. But from what I was told, nobody had been able to do it before, so maybe you're the only one they need to watch out for."

"Them and the rest of the world."

Thane skimmed through the document one more time, not understanding any more than he did the first time. "Don't quote me on this, but they'd probably like to offer you a job there once you're old enough."

"Baby, I want to be *on* TV, not working *for* TV." She gave him a profile angle of her face, then grinned. "So we good?"

Thane slid the paperwork back in the envelope and nodded. "I think we're good."

Cricket stood, walked over, and firmly shook Thane's hand. "Pleasure doing business with you. I sort of enjoyed having my own lawyer. Especially a famous one. I'll bet you're always seeing people take your picture when they recognize you."

"It's happened more than a couple times, yeah."

"That's what happens when everyone has a camera in their pocket." She pulled her phone out and took a picture of Thane, then looked at it and grinned. "Whoo baby, I got me a lawyer for the stars!"

She laughed, then turned and headed toward the door, but something Cricket said suddenly gave Thane an idea.

"Hey, you're obviously skilled at this sort of thing. Does it apply to just cable systems, or are you good at hacking into other things as well?"

Cricket looked at him as if he were testing her, to see

whether she had learned her lesson. He didn't want her to simply say what she figured he wanted to hear, so he continued, "For instance, cell phone companies. Think you'd be any good at getting inside their system?"

She continued studying him, then smiled and slowly walked back to her seat.

"You really don't have kids, do you? You know, don't you, that as an adult, you're supposed to be keeping me out of trouble, not getting me into trouble?"

"I'd pay you two hundred bucks."

Her eyes lit up. "And be my lawyer next time I need one?"

"Of course. We'll consider this task to be your retainer."

"I don't need no retainer—my teeth are beautiful. But tell me what you're needing, lawyer-man." She looked at him again and shook her head. "You crack me up."

After talking more with Cricket, Thane held the door to the main office open for her as she sauntered off to start her new assignment. He couldn't help but admire her confidence.

"I think you'd be a great dad," Letitia said, as Thane turned back toward his office.

"That's funny, I was just thinking the opposite."

He noticed Kristin sitting in her office, staring at the top of her desk like she was burning the wood with her eyes. He walked over and leaned into her office.

"You doing okay?" he asked.

She didn't look up at first, then leaned back in her office chair and put her hands over her face.

"I'll take that as a no," Thane said as he walked in and shut the door. "How's Gus holding up?"

Kristin shook her head. "It's been two months now. He's scared to death to implicate Andre, so Mahone is just going to let him stay there without bail until we go to trial. But if we go to trial right now, he's going to lose since we can't find Andre, even if he was willing to testify."

Thane sat in the chair across from her, once again marveling at the lack of paper on the top of her desk. Maybe all those rumors of moving to a paperless workplace was actually starting to happen, although he knew it would likely be decades before he caught up with it. He needed the hard copy of a document to hold and to ponder. Kristin's desk, on the other hand, looked like it was her first day on the job and she was waiting for her first assigned task.

Except this time, there was a single piece of paper sitting squarely in front of her. Kristin picked up the paper and handed it to Thane.

"Mahone sent me this. It's a copy of a letter someone named Winston sent him from jail, someone who apparently has been spending time with Gus. The letter says Gus told him he might be able to hook him up with a job when he got released, as long as he was comfortable dealing drugs."

"So he's saying Gus actually deals drugs?"

"That's what the letter claims. The hits just keep coming."

Thane skimmed the letter then put it back on the desk. "It's possible this Winston guy knows Mahone is open to dealing in information. Maybe he thinks he can help himself out by testifying against Gus. I'm guessing Mahone has a rep for not caring if something is true or not."

"That has to be it, although I'm not sure why Mahone would send this to me. If I was prosecuting Gus, I'd want to be the one deciding when this got released."

"But Mahone isn't interested in making sure Gus gets convicted. He only wants him to flip on Andre. He wants you to know he has more than enough to send Gus away for a long time, in the hopes he'll change his mind."

"Do you think he should? Gus, I mean. Do you think he should tell Mahone what he wants to hear, even if it's not true?"

"If it keeps him from going to prison?" Thane asked.

Kristin nodded as Thane thought about it.

"I'm afraid I do. I used to think you had to stick up for what you thought was right in cases like this, but people who say that have likely never done time. After a week or two at Forsman, Gus would be rethinking his decision fast."

"So he should just go along with a corrupt system?"

"Whether Gus goes to jail, or he tells a lie about Andre, the system won't be changed by the actions of one eighteen-year-old kid."

"But if more people did the right thing—"

"The jails already hold more than enough people who wouldn't testify against family or friends who had done nothing wrong. How full do the cells need to get before they see a difference?"

"So what's the answer?"

"I don't know. Maybe it's attacking it from the inside. I mean, isn't that we do? We're trying to help people who are in this sort of predicament."

"But getting them freed doesn't change the system.

People like Mahone simply move on to the next case. On to the next kid who doesn't have a lawyer who works hard for him."

It was one of the things Thane struggled with the most. How could he make things better for more people? Unfortunately, the only way he could see to make the system better was to not work within the system, and he didn't want that to be his only answer. It wasn't a good long-term solution.

"Let's focus right now on helping Gus. Maybe afterward we can have a team meeting and figure out how to fix the legal system. I'm guessing Gideon might have some ideas."

Kristin couldn't help but laugh. Thane realized it was the first time he'd seen her smile since she was threatened.

"Have you guys made up yet?" Thane asked.

"Not officially, but I know the person I need to be angry at is that psychopath who barged into my apartment."

"Do you understand why Gideon and I confronted Stick?"

"Yeah, I get it. I just don't want to be the helpless woman."

"I'm sure Stick has intimidated a lot of men as well. Think of it more like a case of someone who has a soul finding themselves face-to-face with someone who is dead inside."

"But you confronted him. Don't you have a soul?"

"I like to think so, but for several years it had been switched off." Thane didn't want to go down the road of sounding like he was feeling sorry for himself. "Gideon has a soul, too. It's just we're both more accustomed to

293

dealing with psychos like Stick."

"It's okay," Kristin finally said. "I'm moving forward. And I've decided that if I need to go at Andre one more time to try to get him to testify, I'll do it, though first I'd have to find him."

She picked up the letter and read through it again, her eyebrows scrunching downward as if something didn't set right with her.

"I checked this guy's record. He's mostly been convicted for petty stuff. He also dropped out of school when he was fifteen." She studied the page a bit more. "Anything about this strike you as off?"

Thane could see her mind starting to fire as she worked through what was bothering her. She was bright and had an attention to detail, so he had no doubt she had come across something in the letter that didn't make sense. He held his hand out to take the letter back from her.

He looked at it for a moment. "Is it that the document isn't stamped?" he asked.

"Stamped? No. What do you mean, stamped?"

Once he explained, her eyes lit up, and she couldn't restrain a smile. He then handed the paper back to her.

"Your turn. What is it you're seeing?" he asked, confident he already knew the answer.

33

Thane entered the Star Bright bar for the second time, hoping to find Stick there. He also hoped no blood would be spilled. Especially his.

Stick was again sitting on his tall stool near the pool table, as though he hadn't moved an inch from the last time Thane and Gideon paid him a visit. Thane wondered if the man lived there.

A couple of Stick's crew were again playing pool. One of the men had a swollen nose and a black eye, the result of his face having been crushed into the pool table. He glared at Thane as best he could through his one good eye, but didn't appear to be interested in a rematch.

"You got balls coming back here without your pit bull," Stick said. "Question now is, will you be leaving with them, or they going to end up in my pocket?"

"That's an odd hobby," Thane said. "Ever think of collecting stamps instead?"

Stick looked at him, puzzled, then laughed. "I'm assuming the only reason you felt comfortable coming back here is 'cause you decided you're open to having another client after all."

Thane leaned against the pool table in front of Stick. "Not yet. I still need to get through the case I'm

295

working on."

"So why you here?"

"I need a favor."

Stick looked at Thane as though he'd just given him an algebra question to solve. He finally shook his head. "Well, I need a L.A. Rams cheerleader, and I'm pretty sure my odds are better than yours. Favor? Why the hell would I want to do you a favor?"

"Because I want to take care of Gus's case without involving Andre."

"Andre ain't gonna get involved in this case."

"He won't if you'll help me. It won't take you long, and it plays to your strength."

"I got lots of strengths. Which one you talking about?"

"Your people skills."

Stick couldn't help but smile, although even his smile looked laced with violence.

"You threaten my brother with a bounty, then you come in here looking for a favor. Shit. You are one crazy-ass fuck."

"Your brother got a bounty on him because you threatened a woman who works for me. This is all on you, so you can either help me finish this so we can all get back to our business, or we can keep having a pissing contest."

Stick stared at Thane.

"How about you tell me what your favor is, and I'll see just how crazy you really are."

Thane brought out a piece of paper and handed it to Stick.

"I'm going to ask three questions of someone, and these are the answers to those questions."

Stick looked at the piece of paper and started reading the answers. "Yes, No, and..." Stick looked up at Thane. "I gotta admit, you sort of got my interest now." He looked back at the answers. "So what are the questions?"

"Not important."

"This guy will know what they are?"

"He'll know when I ask him. Just don't tell him who will be asking the questions. All I need is for you to use your power of persuasion to get him to remember these answers, and to understand that not answering the questions is not an option for him. Think you can get him to understand that?"

"Not a problem. Like you said, I got people skills."

"He's likely going to feel pressured by others to not help out."

"My pressure will be greater."

"That's what I'm betting."

Thane and his team huddled in one of the consultation rooms down the hall from the main courtroom where the defense was about to present its case. Letitia joined the rest of the team to observe both Thane and Kristin in action during what promised to be an interesting day.

"Are you still positive the judge will allow us to call Mr. Winston to the stand?" Kristin asked.

"Well, 'positive' might be a little optimistic, but I believe she will. I had to argue the reasoning for it to her for quite a while, and I'm sure Barry is going to object one more time, but she seemed willing to give me the benefit of the doubt."

Letitia laughed. "The judge probably feels like the system owes you one. You weren't exactly conventional in Mr. Burns's case, either, but you showed you were right in the end."

"We'll have to see how it goes," Thane said, "but we have to go in there trying to save two birds with one trial, and that starts by being able to put Rayvis on the stand."

"The spineless rat," Gideon muttered.

Thane turned to Kristin. "You ready for your day in the spotlight."

"I was born ready," Kristin said.

Gideon guffawed. "That's the first time that hasn't sounded like a corny cliche."

Kristin blushed a bit, but returned Gideon's smile. She reached out and they fist-bumped, apparently back to being on the same team.

"You know what our objective is." Thane said. "And if it turns out your assumption about the letter is wrong, then get him off the stand and we'll regroup."

"And if we're wrong, where does that leave us?"

"Same place we were before. Up against the wall."

Court was almost ready to be called to order. The gallery was packed now that the defense was getting ready to present its case. Thane had obviously gained a reputation for putting on a good show, and people who missed his previous case apparently wanted to see him perform in person.

Thane spotted Detective David Mahone near the back of the courtroom, dressed in a sports coat and tie with his hair slicked back. Mahone chuckled when their eyes met, then offered up a shrug. Thane knew they would have time to talk later, albeit in a more formal context.

Judge Kaelin entered the courtroom and took her place, then signaled the bailiff to start the proceedings.

"Mr. Warlick," the judge said, addressing the Assistant DA. "Before we bring in the jury, it's my understanding you have an objection you want to make?"

Warlick rose. "Yes, Your Honor. I want to enter into the record our objection over the defense's first witness. This individual has absolutely nothing to do with this case. I can see where Mr. Banning might want to call this witness at a different hearing, but this witness is not relevant in the matter before the court today."

Judge Kaelin turned to Thane, who also rose.

"Your Honor, as I've stated before, I am simply asking for a little latitude here. I believe our first witness will speak to the veracity of another of our upcoming witnesses."

"You're expecting this individual to help support the testimony of another of your witnesses?"

"No, Your Honor. I believe he will show that that witness should not be believed."

This appeared to catch the judge off-guard, but she tried not to show it. "So this witness is going to tell us not to believe one of your other witnesses?"

"That is my thought, Your Honor."

She looked at Thane quizzically, then turned back to

Warlick.

"Mr. Warlick, your objection is duly noted, but my original ruling stands."

The jury was brought in and seated, and Judge Kaelin nodded toward Thane.

"You may call your first witness."

"Thank you, Your Honor. My associate, Ms. Kristin Peterson, will be handling the questioning."

Thane could tell the reporters were interested in this development. They had watched Kristin during Skunk's trial, but most of them had next to no exposure to her. There had been some questions asked of her during the earlier trial, and she had given a couple of interviews to local publications, but this was her first appearance as an acting attorney.

Kristin looked at Thane and nodded as she rose. He was struck by how confident she appeared as the witness, Rayvis Winston, was called to the stand.

Winston was brought into the courtroom, escorted by a guard who directed him to the witness stand. He was in his late twenties and looked like a guy who had started smoking when he was five and stealing cars when he was ten. He was still in his city jail jumpsuit—per Thane's request—and looked like he had just awoken from a restless nap. He acted somewhat amused at being there, as if grateful for having the chance to get out into the fresh air, but disinterested in the specifics that got him there.

After unenthusiastically swearing to tell the truth, Rayvis Winston looked at Kristin as she approached the witness box. He raised his eyebrows and offered up a grin, like he had a go-to pick up line he wanted to throw her way.

Kristin looked at him and rolled her eyes, which took away his smile.

"Mr. Winston, you are currently incarcerated at the Los Angeles Twin Towers Correctional Facility. Is that right?"

"Yeah," Rayvis said. "That's home-sweet-home for now."

"And you are looking at the likelihood of being sent to prison for three to five years for distributing cocaine and for possession of an illegal firearm."

"So they claim."

Kristin glanced at a small notecard in her hand. "Mr. Winston, in a letter you recently wrote, you claimed to have information that would evince the guilt of another one of our clients."

Rayvis cocked his head. "What's 'evince'?"

"Sorry. It means to show clearly. You had evidence that you said would show clearly that another of our clients was a drug dealer."

"Okay," Rayvis said, not exactly agreeing with Kristin's statement, but also not disagreeing.

"And you were willing to depose—"

"I was willing to what?" Rayvis asked again with a grin.

"Depose. Testify in court. You were willing to testify in court, and the testimony you were offering was predicated on the fact that you—"

"Whoa, whoa. Damn, girl. What do you mean 'predicated on'? "

Warlick stood. "Your Honor, I understand Ms. Peterson has just recently passed her bar exam, and I

301

welcome her into the legal fraternity, but perhaps you can tell her that we'll believe she's smart even if she doesn't use ten-dollar words."

Several in the gallery chuckled, including a couple of reporters. An older reporter looked like he wanted to pat Kristin on the head and tell her it would all be okay.

"I apologize, your Honor, for my word choices. I only used them because they are words the witness used in a letter he allegedly sent to a narcotics detective, so I assumed he was familiar with them."

The reporters who laughed continued to smile, although now for different reasons. The man who acted like he wanted to reassure Kristin that everything would be alright now looked like he wanted to offer the same patronizing words of support to the prosecutor.

"But perhaps it's best if I just speak plainly, since apparently the witness does not recognize the words he used so eloquently in his letter."

Kristin walked over to the defense table and pulled a letter from a folder sitting in front of Thane, then walked back to the witness stand and handed the letter to Rayvis.

"You supposedly wrote a letter to a narcotics detective saying you were willing to testify against a client of ours, one Gus Cleveland. This is the letter in question."

Rayvis didn't take the letter at first, but when it was apparent Kristin wasn't going to continue until he took it, he grabbed the letter but didn't look at it.

"This letter alleges that Mr. August Cleveland offered you a job selling drugs once you got out of jail. A letter that says you would be willing to testify to this effect. A letter you supposedly wrote, and yet it contains several words which you now don't seem to even know."

Kristin paused and watched as Rayvis stared back at her.

"Okay," he finally said.

"I'm afraid 'okay' is a little vague, Mr. Winston. How did you write a letter using words you don't know?"

Rayvis glanced at the letter, then shrugged. "I didn't write it."

Kristin froze, surprised he would offer that admission so easily. She glanced back at Thane who simply nodded for her to go ahead. They had talked at great length about what to do if she was able to get him to admit he hadn't written the letter.

"So how did a letter with your signature get sent to the police?"

Rayvis glanced at the letter again and grinned. "That ain't my signature. Hell, you wouldn't even be able to make out my name if I'd signed it. This one, you can read each letter."

"Help me understand, then, how is it—"

"Look, I didn't do nothin' wrong. Besides, if I'd sent this letter, it would have had a stamp from the jail showing it had been reviewed before going out, but there ain't no stamp on this. All I know is some detective showed up at the jail and handed me this letter and said he wanted to talk to me about it. "

"And what did he say?"

"That he'd reduce my jail sentence if I testified against this Gus somebody. I don't hardly even know the kid. Maybe saw him across the cellblock 'cause he's in my section of the jail. The cop said he'd help me if I helped him, but I'm not gonna lie in court about it. I didn't claim to write the letter. I'm here because you called me, not because I ever said anything to anybody about writing this."

"But you also didn't say right away that you didn't write it."

"Yeah, maybe, but I also didn't say I wrote it, so I wasn't lying. Look, the narc said he'd help me, so I figured I'd see where things went. But I'm not looking to come into court and lie about it. I may not know your big words, but that don't mean I'm stupid."

"I don't think you're stupid, Mr. Winston. I think you're being truthful. I hope you'll continue that truthfulness with my last question. Who was it that brought you the letter and offered to reduce your sentence if you helped him out?"

Rayvis shifted in his seat, suddenly uncomfortable.

"Ah man, I don't need to be making enemies with no narc."

"Please answer the question, Mr. Winston," said Judge Kaelin.

Rayvis slumped down in his seat.

"Cop named Mahone's the one who gave me the letter. But I didn't ask for any of this."

Thane wanted more than anything to turn around to see Mahone's expression. He assumed the man's lips were tight and perhaps his face was starting to burn, but Thane wasn't ready to deal with the detective just yet.

Kristin said she had no further questions and returned to her seat.

Warlick sat silent for a long moment, then apparently decided he wasn't sure what questions he could ask, so he simply reserved the right to recall the witness if need be.

As Rayvis was escorted back out of the courtroom,

Gideon leaned over from the front row of the gallery behind the defense table and patted Kristin on the shoulder.

"I'm glad my nephew has one tough motherfucker representing him," he said.

Kristin offered up the slightest of smiles, not wanting the jury to think she was doing a victory dance.

But Thane could tell her adrenaline was pumping.

34

Thane recalled Robby "Rabbit" Reynolds to the stand. The young DJ sauntered to the witness box, once again dressed in a coat and tie. He didn't seem at all leery being recalled by the defense. He likely saw it as another opportunity to further his brand. Whatever the case, he all but waved to the gallery as he sat down in the witness box, happy to have been called for an encore.

After being sworn in, Thane rose from the defense table and approached the witness.

"Mr. Reynolds, since your last court appearance, I had an opportunity to look at some of the videos you've posted on your site."

Rabbit grinned broadly, seemingly glad to know the two men were still friends. "I hope you clicked the Like button!"

"You've shared quite an extensive array of video snippets over the past couple of years. There was a brown paper bag floating in the air for at least half a minute, and another of a taxi driver stuck in traffic blasting his car horn, and another of a pigeon perched on the back of a trash can. Your videos do seem to run the gamut of subjects."

"I notice the sights of everyday life. Big, small, I

present my city to my followers, as I see it in real time."

"You certainly do. There was also a video of a mouse on a sidewalk, a hot dog vendor and someone sleeping on a park bench."

Again, Rabbit beamed, then he glanced over at the jury to see if they were impressed. Some of them smiled at his earnestness, while a couple of them looked like they wanted him to stop talking.

"That's one thing about cell phones," Thane said. "We have immediate access to our camera. I know I'm basically strapped to my mobile device from the time I get up until I go to bed."

"And sometimes beyond that," Rabbit said with a grin.

"Your Honor," Warlick said as he stood, "I'm sure we all love our cell phones, but I'm curious if there's a question here that's relevant to the matter at hand."

"Mr. Banning," Judge Kaelin said, "perhaps you could fast-forward to the place where you ask your question?"

"Of course, Your Honor." Thane turned back to Rabbit. "Given the wide—and I do mean wide—range of videos you post on your site, and given the fact your phone is basically a part of you, why is it that when you saw someone carrying a body down the sidewalk, you didn't video that?"

Rabbit paused for an awkwardly long moment, then spoke in a much quieter voice, "Well, again, at the time, I didn't think it was a dead body."

"I understand, but you did think it was someone carrying a friend so drunk the person couldn't even walk. I mean, with all due respect, if you take a video of a taxi driver blaring his horn and a video of a pigeon sitting on a trash can, I would think that someone dragging a body beside him would qualify as an action scene. So why didn't you video what you were seeing?"

Again Rabbit paused, then he glanced over at Warlick. It was obvious he was stumped for an answer until his face lit up.

"I remember now. I left my phone back at my apartment. I remember thinking when I saw the guy with the body that I could have kicked myself for leaving it behind."

"Really? You left your phone? I think you would have noticed fairly quickly and gone back to get it. Like you said, it's with you day and night."

"Objection, Your Honor. The question of where his phone was has been asked and answered."

"My question may have been answered," Thane responded, "but I'm not sure it was answered truthfully."

He walked back to his table and pulled a sheet from a manila folder. He reviewed the document, the contents of which were courtesy of a ten-year-old hacking prodigy.

Thanks, Cricket, Thane thought to himself.

"Mr. Reynolds, I have records from your cell phone carrier that show the location of your phone at the time you were allegedly at the site of the murder. Care to guess where this record says your phone was?"

Rabbit stared at Thane, looking as though he'd rather be DJing at a senior center than be subjected to this particular question.

"Mr. Reynolds? Care to guess?"

Rabbit shook his head.

"That's interesting. I would have thought you'd have guessed your apartment, since that's where you said it was, but that, in fact, would have been incorrect. The phone company says your phone's signature trail put it near PlayPen's Party Palace, a nightclub in the Hills where you sometimes DJ. A place where, in fact, the owner will testify you were DJing at the time you said you saw the defendant dragging the body."

The gallery began to murmur. Thane looked at the jury, then returned his focus to a sweating Rabbit.

"Does your phone have a habit of going out on the town when you accidentally leave it behind?"

"Objection, Your Honor. Counsel is trying to be funny."

"Actually I thought that *was* at least a little funny," Thane said. "But fine, I'll withdraw that question for now and turn to something a bit less funny.

"Mr. Reynolds, you were arrested three months ago for possession of meth. Not a large amount, but large enough to run the risk of the possibility of jail time, assuming the officer in charge wanted to pursue that. Of course, the same officer could likely make the charge go away, assuming you cooperated with this case. But possession of meth is no small matter."

Rabbit looked bewildered that his friend had turned on him like this. He also likely saw his brand taking a direct hit—although publicity was publicity, so there was that.

Thane walked up and rested his hands on the front of the witness box and leaned forward, waiting until he was sure Rabbit was looking directly at him.

"Mr. Reynolds, I'm now going to ask you three questions. Three *important* questions." Thane paused for a moment, hoping his message was received. "And I need you to give me three important answers. Do you understand?"

Rabbit nodded at first out of reflex, then his eyes widened in disbelief as he sat back in his chair a bit, trying to put whatever distance he could between himself and Thane.

"Do you understand?"

Rabbit continued looking at him with a gaping mouth, then he finally nodded.

"Were you told all charges against you would be dropped in exchange for your testimony in this case?"

Rabbit looked down at his lap, but there were no notes there to help him. He finally nodded.

"Is that a yes, Mr. Reynolds?"

"Yes."

Thane could hear members of the press shifting in their seats.

"Question number two: were you where you claim to have been the night of the murder and did you, in fact, see the defendant carrying a body?"

Rabbit started shifting in his seat. He looked over at the judge. "Do I need to answer that? Isn't there something about incriminating oneself?"

The buzz amongst those in the gallery was building. At the same time, unnoticed by to anyone but Thane and Rabbit, one of Stick's right-hand men from the bar appeared in the back of the courtroom. He stepped to the side of the door until he made eye contact with Rabbit, who once again froze.

"Mr. Reynolds," Judge Kaelin said. "Are you asking me if—"

Rabbit waved her off. "Never mind! I can answer the question."

Stick's man standing at the door turned when one of the court bailiffs started heading over to him, then skulked back out of the courtroom.

"Mr. Reynolds, were you in that neighborhood and did you see the witness carrying a body on the night in question?"

"Dude…" Rabbit said plaintively.

Thane wouldn't have been surprised if Rabbit threw up in his own lap, which pretty much would have been the same as answering the question, but after waiting him out, the witness finally squeaked a quiet response:

"No."

Judge Kaelin had to use her gavel this time as the murmuring in the gallery grew louder. Thane saw several reporters rapidly jotting down notes, so he gave them a couple of seconds to catch up before asking his final question.

"And finally, Mr. Reynolds, who was it who told you all charges against you would be dropped if you testified that you saw the defendant carrying a body when, in fact, you didn't?"

"Objection, Your Honor."

Judge Kaelin looked at Warlick, waiting for him to express his objection, something it appeared he was still trying to formulate in his head.

"Your Honor, the DA's office would like the opportunity to investigate this turn of events in more detail. If there is evidence of wrongdoing on the behalf of anyone, I would like the chance to pursue it first before we go any further."

The judge looked at Warlick and cocked an eyebrow. "Mr. Warlick, we have put a man on trial for capital murder. If it's all the same to you, I'd rather have whatever investigation you want to conduct take place after we resolve the matter at hand."

She then turned to the witness.

"Mr. Reynolds, please answer the question. Who told you charges would be dropped if you testified against the witness?"

Rabbit glanced over at the jury, looking as though he wanted to sincerely apologize for what he had done. He then looked at Thane, but no longer appeared to be wanting to get the lawyer on his podcast.

"Mr. Reynolds?" Thane asked. "Who asked you to lie to the court?"

Rabbit hung his head, then leaned closer to the microphone.

"Narcotics Detective Mahone," he finally said.

Thane turned and looked out into the gallery. Mahone was starting to rise, ready to object, but once their eyes met, Mahone could only stare coldly at Thane.

"No further questions, Your Honor."

Judge Kaelin looked at Warlick and nodded for him to proceed. Warlick sat at his table for a long moment. Finally, he shook his head.

"I, uh… no questions, Your Honor."

35

As soon as Detective Mahone's name was called, he power-walked to the witness stand, a man ready to do battle.

Thane could tell Mahone was trying not to look hostile, likely in an effort to sway the jury, but he wasn't being successful. His lips tightened while being sworn in, and his fists were clenched.

"Do you swear to tell the truth, the whole truth, and nothing but the truth?"

"I do," Mahone said, then sat down and added, "and the truth is, I've never seen Mr. Reynolds before in my life."

Thane headed toward the witness chair.

"Actually, Detective Mahone—"

"And Rayvis Winston told me he wrote that letter. He was lying when he said—"

"Detective, none of those are answers to the questions I have for you."

"I figured. That's why I'm saying right now that both of those guys were lying about—"

"Your Honor," Thane said, turning to Kaelin.

"Detective Mahone," the judge said, obviously unimpressed with the man's hijacking of the proceedings, "you know how things work in my court as well as anyone.

313

The lawyers ask the questions, and the witness answers them. I understand you'd like to talk about what you want to talk about, but that's not how things work here. Do you understand?"

Mahone all but waved off the judge as he looked over at Warlick. "I understand someone better ask me questions about the last two witnesses."

"Detective," Judge Kaelin said, her tone sharp.

Mahone raised his hand up halfway as if he was willing to humor the judge. He turned his attention to Thane, with no hint of amusement in his eyes.

"Detective, did you offer to help Rayvis Winston with his sentencing if he cooperated in the case against Gus Cleveland."

"He reached out to me. I didn't write that letter for him to sign. I thought it was real, which is why I offered to work with him."

"And did you not also tell Gus Cleveland—and my colleague, Ms. Peterson—that if he helped you out on another case, that you could get charges against him dropped?"

"Police work is often achieved by working with people accused of lesser crimes in exchange for their cooperation in helping arrest others who have committed more serious offenses."

"So you offered Rayvis Winston a reduced sentence— and possibly no sentence at all—if he testified against Mr. Cleveland."

"When I thought he had something of importance related to the case, yes."

"And you told Mr. Gus Cleveland the same thing, because you thought he might be able to help you convict someone who was more important to you."

"That's correct. He could help me put away a major drug kingpin responsible for ruining the lives of thousands of L.A. citizens."

"Your Honor," Warlick said as he rose. "Once again, we seem to be litigating a case other than the one we are here for."

"Mr. Banning," the judge said, "I believe it's time you start bringing this back to the case at hand."

"I agree, Your Honor." Thane turned back to Mahone. "Is it not correct, Detective, you also told the defendant, Kyle Miller, the same thing? That you could get his sentence reduced if he cooperated with you on a case you were trying to make against that same major drug dealer?"

The gallery and the jury once again began murmuring. Mahone glared at Thane. Warlick rose once again.

"Objection, Your Honor. Counsel knows full well only the DA's office can offer reduced sentences."

"I'm not saying Detective Mahone was able to promise anything. I'm simply asking if he did so."

"Overruled."

"Detective, did you tell Mr. Miller—and, again, did you also tell *me*—that if Mr. Miller helped you with your case against this drug dealer, that you would be able to significantly reduce his sentence, even though it was a high-profile, felony murder charge?"

"Sometimes a detective will say something in the hopes that it will get a felon to offer up information. I didn't promise him anything."

"Actually you said you guaranteed it. *Guaranteed.*"

"But I didn't put anything in writing. As Mr. Warlick

said, only his office is able to do that."

"So you lied."

Mahone shook his head.

"I may have misled, but when dealing with felons like Mr. Miller, being a little misleading is not an uncommon tactic. It's also perfectly legal."

"So, misleading is different than lying?" When Mahone didn't answer, Thane continued, "I'm going to guess it's a very subtle difference, but be that as it may, let's continue." Thane paused and glanced over at Letitia, who was sitting on the edge of her seat next to Gideon. He was ready to introduce into court her observation from the other day. He turned back to the detective.

"But what if you were telling the truth about being able to get his sentence reduced? Not because you can make such an offer, but because you were able to prove he didn't murder Joseph Crowell?"

Thane could feel the gallery and the jury starting to pay closer attention. The cockiness Mahone was displaying was likely not helping how he was being perceived by the onlookers.

"A couple of months before the murder of Joseph Crowell, you and two of your fellow detectives were watching when the defendant, Kyle Miller, received a package from a neighbor. The minute this package exchanged hands, you and your detectives appeared and apprehended Mr. Miller and the other man, but it turned out the package simply contained tools the neighbor had borrowed from the defendant. How is it you happened to be in a position to witness this exchange?"

"Mr. Miller was a known drug dealer before going to prison. We believed that after being released, he was going to resume dealing."

"So you had him under surveillance."

"Yes."

"And if you caught him dealing drugs, is it safe to assume you would have used that arrest to pressure him into cooperating with you as you pursued this other drug kingpin. I mean, that's what you did with Rayvis Winston, and with Gus Cleveland."

"We didn't get to that point."

"But it feels like a pretty safe bet that that's what would have happened."

"Objection, Your Honor. Defense is speculating," Warlick whined.

"And probably speculating fairly accurately," Thane responded.

"Mr. Banning—" the judge started, but Thane smiled and nodded.

"I know, Your Honor. My apologies." Thane returned to his table and retrieved an enlarged color photograph of a disheveled blond man with a handlebar mustache and a nose that was slightly off-kilter. He looked like someone who worked at the docks, wearing an unbuttoned flannel shirt with a ripped t-shirt underneath it. Thane walked back to the witness stand and held up the photograph to Mahone. "Detective, is this one of your men?"

Mahone nodded. "That's Brian Murphy. Murph's part of my team."

"A detective?" Thane asked as he walked the photo over to show the jury. "He's dressed a little rough. Do you not pay well?"

"I'm sure he was working undercover when that picture was taken. Narcotics detectives try not to stand

317

out when they're on the job. I sort of assumed everyone knew that."

"And do you usually work with the same team of detectives?"

"Yes, I have five men assigned to my team. We work as a unit."

"Did you know that Detective Murphy is a recovering alcoholic?"

"Objection, Your Honor," Warlick called out. "How in the world is talking about an officer's private health information appropriate, let alone relevant?"

"Your Honor, I would request a little leeway here, if you would. I promise this will become relevant. As for Detective Murphy's alcoholism, I learned about it from an impressive interview he did with the *L.A. Times* several months back. He's been a vocal advocate for seeking help for drinking problems, so it's not as though I'm violating some sort of trust here."

"You have some leeway here, Mr. Banning, but I'd like for you to try to make your point fairly soon. The witness will answer the question."

"Yeah, I knew. Like you said, he's open about it."

"Your Honor, what I'd like to do now is show the footage again from the bar the night of the murder."

The video monitors in the courtroom began to glow blue, and Thane picked up the remote control. He found it ironic that once again, it was the constant surveillance of video cameras that provided a key part of his defense.

As had been seen previously, Kilo walked up to the bar and ordered a drink, then after being served, he turned and walked out of view.

"As the prosecution pointed out previously, Mr.

Miller was at Gulliver's Bar the night Joseph Crowell was murdered, but this is where the footage for the jury was stopped."

Thane continued watching the video for another minute until another man holding a bottle of beer walked into view and took a seat at the bar. He faced forward for a couple of seconds, then turned slightly on his barstool so that he was looking in the general direction that Kilo had gone.

Thane froze the video footage.

"This is Detective Murphy, am I correct?"

Mahone stared at the video, not answering.

"Detective Mahone, is this—"

"Yeah, that's him," Mahone finally answered.

"He looks like just another guy at the bar, which, as you mentioned, is probably the goal when someone is being followed. Just as you all were dressed for undercover work the evening you thought you had caught Mr. Miller receiving a bag of drugs. Although, I don't believe Mr. Murphy was part of that first surveillance team, which is probably why he was assigned to the stakeout at the bar."

Thane restarted the video and let it run.

"Or at least, it appears to me that once again, someone on your team had Mr. Miller under surveillance."

"Or it's simply a coincidence that Murph was there that night," Mahone scoffed.

"Do you suppose he often goes to a local bar and orders a bottle of beer that he doesn't drink? He's not facing the TV above the bar, he doesn't talk to anyone else, he just sits there, constantly looking in the direction in which Mr. Miller walked, and holding a beer. If we were to watch the entire video, he never takes a drink, which makes sense, given his situation with alcohol."

Thane put the video on pause.

"Detective, when there is a major crime that has taken place, do all L.A. detectives get an alert sent to them, or only those detectives who work those types of crime? In other words, do narcotic detectives only get an alert when it's drug-related? If another serious crime has taken place, are you also notified if you're in the area?"

"Yeah, we're all notified if there's a serious crime in our general vicinity."

Thane took the remote and fast forwarded it to a specific point on the video footage, then stopped it again.

"I'd like the jury to note the time. It's 9:35 P.M., which is when the police sent out the alert to all detectives in the general vicinity that a body had been found. The body of Joseph Crowell."

Thane started the video and pointed out to the jury that at the exact time the alert went out, Detective Murphy reached into his jacket, checked his phone, looked back in the direction that Kilo was apparently sitting, then got up and quickly walked out of the camera's view.

"Detective Murphy gets a call at the exact same time the alert was sent out from the station. He's only a couple of blocks from the murder site. He responds and records show he was one of the first detectives on the scene."

Thane stopped the video.

"Detective, you once again had Mr. Miller under surveillance the night of the murder. You knew he didn't commit the murder, and that's why you told him you could guarantee you could get his sentence reduced. What you meant was that you could get the charges dropped, although he never would have believed that without asking questions. But once you got his cooperation on your other case, you would have conveniently come across the records that showed he was actually being watched by one of your men."

Mahone didn't answer. He glared at Thane.

"Detective?"

"I don't recall. It was a few months ago. It looks like you might be right that Mr. Miller was being watched that night, but I'd have to check. I can ask Murph what he remembers. If so, then I'm sure he would be happy to testify to that fact. We always want to do what's right."

"Yes, of course you do. I only wish I had the phone number of the person who called in the anonymous tip saying Mr. Miller was at the bar the night of the murder and claiming he had committed the crime. Whoever called it in certainly helped you have leverage over Mr. Miller, but I'm sure that person didn't use their actual phone."

"Objection, Your Honor. Defense is implying something that hasn't been established."

"I didn't mean to imply it, Mr. Warlick. My intention was to say it outright, but I'll withdraw my statement."

"Your Honor," Warlick cried.

"We can call Officer Murphy to testify he had my client under surveillance the night of the murder," Thane continued, "if the District Attorney's office doesn't decide to drop all charges immediately. I only wanted to start with you, Detective, since your name keeps coming up. I mean, if you thought catching Mr. Miller with drugs might be enough to pressure him into helping you, imagine what having murder charges hanging over his head would do. And if you're willing to get someone to write a false letter implicating someone else in a crime, and you get a witness in a murder trial to lie, then why not go ahead and see the case through until the end?"

"I didn't do those things. That's not true."

"But what is truth, Detective? What is truth?"

Thane paused as he stared down Mahone, then turned to go back to his seat.

"I withdraw the question, Your Honor. It's obvious the witness has no idea what the truth is. No further questions."

Warlick stood, but decided he had no questions for Mahone.

Mahone glared at Warlick, but Thane wasn't surprised the Assistant DA didn't want anything to do with him.

When Mahone was dismissed, he didn't appear to want to leave the witness box, but finally stood and walked back toward the gallery, where a couple of reporters had already scurried outside the courtroom, likely hoping to be the first to catch the detective when he left.

Kristin sat at the end of the defense table close to where Mahone passed. The detective glared at her. She looked up at him and smiled.

"Ah, you're not going to cry, are you, little boy?" she whispered.

36

Court was adjourned following Mahone's testimony. The judge ended the day's proceedings early, most likely to give the DA's office an opportunity to drop all charges against Kilo.

Most of the people in the courtroom gallery filed out, but several of them—mostly reporters hoping to catch Thane—stayed around. Kilo's wife, Ana, also hung back, a beautifully huge smile on her face and tears in her eyes.

A guard came to get Kilo, but Thane held up his hand and asked for a couple of minutes with his client. As Kristin walked over to Warlick, who was ,

Thane pulled Kilo to the side so they could talk.

"Is it just wishful thinking," Kilo asked Thane, "or was today a pretty good day for us?"

"Today was an excellent day for us."

Kilo looked over at Barry Warlick.

"Do you think he'll drop the charges?" Kilo asked.

"I have no doubt. The video of Detective Murphy having you under surveillance is more than enough to raise reasonable doubt. Add to that their witness saying Mahone got him to lie, and they don't have a case."

Kilo glanced around, then leaned closer to Thane.

"Ol' Rayvis did pretty good, didn't he?"

"He was perfect. How do you know him?"

"From when I was dealing. I got him out of a big jam years ago, so he owed me. Think that's going to help your other client?"

"I do. And thank you."

"Funny thing is, he actually knew a couple of those words, so I had to keep reminding him to play dumb."

A couple of the reporters started calling out to Thane, apparently anxious to file their report, and not wanting to wait any longer to get him to answer their questions.

"Let me go talk to the press. I want to make sure they understand what happened here today." Thane started to turn to walk over to the reporters, but Kilo put his hand on Thane's shoulder.

"Thank you for everything you did for me. I know I didn't deserve it, but I appreciate it."

"You didn't deserve any of this. I'm confident you'll be going home very soon. I'll tell your wife to buy a couple of steaks."

The guard led Kilo away as Kristin returned from talking with the Assistant District Attorney. Warlick wasn't making eye contact with anyone else at the Defense table, and appeared to have deflated considerably over the past hour.

"Tell me you didn't go over to gloat," Thane said with a smile.

"I don't gloat. I just asked him—very politely—to consider dropping all charges against Gus. Given what came out about Mahone today, it seemed like a reasonable request."

"Did he say anything one way or the other?"

"Just that he'd consider it, but I'm ninety-nine percent

sure he doesn't want to have to go through another day like he had today." Kristin leaned over and picked up her briefcase, then looked back up at Thane with her megawatt smile. "But man, I'd be happy reliving today a hundred times."

Thane and his team regrouped back at the office following the trial. He had picked up a couple six packs of beer on the way back from the courthouse, and everyone now had an open bottle as congratulations were passed around.

Gideon's phone rang, and when he saw who was calling, he got up and walked into his office. After a couple of minutes, he rejoined the group with a smile on his face.

"That was Pearl. Gus is getting released as we speak. All charges dropped, just like our spitfire here predicted."

Kristin beamed as she stood and pumped her fist. Gideon walked over and the two of them lifted their hands and slapped them together, looking like a quarterback and wide receiver celebrating after a touchdown.

"You did good," Gideon told her. "No, actually you did great. I appreciate it more than I can say. You are one hell of a lawyer, girlfriend. Or woman-friend. Whatever."

She gave him a big hug, his eyes opening wide. He left his arms by his side at first, uncertain what to do with them. He then patted her back softly, likely in an attempt to wrap up the display of emotion as soon as possible.

"They going to have a welcome home party?" Thane

asked.

"Yeah," Gideon said. "Pearl invited me to join them for dinner this evening. But I don't know."

"What do you mean you don't know?" Letitia said. "Of course you should go."

"Maybe," Gideon responded, still sounding uncertain.

The conversation was interrupted as District Attorney Day entered the office. Kristin quickly hid her beer behind her back, like she was about to be busted by a teacher.

Gideon didn't acknowledge Day, but instead said he had some work to do, then went back into his office. Kristin said hello, and said that she, too, had to make some calls. She backed up into her office, keeping the beer out of sight, but not fooling anyone. Letitia went back to her chair behind the front desk.

"Sorry to stop by unannounced," the DA said. "I didn't mean to spoil the party."

"Not a problem. Can I offer you a beer?"

"I'd love one," she said with a smile. "But I'll have to pass."

"I understand."

"I just have a minute. I wanted to let you know we will be dropping all charges against Mr. Miller. We'll review the security footage from the bar again, but in light of what came out today in court, it's more than likely it will show he had nothing to do with the murder of Mr. Crowell."

"I'm glad to hear it. More importantly, Mr. Miller and his family will be glad to hear it."

She looked at Thane for a long moment, then walked over and grabbed herself a beer.

"Ah, what the hell?" she said as she slapped her palm against the top of the bottle, sending the bottle cap flying across the room.

"Impressive," Thane said.

"It's good to have a skill," she responded. After taking a long drink, she again looked at Thane. "You seem to have a penchant for representing clients who have not seen law enforcement at its best. Your last case had a client being framed by the ex-District Attorney, and now you appear to have had two clients who may not have been done right by law enforcement."

"*May* not have been?"

"Detective Mahone is claiming not to have knowledge about the falsified letter he received, or about the witness who testified falsely against your client." When Thane started to protest, the DA raised her hand. "I know. I'm not saying I believe him, in part because I've heard rumblings before about his tactics. I'll be talking with the Chief of Police about where we go from here, but it's not a given he was behind all this."

"He's a cancer. I have a tremendous amount of respect for the police, but he's one of the bad guys. A lot of people are likely in prison who shouldn't be, because of Detective Mahone."

"As I said, I promise you we'll be looking into it further. I've already requested his case files be sent to my office, and if there's a pattern of abuse of power, I'll find it. I'm just saying it's not a given we can prove what you feel came out in court today."

Letitia stood up and addressed Day.

"You just can't afford to keep giving Mr. Banning millions of dollars for abusing people like Gus Cleveland."

Day looked startled as Thane walked the DA over to the front desk.

"This is Letitia. She's part of my team. She's very shy."

"I can tell," Day said.

"Gus Cleveland was just another example of a Black man being sent to prison for a crime where white people would just get a slap on the wrist," Letitia said. "As a Black woman, are you going to try to fix things, or are you only going to focus on being re-elected?"

"Well, I've only been in the office for about an hour and a half, so give me some time."

"A lot of people don't have time."

"I recognize that. And I promise you I'm going to do what I can to help fix some of our systemic problems."

"Letitia is planning on going to law school," Thane said, wanting to keep the conversation from getting too heated.

"I'm glad to hear that. We need more people like you to be involved."

"Oh, you don't need to worry about me being involved," Letitia said.

"I understand you don't want the city to have to keep giving me and my clients millions of dollars to address abuses of the system," Thane said, "but the fact remains I'm convinced Detective Mahone did some pretty heinous things here. Two men spent a couple of months in prison. One of whom was a young man with no previous record. And to be honest, the press seems to be interested in my thoughts on this case."

"That sounds like a prelude to wanting more money, but this case isn't as clear cut as it was with Brad Stone."

"I understand that, and I'm not asking for money. I

would, however, like for you to consider doing two things to help make things right, albeit informally."

"You're not blackmailing me here, are you?"

"What? That sounds illegal. But I do feel like what I'm going to ask is pretty reasonable."

"And that is?"

"You are one of UCLA's star alumni, and I'm sure you have strong connections there. I have a young woman here who is determined to make a difference in the world, and I have a young man now being released from jail who is hoping to go to college. Neither one come from a family of means. If there was any way you could put a good word in to the scholarship committee and help them get their degrees at no cost, I would appreciate it."

Day looked first at Thane, then at a startled Letitia.

"Given the circumstances and everything that has happened," Day said, "that is probably do-able. I can't promise anything, but I'm confident I can figure something out."

"I appreciate it. The other request is a little trickier. You said you had requested Mahone's case files. When you receive them, I'd appreciate it very much if you could start with a young man by the name of Lawrence Woods. I met with him in prison, and he's a prime example of someone who was victimized by Mahone's tactic of trying to pressure people into testifying falsely against someone else. All I'm asking is that you at least be willing to talk with his public defender—a Sheri Basten—and with Mr. Woods. That's all I ask. If you do that, I'm confident you'll feel he should be released for time served."

DA Day nodded as she took her phone out and made a note of the name. "I will start with Mr. Woods. If things turn out to be as you say, I'll do whatever I can to make things right. But I'm afraid I have to get back to the office now, and not just because I'm concerned you'll think of a third thing."

Thane shook Day's hand and walked her to the front door. She stopped and looked at him.

"You've now had a couple of clients whose guilt seemed pretty certain. Your faith in their innocence has been impressive. And a little surprising. Are you this way with all your clients, or is there more to the story here?"

Thane wasn't sure if she was only saying what was on her mind, or if she was trying to imply something.

"I have a good sense about people," he finally said. "I also have a good sense about you as well. I get the feeling we're going to work well together."

"I'm glad to hear that, because I get the feeling I wouldn't want to be working against you."

Again, Thane wished she had worded that differently. It was hard not to take everything she said as a hint that she felt something was astray. When she left the office, Thane turned to go back into his office, then saw Letitia staring at him, looking stunned.

"You talked with my brother?" she asked.

"Yes. And his public defender."

"Why didn't you say something?"

"I wanted to see if there was anything I could do to help him. I now feel like there's a very good chance you'll be getting him home sooner rather than later."

When Letitia didn't appear to know what to say, Thane thought he should take advantage of this rare occurrence, so he grabbed his beer from the front desk and walked on back to his office.

Thane half-closed his office door then leaned back in his desk chair and stared at the ceiling, relieved at the thought of being able to put all this behind him. Or at least able to put Kilo's and Gus's cases behind him.

He heard a soft knock on his door as Kristin entered.

"Next time you talk with the DA," Kristin said, "what would you think about requesting that Gus's record be totally expunged?"

"Good idea. I think she's pretty open to helping me, as long as I don't ask for another big check."

Kristin offered a smile, but it slipped off her face quickly. She looked at Thane, her lips starting to move like she had something else she wanted to say, but it wasn't coming out easily.

"You did a great job on Gus's case," Thane said, in case she was still being hard on herself. "It's hard enough going up against the police, but when a cop isn't playing fair, that makes it all the more challenging."

"Thanks," Kristin said. "I hope that detective gets run out of town, but slime like him will probably just find another place to be slimy."

She turned to leave, then paused before turning back to him. "I just want to say something." After a long sigh, she continued her thoughts. "I don't want to be used, okay? I'm not saying I was, but I need you to respect me. I may be young, but I hope you know I'm nobody's fool."

Thane wasn't sure where this was coming from, but he was surprised.

"Kristin, you are the least foolish person in this firm. Granted, that may be placing the bar pretty low, at least where Gideon and I are concerned, but you far surpass it nonetheless."

"I know you can be a little unconventional," Kristin said, "and maybe that's how things work in the real world. I don't know. But I do respect the law, and I don't want to be part of anything *too* unconventional."

"What's on your mind, Kristin?"

"Getting the phone records that showed where the witness's phone was. That's not something you can just get without a court order. I'm pretty sure I know how you got it—which is a totally different conversation—but that's not what I'm talking about. I mean the letter that Rayvis wrote. Having him recant on the witness stand."

"You did an incredible job with that."

"Did I really? That's what I'm not sure about. I mean if Mahone really did write the letter and signed Rayvis's name, why in the world would he include those big words in the letter? Wouldn't he know that would make it suspicious?"

"I don't know how that man thought, although he didn't strike me as being someone who thought things through. All I know is you questioned Rayvis perfectly and got him to admit he hadn't written the letter. The how and the why of the letter is something I can't speak to."

"And he certainly did admit he hadn't written it pretty quickly, didn't he? He ended that charade right quick."

"Because someone who has done as much time as he's done understands perjury is something judges take seriously. Cons with half a brain in their head know to avoid perjuring themselves unless that's the only option left to them. Plus don't forget that Rabbit also testified that Mahone tried to get him to lie as well, so there's a pattern there."

Kristin seemed to think about that. Thane could tell from her slightly furrowed eyebrows that she wasn't totally convinced, but she appeared to at least be open to that possibility.

"You're right," she said. "I just don't want to be used if something inappropriate is going on. I hope you know I love working with you, and I want to be a part of what this firm is doing, but if I ever feel like we're going too far beyond the boundaries of what's legal, then I'll be leaving. I just want you to know that."

"And that's one of the reasons I told you the other day you are one of the strongest people I know. You have faith in yourself, and you have faith in the system. And that's why I hope to hell you never leave here. Gideon is always going to advocate for ignoring all rules and laws, and I need you to help keep us in the guardrails."

"And where do you find yourself on that spectrum?"

"I'm a lawyer. I've been a lawyer for many years, and even though the vast majority of my years was in real estate law, I always had respect for the legal system."

"You say you 'had' respect for the legal system. Do you still have it, or have things changed?"

"My view was shaken pretty seriously when I was sent away for five years for a murder I didn't commit, but that doesn't mean I don't want to get back to where I was before. It's the right place to be."

Kristin smiled and appeared satisfied with that answer.

"I'm glad to hear it. That's all I needed. It's just I sensed something wasn't quite right with how things played out, and my sense is usually correct, but I know I also may be a bit messed up right now. I may still be a little traumatized from what happened with Stick, so I apologize if I'm looking for fights where there aren't any."

She once again turned and started to leave, but Thane called her back. "Can I ask you something?"

"What's that?"

He thought about it for a moment, wondering whether it was best to leave it alone, but he really wanted to know.

"Do you feel like justice was done in this case?"

"With Gus, or Kyle?"

"Either. Both."

"Yes, I'm sure justice was done. I'm convinced both of them were innocent."

Thane nodded his agreement. "If you had been right about Rayvis's letter, would you have said it was better to have Gus stay in jail than to have had someone set up Mahone? That didn't happen, but if it had, would you have felt that justice was done?"

"If Gus ended up spending years in prison? No, that wouldn't have been justice. But manipulating the law also isn't right. Isn't the goal to win the case on its merits?"

"Yes, and that's what we will do. What I struggle with from time to time is what happens when the other side isn't playing fair."

"If they're not playing fair, then we expose them, but we do it the right way. Like we did this time. We're the good guys. I mean, aren't we? I guess maybe that's what concerns me. We need to be the good guys."

Thane smiled at her response. She was everything he wanted to once again become. He just didn't know if, given his experiences, he'd be able to get there again.

"And we are. We exposed them, and we did it the right way."

Kristin looked pleased. "And that's how I'm always going to want to do it, because I don't want to leave you and Gideon on your own. God knows what sort of trouble the two of you would get yourselves into."

"And we don't ever want you to leave."

"Then don't ever play me for the fool. That's all I ask. And I'll take you at your word that you didn't."

She once again turned and headed toward the door.

"So we're good?" Thane said.

"We're damn good," Kristin responded. "Or at least I am," she added, laughing at her own cockiness.

Thane had a tremendous amount of respect for Kristin, but he *had* played her, and he needed to never do that again. He was sure she'd pick up on the arcane language in the letter he wrote under Rayvis's name, and even though Rayvis had played it exactly as Kilo instructed him, Thane had sold Kristin short by not thinking she would easily see how suspicious the whole thing was. As she said, she wasn't a fool. And if she ever learned about Stick's involvement in Rabbit's revised testimony, she'd be out of there without a word.

Or if there were words, they would be profane.

He also wasn't kidding when he said he needed someone like her in the firm. He knew he couldn't keep doing whatever it took to win a case. He was turning into a vigilante. Hell, he had already become a vigilante. What was meant to be a one-time thing was now a two-time thing. He tried rationalizing it by saying it was all connected with the first case, but he knew what he was doing.

At least he was still honest with himself.

Yet at the same time, a man who was falsely accused of murder was going to be freed, and a young man who didn't want to falsely testify against a friend wasn't going to go to prison for doing the right thing. A detective who sent a number of people to prison for not telling him what he wanted to hear was now under investigation; a detective who justified the wrongs he did by believing they served the greater good.

The same thing Thane was doing.

37

Thane sat in his backyard, relaxing in his favorite dark green Adirondack and looking up at the beautiful twilight sky. Hannah appeared and handed him a glass of whisky on ice. She sat in the chair next to his and took a sip of her water.

"You're not joining me in a celebratory cocktail?" Thane asked.

"I told you before I need to start eating healthier, so I'm going to start by drinking more water."

"Me too," Thane said. "That's why I asked for ice."

"You're such a health nut."

They sat in silence for a couple of minutes. A light breeze blew across their lawn, and Thane felt he could sit there for hours. He reached over and held out his hand, which Hannah took.

"I know I say this a lot, but I'm very proud of you," Hannah said. "Most people wouldn't have done what you did, helping out someone who tried to kill them."

Thane didn't respond. If she only knew how tempted he had been to let Kilo take the rap for the murder Thane orchestrated.

"The other night at the bookstore," Hannah said. "I'm sorry to have burdened you with my concerns about our communication."

"Don't apologize. We need to be able to talk about that sort of thing."

"But we didn't need to right in the middle of your case. It's just—I get scared of losing you again. Losing yourself to these cases. But then you do something like this, and I realize you are still the man I married. You are the man I want in my life, forever."

"I know I can do better. It's just after so many years of closing myself off while in prison, it's not as easy as flipping a switch. But I'm working on it."

Thane wanted to put the trial and the investigation behind him, although he knew it wasn't going to be up to him. But at least for this evening, he didn't want this to be their main topic of conversation.

"Have you heard anything about the position at the Shelter?"

"Nothing official, but I've heard informally that I'm going to be offered the job."

"Really? That's terrific. I'm assuming you'll take it?"

"I need to talk with them about something, but it's likely I'll accept it."

He pulled her hand over to his lips and kissed it, then released it. He raised his cocktail glass in the air.

"I am equally proud of you," he said, as Hannah reached over and clinked her glass with his. "What do you need to talk with them about?"

She didn't answer at first, then shifted in her chair so she was turned facing him more directly. "You know we've been dancing around the question of having a child for a while now. You know that I'm ready, and I understand your hesitancy. I also hope that you trust me.

That you know I would never do anything to deliberately undermine this trust. Never. It's important to me that you trust me."

"I trust you completely. You are the one person I truly believe in."

She paused, as Thane wondered where this was going, but he didn't have to wonder much longer.

"And I hope you understand that while birth control is about ninety-eight percent effective, that means that two percent of the time—it fails. Through no fault of the person, I might add."

She looked at Thane and offered him a partial shrug. He smiled.

"I might need another whiskey," he said, his head spinning. "I'm guessing it's safe to assume you're going to be sticking with water for a while?"

"For the next few months, anyway."

Thane again reached over and took her hand, this time holding it tight. His eyes watered, the reality hitting him harder than he thought it would. He thought if this moment came, he would be filled with the fear of possible loss, but instead he felt nothing but love. He could only think of creating a family with this woman he cherished. And about the need to do better.

The need to *be* better.

Gideon sat on the curb outside his sister's house, looking at the small image of a car on his ancient iPhone screen. Uber told him his ride was still twelve minutes away.

Pearl's living room window was brightly lit as she and her family celebrated Gus's return. He was tempted to get up and actually go to the door, but his ride was now arriving in eleven minutes, so he decided it was too late.

He heard the soft squeak of the front door opening, and then the tap of a woman's shoes walking down the sidewalk. He continued looking out at the street until Pearl was standing next to him.

"I saw you sitting out here. Aren't you going to come in?"

Gideon shook his head. "No, probably not tonight. Sorry about that. I appreciate the offer, but I don't feel comfortable doing that just yet. I came close, though. Almost even knocked on the door."

Pearl slowly lowered herself onto the ground next to Gideon, their feet extending out in the street as they sat on the grass. She had a small canvas bag that she placed next to her on the ground.

"Gus would love to see you. He owes you so much. We all owe you so much. Is that what makes you uncomfortable?"

Gideon thought about it.

"Maybe. The fact is, no matter how hard I try, I usually end up behind bars. In the past, I didn't have much of a life when I wasn't in jail, so it wasn't as though there was all that much I was going to miss when I got sent back. I just think it would be hard gettin' too close to people and having an actual life, then having that all taken away from me again."

"It doesn't have to play out that way."

"I know, and I'm trying my best to do things right

this time, but I also know myself pretty well. My track record ain't that great."

They sat silently together for a long moment. Gideon glanced at his phone; the little image of the car was supposedly four minutes away. He was torn between wanting it to speed up and wishing it would slow down.

Pearl reached over and lifted the canvas bag.

"I figured you probably weren't going to come in, so I'm sending some food home with you. You can bring the containers back some other time. Gus wants to see you. You're kind of a hero to him right now."

Gideon laughed and shook his head. "Oh good god, that's a mistake. You need to tell him to aim a little higher. I ain't no one's hero."

Pearl put her hand on Gideon's shoulder and squeezed it.

"That's not true. You're my hero, and it pleases me to no end that my son has a chance to get to know you."

"That's nice of you to say and all, but—"

"No, there's no 'but' to it."

She paused, and Gideon could tell she had something she wanted to say. He hoped against hope his ride would get there before she could say it, but it wasn't fast enough.

"That night. At the house. You knew what dad was doing to Rose. I mean, the beatings and the verbal abuse, that was one thing, but what he was *doing* to Rose—that was nothing but evil."

"Pearl, you don't have to—"

"You might have only been thirteen, but you knew what was happening. Just like you also knew that once Rose left for college, I was probably next." Her voice caught hard in her throat. "Oh God, I never really let myself think about that, but it's true. I would have been next. I could have handled the beatings if they continued, but—"

"Pearl, we don't need to talk about this."

"But we do, Gid. I do. You took care of it. You took care of all of us, and then I think maybe we got a little scared of you, even though you didn't deserve it. And as you got older, the anger got bigger, and it never occurred to us that you weren't really that way before that night. You always stuck up for the person being bullied. Always. And then a couple years later when you went to jail, we weren't there for you."

"You had your own lives to live."

"Because of you. We had our own lives because of you. But I'm telling you right now, you're going to be a part of our lives from here on out, whether you want to be or not. And when Gus graduates high school in a few months, you damn well better be there."

Gideon looked at Pearl, his mouth dropping open in an exaggerated display of shock. "Pearl Louise! I don't think I've ever heard you swear before."

"Well," she said, "you have a way of bringing it out of me. And when they call his given name to get his diploma, I don't want to see no eye rolling."

They started laughing as Gideon's ride turned the corner a couple of streets up and headed their way. They leaned against each other for a moment, which felt like heaven to Gideon, then they stood as the car pulled up to the curb a few yards away.

Pearl hugged Gideon tight, and handed him the bag of food.

"Thank you for everything," Pearl whispered in his

ear. "Again."

He started walking toward his ride, then turned back around.

"Hey Pearl, I always wondered: you think them social services people really believed our old man broke his neck falling down the steps?"

She thought about it for a moment.

"I don't know. But even if they had figured out what had been going on in that house, I'm guessing they wouldn't have asked too many questions."

Gideon thought about it, then got in the car. He waved at her as the car drove away, holding the bag of food on his lap.

"That smells good," the driver said. "What is it?"

"I don't know, but you're right about it smelling good. You ain't getting none, though."

He looked in the bag. On top of the Tupperware containers of food was a beautifully framed picture of Pearl standing between her husband and Gus, all of them flashing their happiest smiles.

The bottom of the frame had the word 'Family' carved into the wood.

38

Thane jogged down the Venice Beach boardwalk, although it was considerably more crowded than during his usual run. He didn't like running there on the weekend because of all the tourists crowding the streets but today he decided to risk it. Near the end of the run, he saw that his bet had paid off.Sitting on a bench, looking out at the ocean, was Bradford Stone.

Thane slowed his run about fifty feet from Stone, giving himself a chance to catch his breath as he approached. Stone turned and saw him as he got closer, displaying what Thane thought was a surprised expression.

"You're running on the weekend," Stone said. "I've not seen you running on a Saturday before."

"That's because I haven't seen you around lately. I thought you said you were down here most days, but you'd disappeared, so I thought I'd try a Saturday. See if you were avoiding me."

Stone looked at him in a noncommittal way, then looked back at the ocean. "I saw you made the news again."

"That seems to be what I do."

"That, and you also always seem to end up with

someone trying to frame your client, although I guess this time it was a detective setting him up to take the fall."

Thane looked out at the ocean and at the people meandering along the beach, doing nothing but enjoying their lives.

"Think they'll be able to prove he got that witness to lie about seeing your client the night of the murder," Stone asked, "or will it just be the detective's word against the witness's?"

"I don't know. I like to think Mahone will be removed from his job, but if he manages to hold on to it, at least he'll hopefully be under the spotlight with how he operates in the future."

"So you think he might get away with it?"

"Maybe. In part because he didn't do it, but that doesn't stop me from hoping people assume he did."

Stone cocked an eyebrow. "What do you mean he didn't do it? You don't believe the witness?"

"The witness said your former colleague Barry Warlick coerced him into lying about having seen Kyle Miller with a body. Or at least he said that off the record. What he said in court was simply another lie."

Thane watched Stone for a reaction, but he wasn't surprised to see the man's face continue to look as though it was carved in granite.

"Rabbit—yes, the witness actually goes by the name Rabbit—said Warlick agreed not to press charges on the meth rap in exchange for false testimony. Warlick also told him his testimony wouldn't actually send anyone to prison for murder, because there was visual evidence that would be introduced later that would set him free."

Stone still didn't say anything at first, but instead just

watched Thane.

"So why did he say it was Mahone who told him to lie?"

"Maybe Mahone was causing a lot of damage to more people's lives. Maybe there were other people who could be set free if Mahone's pressure tactics were exposed, such as allowing Kyle to be locked up even though Mahone knew he didn't do it."

"Maybe it helped you and your clients more if the witness said Mahone was behind it."

"I'm confident Mahone had a lot of witnesses lie, even if that DJ wasn't one of them. That's the funny thing about karma. But Warlick is the one who told this particular witness to lie."

"Why?"

Thane looked at Stone, disappointed they couldn't talk more candidly and move away from the charade, but he also understood the danger of either one of them being too direct.

"For you. You said yourself he was always extremely loyal to you, and I experienced firsthand his resentment of me. I'm not sure why he thought arresting Kyle would bring me hardship, but apparently he did."

Stone appeared to think long and hard about Thane's assessment of the situation.

"Maybe he thought you were somehow involved in the death of your friend. Maybe he thought you were putting yourself on a little too high of moral high ground saying that people should just do what's right regardless of the cost."

"You mean like I accused you of doing?"

"Exactly like that. You put me in a difficult position

and ridiculed me for not doing the right thing. I had my reasons for doing what I did to you in your original trial, and as I've said before—and as I'll hopefully say until I die—in retrospect they weren't good reasons. But at the time, I felt like I was doing what was right for the greater good. But you called me a hypocrite for rationalizing an immoral action, as if doing the right thing was always a simple thing. Maybe Barry was seeing if you would do the right thing when your client was charged with the murder of your friend."

"But he couldn't have known I'd end up representing him."

"And yet, there you were, actually seeking out Mr. Miller, if my understanding is correct. Maybe as soon as that happened, Barry was sure his theory was right, and he wanted to put you in a position to have to do the right thing, to see if that's what you would actually do, or if you, too, would rationalize a different strategy."

"By putting a man in jail for a murder he didn't commit?"

"By charging a man who had been in prison several times before, for a murder Barry could then prove he didn't do. I'm just hypothesizing here."

"Of course."

"When Barry watched the security footage from the bar, he likely recognized Mahone's man. The DA's office works a lot of with undercover detectives. And he would know that Murphy responded to the murder, so maybe he always had that card he could play."

"That sounds inappropriate."

Stone looked at him directly. "Or maybe it sounds familiar."

Thane didn't know how to respond. He knew Stone had something he wanted to say, but after having sought out the former DA, Thane now wished he had kept on running.

"After our case was over," Stone continued, "and I was sent out to pasture, you know what suddenly occurred to me? At no point during your representation of Scotty Burns did you ever ask me if there were any plea agreement options. Maybe you figured I wouldn't be willing to offer one, but still, despite all of the evidence that pointed to Burns' guilt, you never once asked if there was even the possibility of pleading to a lesser charge. At first, I thought maybe it was because you hadn't really practiced criminal law, but any lawyer knows to do that. So then I thought, maybe there was more to this case than met the eye."

"I'll be the first to admit I made mistakes, but it was my first criminal case."

"But I don't think you did make any mistakes. I think you knew your client was innocent, and you knew you had evidence that could free him at any point. Maybe you let an innocent man spend time in jail because you knew you could get him out. So when you look at Barry, you can be critical of what he did, but maybe it's harder to point your finger at him. I can't say for sure."

"For what it's worth," Thane said, "I don't think Barry was sharp enough to come up with this on his own. I think his idea of getting even was to yell at me at a fundraiser a few weeks ago, and that was only after having had too much to drink. So, if whoever helped him figure this whole thing out did so to test my moral fiber, I wonder if they're satisfied with how it turned out."

Stone didn't make eye contact with Thane, but also didn't appear to be too offended by the implication that perhaps he was involved in it.

"So are you?" Thane continued. "Are you satisfied?"

"I'm not saying I had anything to do with this," Stone said, "but I don't know that the results would have confirmed much of anything, at least as far as proving you would do what was right. From what you've said, it sounds like you set up a detective who was taking the law into his own hands. And if there was, by chance, more than meets the eye with your involvement in the previous case, then no, you didn't step up and do the right thing, even though you always talk like you would. It's possible you simply went outside the rules once again, to get what you wanted. Like I did."

Stone paused and gathered his newspaper and water bottle before standing.

"I'm assuming you made your choice," Stone said, "by going after Mahone instead of promoting your theory— correct or incorrect—about Barry Warlick. About me. Mahone, I might add, is a pompous, condescending prick who has likely hurt a lot of innocent people, so please don't let anything I say be interpreted as feeling sorry for that asshole. The force would be better with him out of it, in part because he's called in 'anonymous' tips before, to pressure a suspect. But Barry is retiring soon. Going after him would not make a dent in how things work in our legal system. And despite what you think, Barry is actually an honest man. I'd hate to think of you holding a vendetta against him. I think I've seen what you're capable of doing when you have a vendetta."

Stone was correct about that. The death of Detective

Gruber, the death of his friend Joseph, and the fact that Stone had been exposed, fired, and humiliated was evidence of what he was able to do.

"I do think, though, that it will be good if Barry follows through on his plans to retire," Thane said. "Sooner rather than later."

Stone nodded in agreement.

"So where do things go from here with us?" Thane asked. "Am I to assume you're going to continue testing me? That you're going to keep trying to prove to me that I was unfair in how I judged you?"

Stone looked back at the ocean, as if the answer might float in on one of the waves.

"As far as I'm concerned, we're done. I did something unforgivable to you years ago. And maybe things were set up to have Mr. Miller look guilty, but perhaps evidence existed that was guaranteed to have the case eventually dropped, ensuring he would never go to jail. And maybe you set up your previous client so that he went to jail on a murder charge, but evidence existed that would free him.

"Maybe we're not all that different, and to be honest, that's why we're now done. I don't want to become like you. I need to move forward. I have my own sins to confess and my own penance to serve for what I did to you, and that's something that will be with me the rest of my life. I can't keep perverting the law in the name of justice, or to try to show you are a hypocrite when it comes to doing the right thing. Besides, if you did play any part in the two murders that took place in the past, I believe Detective Struthers is still working this case. So if there's anything there, he'll find it, of that I'm certain. Either way, I need to focus on my own moral reformation."

Stone offered a half-wave and turned to leave.

"I wish you well," Thane finally said. "I really do."

"I hope you find peace, Banning. I'm just not sure you're going to find it in the direction you're heading." Stone tossed his plastic water bottle into the trash and headed on down the Venice Beach boardwalk.

Thane watched him go, then sat down on the bench and watched the waves.

The former DA was right: Thane wasn't going to find peace if he continued on this path. But peace was going to be elusive for him anyway, at least as long as Detective Vince Struthers was still working the case.

But Thane had to try. It was time to do things the right way, and not just for himself, and not just for Hannah. Things had changed.

He was going to be a father.

ACKNOWLEDGEMENTS

First, I'd like to thank all of the people who took the time to write so many positive things about my first novel in this series, *Contempt*. The response was unexpected...and a bit stunning...and I appreciated all of the kind words. A couple of the negative reviews also made me smile (especially the one that said if I was a lawyer, I "should be disbarred for being an idiot." Well played, sir.)

I'd also like to thank Donna Spearman for being an early reader and providing numerous suggestions and corrections; Valerie Williams for her input and encouragement about my writing; my weekly author group (Angelina, David, Don, Rochelle, and Shai) for providing me with a bit of human interaction on a regular basis; Melinda Lee for being an enthusiastic cheerleader; Anne McAneny for being Anne McAneny (and all that brings with it); and to Bill Archambault and Bruce Gehle for answering some of my legal questions, however naïve they may have been (the questions, not Bill or Bruce). And thank you to Kate, if for no other reason than out of reflex (although there are other reasons).

Thanks also to Nicholas Holloway, editor extraordinaire and terrific author in his own right.

And, as always, a big thank you to my family and closest friends. Your response to my work always means the most to me, even if I suspect you're just being kind.

And a final shout-out to my dog, Trolley, because she's a very good dog. Good dog, Trolley, good dog!

ABOUT THE AUTHOR

Photo by Sabrina Hendricks

Michael Cordell is a Silver Falchion Award-winning novelist, playwright and produced screenwriter. His first novel, *Contempt*, was a Top 10 Amazon Kindle legal thriller. He has sold three screenplays to Hollywood, including *Beeper*, an action-thriller starring Harvey Keitel. Michael currently lives in Charlottesville, Virginia, where he has taught screenwriting for over fifteen years.

CONNECT WITH MICHAEL CORDELL

Sign up for Michael's newsletter at
www.michaeljcordell.com/newsletter

To find out more information visit his website:
www.michaeljcordell.com

Facebook:
www.facebook.com/michaeljcordell

BOOK DISCOUNTS AND SPECIAL DEALS

Sign up for free to get discounts and special deals
on our bestselling books at
www.TCKpublishing.com/bookdeals

9 781631 611902